I0594485

α ω α ω α ω α ω α ω α ω
ω α ω α ω α ω α ω α ω α ω
α ω α ω α ω α ω α ω α ω
ω α ω α ω α ω α ω α ω α ω
α ω α ω α ω α ω α ω α ω
ω α ω α ω α ω α ω α ω α ω
α ω α ω α ω α ω α ω α ω
ω α ω α ω α ω α ω α ω α ω
α ω α ω α ω α ω α ω α ω
ω α ω α ω α ω α ω α ω α ω
α ω α ω α ω α ω α ω α ω
ω α ω α ω α ω α ω α ω α ω
α ω α ω α ω α ω α ω α ω
ω α ω α ω α ω α ω α ω α ω
α ω α ω α ω α ω α ω α ω
ω α ω α ω α ω α ω α ω α ω
α ω α ω α ω α ω α ω α ω
ω α ω α ω α ω α ω α ω α ω
α ω α ω α ω α ω α ω α ω
ω α ω α ω α ω α ω α ω α ω
α ω α ω α ω α ω α ω α ω
ω α ω α ω α ω α ω α ω α ω
α ω α ω α ω α ω α ω α ω
ω α ω α ω α ω α ω α ω α ω
α ω α ω α ω α ω α ω α ω
ω α ω α ω α ω α ω α ω α ω
α ω α ω α ω α ω α ω α ω
ω α ω α ω α ω α ω α ω α ω
α ω α ω α ω α ω α ω α ω
ω α ω α ω α ω α ω α ω α ω
α ω α ω α ω α ω α ω α ω
ω α ω α ω α ω α ω α ω α ω
α ω α ω α ω α ω α ω α ω
ω α ω α ω α ω α ω α ω α ω
α ω α ω α ω α ω α ω α ω
ω α ω α ω α ω α ω α ω α ω
α ω α ω α ω α ω α ω α ω
ω α ω α ω α ω α ω α ω α ω
α ω α ω α ω α ω α ω α ω
ω α ω α ω α ω α ω α ω α ω
α ω α ω α ω α ω α ω α ω
ω α ω α ω α ω α ω α ω α ω
α ω α ω α ω α ω α ω α ω
ω α ω α ω α ω α ω α ω α ω

BLUE JUSTICE

by

Phil Copsey

in case of emergency press
http://www.icoe.com.au
Travancore, Victoria
Australia

Blue Justice

by Phil Copsey

This novel is inspired by true events that have been recombined into elements suitable for narrative storytelling. Any correspondence with actual events or characters' names is purely coincidental.

Published by **in case of emergency press** 2020

ISBN 978-0-6485571-1-1

Dedication

To the most patient of families: Liz, Daniel, Nathan and James.

Contents

Chapter One

Tony Signorotto slouched inside the darkness of his parked sedan. He had one friend with him. A can of Jim Beam bourbon and coke nestled in his large right hand. Three-quarters drained.

He sucked down the last mouthful, feeling the fiery liquid burn into his gut like a nine-millimetre bullet. It was enough to give a black dog heartburn.

Throwing the crushed empty out the window, he wiped the sleeve of his police jacket across his mouth and thought about the night ahead. Alone. He knew the booze was slowly killing him. On duty he never hit the turps in front of other police staff. Besides, it was *because* of his job he had the problem. It wasn't his fault. Never had been.

Tony had parked his patrol car down a dead-end alley in the heart of Melbourne's all-night strip of Italian restaurants along Lygon Street, in the inner-city suburb of Carlton. He just wanted some peace and quiet. Not too much to ask for, was it?

His raw nerves screamed when his mobile phone rang, breaking the beautiful silence. Picking it up, he just hoped it wasn't work ringing him. The name 'Dom' flashed in the display. The number belonged to his long-time friend Dom Santino, the owner of the restaurant by the same name in Lygon Street. Tony raised the phone as he pressed the talk button. Before he put it to his ear, he could hear a female scream erupting from the speaker.

'Dom, what's wrong?' Tony asked loudly.

'Tony, Tony, there are two men in the kitchen. They're both drunk and going to hurt Gina. They've got knives. They went mad after I told them to leave. They wouldn't pay the bill and now they attack anyone. Quick, my friend, hurry!'

'I'm just around the corner, mate. Hang on,' Tony replied, as he struggled furiously with the ignition, dropping the phone onto the passenger seat. It was only thirty seconds to Dom's bistro, but he could imagine what two doped or piss-fuelled hoons could do to Dom's youngest daughter Gina in that time. She was only sixteen but looked much older with her olive Italian complexion and long dark hair. Tony's blood boiled at the thought of them touching a member of his old friend's family. Dom would defend her to the last drop of his blood but, at the end of the day, he was over sixty.

This was happening to a friend and Tony would deal with it in his own way.

Justice would be served with all the Italian trimmings!

Tony drove quietly up the back lane to the rear entrance of Santino's family bistro. He grabbed a torch from under the seat, slipped out of his car, then pulled on a pair of black leather gloves as he silently entered through the kitchen door.

Inside he could see Dom slumped against one wall with blood flowing freely down his fat Italian face. One young punk with spiked hair was standing over him with fists clenched. Next to him was his associate who had Gina bent backwards over a steel kitchen bench.

He had a gleaming knife in one hand, while the other hand was high up under Gina's T-shirt. Her jeans had been ripped open and pulled down over her slim, olive-skinned hips.

As Tony quickly took in the scene, the second hood moved his long-bladed knife under Gina's T-shirt and, with a fast upward thrust, slashed it and her bra open, leaving a thin red line of droplets running downwards from between her breasts to her navel. Gina's scream filled the air.

A red mist descended over Tony as his left hand moved to the light switch. The kitchen was immediately thrown into darkness. Gina's screaming went up an octave.

Tony knew his way around the kitchen only too well. He had been to many a celebration with friends and family over the years at Dom's. Celebrations that had spilled from the restaurant into the kitchen at closing time with much laughter and too much booze.

For a big man, he moved deftly around the freezer to where he knew the two low-lifes to be standing. Hitting the switch on his torch, the blinding halogen globe threw an arc of light across the kitchen.

'What the fuck?' one of the punks yelled, as the eerie torch light bounced off the white walls like a disco ball at a night club. Tony grabbed the punk who still had a hand firmly over Gina's left breast, and slammed his head into a stack of plates next to her. Crockery splintered everywhere as the first piece of shit slid to the floor groaning. Gina threw herself away from the bench and ran to her father.

Tony held the torch blindingly in the face of the second shell-shocked punk, before flipping it over so the steel end became a weapon of mass destruction. The WMD hovered above the punk's nose.

'I didn't fuckin' touch her, man, I swear. I wasn't going to do anything. It wasn't me, it was him!' The punk pointed a shaking hand at his mate who was lying on the floor, groaning between picking pieces of china from a mouth that was now displaying a bloodied set of broken front teeth. 'You can't do fuckin' nuthin' to me. Fuck off, prick.'

As the last sentence came out of the punk's hysterical mouth, Tony brought the end of the torch down viciously across the bridge of the punk's nose, shattering bone and cartilage, and causing a torrent of claret.

Tony's voice turned into a growl. 'This fella's gonna make you wish you'd stopped in Little Bourke Street for Chinese. I don't think you'll ever want to go Italian again when I'm finished with you.'

Gina stood up and came towards Tony, one arm across her sweat-soaked breasts with the other trying to hold her torn jeans up. Tony put out his arms, then held her tightly against his jacket. Leaning down, he helped Dom off the floor.

'Dom, take Gina into the office and don't let anyone else in here. On your way out, turn on the lights. These boys are going to get a close-up tour of the kitchen.'

Dom nodded, his face rigid.

Tony took off his jacket and put it around the near-naked Gina. On her it looked like an overcoat. She shrugged off the torn jeans and kicked them away.

Seconds later the lights came back on, as Dom ushered his sobbing daughter out of the kitchen, leaving Tony standing over the two punks who were both holding their shattered heads, tears streaming down their faces.

'Roles reversed now, eh, boys?' Tony said, looking up to see Dom's large frame blocking the entrance to anyone thinking of entering the kitchen.

Concentrating on Gina's attacker, Tony whispered in his ear, 'Let's see what sort of a hero you are now.' Tony reached up to the radio on the shelf above the stove and turned the volume to loud.

'Fuck off, you arsehole,' the punk yelled, as he spat broken teeth, china slivers and blood over the floor, before grabbing his mouth with both hands to stem the pain.

Tony took the torch in one hand and yanked back Broken Tooth's head so the bloodied hole of a mouth opened with a scream. Before the punk realised what was happening, he was gagging on the end of the torch that had been shoved down past his tonsils. Broken Teeth's body began to twitch and jump like a headless chicken. Choking sounds began to bubble up from within his chest.

The would-be rapist desperately pulled the torch from his raw throat before throwing up all over himself.

A nearly inaudible sound croaked from the punk's mouth, 'You're a fucking dog.'

'I'm not the one sitting in my own vomit, arsehole,' Tony replied, as he gently tapped the torch into the side of Broken Teeth's head, forcing him to crawl backwards and sit in a large container of fat nearby.

'Be careful down there. You'll get dirty,' Tony said, as he placed his shoe across Broken Tooth's foot to hold him in place on the greasy floor. 'You scrawny prick. You look like you could do with a good feed. Tell you what, how about a nice bowl of minestrone soup? On the house.'

Tony grabbed a soup ladle and then, quickly taking his foot away, lifted Broken Teeth onto his shaking feet. 'Take your jeans off, hero. I don't want you to spill any of this on your clothes.'

Broken Teeth didn't move.

Tony's gloved hand reached down and ripped away the front button and zip. He dipped the ladle into the boiling soup. With his free hand, Tony pulled the elastic of Broken Teeth's underpants towards him and quickly poured the entire ladle of minestrone soup onto the punk's balls.

Broken Teeth collapsed, writhing onto the floor, hands buried between his legs, screaming in agony.

'You scream louder than the girl you attacked,' Tony remarked. 'Good, that's the way it should be. The next time you want to get into a girl's pants without asking, just think what she might say when she sees that pathetic scarred pecker.'

Tony turned his attention to Shattered Nose, whose eyes were the size of dinner plates. 'Your turn now, hero. You want to knock old men about? Well, let's see how hot you are.'

'You can't do this. You fucking can't. You'll go down for this,' Shattered Nose croaked, blood still pouring from his nose.

Lifting him up to eye level, Tony replied, 'Wrong on both counts, prick.' With that, he brought his knee up swiftly into Shattered Nose's crotch. Letting go, the punk fell to the floor in a foetal position, gasping for air and, like his mate, buried his hands between his legs.

'Don't you have the balls to play the game anymore?' Tony said, as he leant over the twitching Shattered Nose. 'Come on, time to play. Let's see your big weapon. Give me your fucking hand.'

Shattered Nose slowly removed his right hand from between his clenched thighs. His balls would have to survive with one hand holding them for the moment.

'Good boy,' Tony said, as he adjusted his gloves ever so slowly.

'Don't fucking touch me again,' Shattered Nose's voice rasped, in between sucking gulps of air.

'Don't worry, I'm just going to give you a hand. A fucking red-hot hand.'

Tony dragged Shattered Nose to his feet, gripped his right hand with his leathered glove and plunged the raw hand into the bubbling deep fry up to the punk's wrist. Tony could see the hissing, spitting fat leaving small smoking holes in the stretched leather of his glove. He gave a slow count back from three.

Tony pulled the red raw excuse for a hand out of the liquid hell, but Shattered Nose fainted before he could work up even a half-decent scream.

A sweet smell like that of overdone boiled pork enveloped the kitchen.

'There, you won't be hitting defenceless old men again,' Tony said. 'And your mate there won't be showing his cock in public ever again.'

Broken Teeth looked up as he cradled his cooked balls and spoke between huge, shuddering sobs, 'You're f-fucking mad. Fucking mad.'

You're probably right. I probably am mad, Tony thought.

Tony then took hold of both punks and dragged them by their hair, kicking and shouting, out the back door to the alley, dumping them on the cobblestones among the potato peelings and fish heads that had spilled from the overflowing garbage bags. A mangy-looking dog padded up to Broken Teeth and began to sniff at his crotch. The air was filled with the smell of soup and rancid overcooked meat.

Tony walked back into the kitchen, went over to the first-aid cabinet, took out two bandaids, then crossed over to the restaurant door where Dom was standing guard. Tony said gently, 'Send my goddaughter out to me, my friend.'

A minute later, Tony and a now-dressed Gina stood in the back alley over the crying, cringing punks. Tony handed the bandaids to Gina.

She leant down and spat in both punks' faces before placing a bandaid on the chest of each, not unlike you'd place a rose on the coffin at your Italian grandmother's funeral. Gina then stepped over to Broken Teeth and slammed the spiked high heel of her right shoe into his crotch, sending a falsetto scream into the night. She smiled at both, handed Tony's jacket back to him, kissed him on the cheek and then went back inside.

'A little first aid, my friends,' Tony said, with a grin. 'Don't say we don't look after people in Carlton. Of course, you'll never find this hospitality again, because you'll never come this way again. And if you do, you won't get the chance you're getting now, to slink out of this alley like the dogs you are. Now that you've had a dose of real justice, you can crawl your way to freedom down the alley along with the other vermin that inhabit this area.'

An insult to the rats.

Tony leaned down and removed both of their wallets. At the same time, he took a pistol from the small of his back, jammed it in Broken Teeth's mouth, breaking the stumps of whatever ivory he had left hanging from his swollen, bleeding lips.

Tony withdrew the barrel from the bleeding hole, swung the weapon around and fired one round into a garbage bag right next to the punk's ear. Both scumbags cowered face-down in the alley with their hands over their heads and ears ringing. If they could have dug their way through the cobblestones, they would have.

Tony removed three hundred dollars in total. Then he threw the wallets into a pool of grease-covered water.

'That's robbery, you fucking prick,' cried Shattered Nose. 'That's theft. That's our money.'

'No, no, my friends. No offence to your family jewels, son, but you've got it all cocked up. I'll give some of this to the owner to pay for your meals. The rest will go to the girl you attacked. It will buy her a new pair of jeans, T-shirt and underwear. She wouldn't want anything next to her lovely skin that you two pieces of shit have touched. By the way, don't expect a receipt.'

Tony let them crawl away with a final warning. 'Don't even think about revenge, boys. You almost made a fatal mistake in visiting the favourite eating place of the biggest mafia name in Melbourne – Benny Illarietti,' Tony lied. 'He's a very good friend of the owner. If he hears what you two tried, you will be found face-down in the Yarra River. But first he'll remove your hands and feet while you are still alive. Think long and hard, boys. You probably think this is rough justice. I prefer to call it Carlton justice.'

Looking at both of them while they dragged themselves along the alley, Tony was glad that Dom Santino didn't hear him say that. The last thing Dom needed was Tony's uncle, Benny Illarietti, using his bistro as his nine-to-five headquarters.

Turning around, Tony shrugged on his blue Victoria Police Sergeant's jacket, strolled back to his patrol car and drove slowly out of the alley into the Carlton night. He mulled over the modern-day police service looking after its 'clients'. Always more service than force these days. After all, too many clients didn't get locked up.

Chapter Two

'Sarge, Sarge,' a male voice yelled.

Sergeant Tony Signorotto snapped himself out of his reminiscing and looked at the young uniformed member trying to pass a Sammy Special through the passenger window of the police vehicle.

Tony's view of the young police officer was partially blocked by the giant triple-decker salami-and-cheese cholesterol mountain that was occupying every square inch of the lad's hands.

The kid wouldn't be more than twenty and he's as skinny as a rake, Tony thought, as he took the feast.

The police vehicle was double-parked outside Sammy's Deli of Delights in Rathdowne Street. It was a popular eatery with the boys in blue from the Carlton Police Station, mainly because Sammy gave them all a fifty-percent discount, which in turn gave him a virtual twenty-four-hour free foot patrol of his premises. One day Sammy would sell up and retire on the money he had made from the long arm of the law. A modern-day juice shop would probably open up and, God forbid, the world would see some fit police. It didn't faze Tony, though, because by that time he hoped to be long retired.

His young offsider fired up the patrol car and pulled back into the traffic.

'Where's yours?' asked Tony.

'I've got a focaccia and green salad back at the station, Sarge,' the young constable replied, as he quickly pressed the button to lower the window so he didn't gag on the smell coming from Signorotto's lunch wafting perilously close to his sensitive, young nostrils.

Tony sank down in his seat and eyeballed the constable. It was all starting to get to Tony these days. He ruminated while he ate. *If you'd said 'focaccia' to a cop ten years ago, you'd have been belted around the head and then arrested for indecent language. As for a 'green salad', well, what other colour was a bloody salad meant to be? Didn't anyone just eat bread and lettuce anymore? Probably goes to the police gym, too. Bloody hell. Wouldn't weigh more than seventy kilos, wringing wet.*

Tony adjusted his seatbelt over his expanding waistline. It wasn't that he was overweight. He was just *solid*. Italian solid, as many a hoon had found out around the traps when they hadn't taken notice of his requests the first time. Tony never asked twice.

His gaze tracked from his Sammy's across the wide panorama of Rathdowne Street. Everything in Carlton was set out in squares with wide streets and beautiful Victorian-era houses. They had vision when they designed Carlton. No matter what the university kids did to this suburb to make it look bad, from hanging washing from the verandahs to dumping broken couches on the porches and slapping anti-uranium stickers all over the street-facing windows, they couldn't succeed. Carlton would always be Carlton. The grand old lady would live on from the San Remo Ballroom to Trades Hall. Was he a cynic after all his years in 'The Job'? The answer was an unequivocal 'Yes!'

Tony's mind detoured from the real truth. The kids at the station who had been out of the Academy for only a few months thought Tony was a hero. He was what they all aspired to be. The big Sergeant with the three stripes. What did they know?

They fought over transfers to Carlton these days. It was the place to be for a young copper all of a sudden. Christ, ten years ago you had to be dragged to the place. The streets were different then. Italians, Turks, Lebos. You name it. Wogs just like him. Back then they drove black Holden Monaros, purple GT Ford Falcons and drank real beer like Vic Bitter and took no crap from any young cop. You never cruised Carlton in those days in a two-litre 'buzz box'. On the rear bumper of every local V8 was the sticker: 'The only things that come in two litres are milk and juice.' Hell, nowadays they shot up and down Lygon Street in their Ferraris and Lamborghinis like they were piloting Exocet missiles, and argued at the top of their voices over the right to park outside their favourite latte café. The big difference, though, was that they were carrying shooters and deadly drugs now. Everything was changing. Yep, Carlton was now the place to be and be seen, all right. Not just for the boys in blue, though. The old saying of a recently retired detective sprang readily to mind: 'Legality comes out of the barrel of a gun.'

Did it have anything to do with his attitude now? He tried to forget, but the last couple of months the only way he could forget was by looking through the bottom of an empty bourbon and coke glass up at the Sarah Sands Hotel in Sydney Road or the Carlton Inn on Drummond Street. Or, more recently, in the bottom drawer of his desk. He hadn't always been a drinker. It was just the last six months he had been hitting it more and more.

People still told Tony it wasn't his fault. The chase, the crash, the death. His mind flickered. The black Nissan sports. Black and yellow. Yellow flames and that arm waving frantically out of the driver's window. He could see the look on the young boy's face in the driver's seat turn from one of hope of rescue to total screaming fear as the flames engulfed his body and licked around his head and arm.

It hadn't been a long chase. Just a couple of blocks. He had been cleared of blame by both the Department and the Coroner. They said he'd done the right thing in backing off from the chase, and there was a lot of time between the backing off and the sickening crash.

Tony was steering his patrol car around the corner into Pelham Street when he saw the black smoke and the bright yellow flames. The 'lights and bells' of the pursuing police vehicle had been switched off two streets earlier. Could he have helped? He still didn't know.

He could remember jumping out and running towards the car. The flames weren't that bad, but all of a sudden there had been an air-sucking 'whoosh'. They later discovered a nitrous-oxide bottle, used for supercharging, had erupted vertically for about three metres at the rear of the crumpled, black, flame-shrouded mess of what used to be the pride and joy of the young driver now being seared into the driver's seat by the ever-increasing inferno. He remembered the acrid fat-like smell of burning flesh as he stood there powerless to help that young life. The thought of that blood-curdling scream emitting from the blackened interior sent horrific chills down his spine to this day.

One thought that stood out at the time was what his long-time girlfriend, Susie Doherty, had said to him the night before the accident when he'd gone to her Canning Street flat, 'Be careful, Tony. Don't do anything stupid out there and get hurt.'

No, *he* didn't get hurt. Because he didn't do a damn thing.

Two road warriors from the Traffic Branch had arrived with fire extinguishers, but it was too late. He kept telling himself that, as he stood there, paralysed and staring at the ever-blackening shape of the young boy's head and arm highlighted in the paint-blistered framework of the driver's window. The arm suddenly dropped and the bone of one finger pointed directly at Tony as it dripped crackling, stinking flesh onto the bitumen.

An accusation from the gates of hell!

Yes, they all told him it wasn't his fault, but he looked back at the start. He knew where the boy came from. Knew his address. Knew he was unlicensed because he had taken him before the courts only two weeks prior on a speeding charge. Been there when the Magistrate cancelled his licence for six months.

Did he have to chase? He wanted to show the kid it was Tony Signorotto's patch and that he and his mates were very low on the food chain in Carlton. If you negotiated with these idiots you legitimised them.

It seemed like eons since he had first been sent to the Carlton Police Station. Ten years. Ten long years. He was tired now. Tired of it all. He sat slouched in the passenger seat, left boot propped up on the dashboard, adding more dirt and grime to the already shabby appearance of the interior of the worn-out vehicle.

Chapter Three

The kid was pulling into the old, run-down red-brick Carlton Police Station in Drummond Street when the black Nissan blasted past. Tony dropped the Sammy Special all over the floor of the car and inhaled deeply.

'His licence is mine,' said the young member, as he went to swing back onto the street, making a little old Italian mama pushing her shopping cart perform an Olympic long jump to get out of the way.

'Forget it,' Tony snapped. 'Just hit the kerb and let me out. Clean this up later.' He jumped out of the car and hurried inside. Tony was sweating on this cold winter morning.

The young constable's jaw dropped in disbelief – or was it disgust?

Going straight to his sergeant's office at the back of the decrepit building, Tony closed the door and stood with his back against it. He shook from head to foot.

Being the only sergeant on that morning, he locked the door and headed to his desk. His hand darted into the bottom drawer and whipped out a silver hip flask, hidden under a pile of conveniently placed paper work. Ironically, it was under a stack of court papers for drink-driving offences.

Tony had practised this routine many times now. The top was unscrewed and the flask went to his lips like a silver bullet. His mouth was open and waiting like a porn star's pose. He gazed around the room and back to the door, waiting for a sound other than the quick gulping noises he made as the Jim Beam slid blissfully down his throat and formed a burning whirlpool in his waiting gut.

From the time he got to his desk until he unlocked the door again was now under thirty seconds. Sitting down, he stared at the blank computer screen in front of him. It all meant nothing. He needed air – quickly!

He darted out the door, through the watch-house, signed his firearm back in with the Senior Constable in charge of the area, then headed outside to where the small park and its bench waited for him like a long-lost lover. This haven had saved him many times recently. He sometimes thought about taking his firearm to the park, but he hated the thought of a mother or child finding him after he had 'eaten' his gun.

He sat and let it all wash back over him. They knew inside. They'd leave him alone until he wandered back in looking a lot more tired than when he had gone out. The more senior ones knew the story. He'd heard Inspector Phil Stone telling the shift changeover months ago to go easy on him, to cut him some slack because of who he was. It was a request, but because it came from Phil Stone there were to be no questions asked. Phil Stone's word was final.

Good old Phil. Everyone respected him. Everyone knew Tony and Phil had been long time mates since their Academy days, years ago. Tony was seven years older than him, but they were squad mates and that equalised everything. Squad mates were squad mates until the last police funeral had been held and the final salute given. You were still squad mates long after retirement.

They had taken much the same path through the Department: Russell Street Headquarters, outer stations, then both to the CIB as Detective Senior Constables. Tony had come back to the city and Carlton, while Stone had gone on to the 'Armed Robbers', a stint with the Homicide squad as a Senior Sergeant, then promotion to Inspector, and back to Carlton as the Divisional Inspector. The world had turned full circle – and what a world they had seen over their time. Choices and decisions had long ago been made and lived by.

Phil Stone was aiming for the top and everyone knew he'd get there. Forty-two years of age and the corridors of power were beckoning. Married to a doll who put up with all the crap that the Department could throw at an up-and-coming officer. Two nice children. Yep, he'd be good for the future. He had to be. Someone had to look after the kids the job was putting out today. Cannon fodder. Lambs to the slaughter. Kids who had degrees and certificates in everything from diplomas in writing to forensic science… and none of them could recognise a crook if they found one floating in their ninety-eight-percent fat-free lentil soup – or skinny latte for that matter.

Chapter Four

Inspector Phil Stone looked out the second-storey window of his office at the lonely figure of his old friend sitting with hunched shoulders on the park bench. Watching members sitting by themselves on park benches always filled him with dread. More often than not, the beginning of the end. He saw both of Tony's hands were on his knees and then glanced at his equipment belt, breathing a sigh of relief on seeing an empty holster.

As the Inspector in charge of the Division, Phil was not only responsible for the station houses of Carlton, Fitzroy and Collingwood, he was also accountable for the welfare of the members who worked in these run-down inner suburban, rodent-infested slums they called police stations. If all the people working under him were making money for the government – instead of putting the area's pond scum in jail and costing the same said government about $100,000 a year per low-life in keepers' fees – they would be working in state-of-the-art buildings. That was a policeman's lot, though, as Gilbert and Sullivan once said.

Susie had come to see Phil many times about Tony during the last few months. Everyone at the station knew she was Tony's girl. They had either met her at the station, a social night or at the Police Credit Co-Op where she worked. Thirty-six years old, Susie had been dating

Tony for quite a few years. Down to earth and someone you could always rely on. Phil would see red when Tony sometimes took Susie for granted.

Phil Stone and his wife Mandy were happily married with two little girls, but the thought had crossed his mind, only fleetingly of course, that Susie could 'park her slippers' under his bed anytime she wanted. Coppers. Always wanting more than what was good for them. No, he was very happy and contented. Unlike his mate sitting on the bench.

Phil put down the monthly arrest reports and headed downstairs. As he passed the watch-house keeper, he said, 'Anyone's looking for me, I'll be outside, Jill. Get it?'

Senior Constable Jill Norton, an old hand at running the station by herself when people above her were otherwise engaged, nodded like the wise sage she was. 'Not a problem, Boss. Look after him,' she said quietly. Jill glanced sideways at the young probationary constable nearby who was glued to his computer screen. Why bring him into it? Let him believe for a while that his bright, new, shiny uniform could solve all the problems of the United Nations of Carlton. He'll learn.

Phil nodded and winked at Jill. They both looked after each other in their jobs.

Phil didn't smoke and he knew that Tony had given it up a long time ago. Up until after that car chase. Phil picked up a packet from some prisoner's property on the way out. He'd replace it later. There were prisoners inside and outside the station at the moment and the ones outside needed his attention right now.

'Smoke?' he said, as he flipped open the packet of Marlboro and put it in front of Tony.

'Thanks, Phil. Got a light?'

'Christ, want me to smoke it for you, too?'

Phil flicked the throw-away Bic with his other hand, and could see the cylinder of tobacco collapse under the long breath that Tony drew.

'How's Susie these days?'

'Yeah, okay, I guess. Saw her for a minute at her place last night.'

Phil grinned. 'Mate, you two are an item. For Chrissakes, marry her, will you? Mandy is driving me mad. Because I'm the Inspector, she reckons I should *order* you to propose.'

'Should, I suppose,' Tony replied, as he looked around, purposely avoiding Phil Stone's glare.

The air hung heavy with silence.

Stone broke it. 'Listen, pal. You've got to snap out of it soon or get some professional help. It wasn't your fault back then, so it's no good going downhill about it now. Susie is frantic about you and I'm getting a bit that way, too. She loves you and one day you'll turn around and she'll be gone. Wake up! This is your mate telling you, not the bloody Inspector.'

Tony said nothing and wouldn't look at his mate.

Phil hesitated, then continued. 'I'm going to give you a serve right now, Tony. I've got complaints from the Sarah Sands and the Carlton Inn about you getting pissed in there and making a bloody idiot of yourself. I can't keep protecting you. Someone will tell the Superintendent and then we're both up shit creek without a paddle. I'm not giving you a choice this time. This is an order. I'm giving you one of the cleanskins who are arriving next Monday from the Academy. He's going to be yours to love and cherish for the next few months. Understand? No excuses. You are going to tell your other mate, Jim Beam, to get out of the station and stay out. I've had enough and so have some of your fellow workers.'

Tony's head snapped around and his dark eyes bore into Stone.

'Yeah,' Phil said, pushing on, 'I know about your desk, too. You can't put anything over on me. Christ, you're the one that taught me all I know.' Phil hated doing this to his old friend, but he had tried everything to help Tony. If he could have done it any other way, he would have, but it was now or never. He had been dragged out of trouble on the streets too many times over the years by his mate to let him down now.

Phil could see tears welling in Tony's eyes and the shudder starting in his shoulders.

The flood started.

The pale winter sun trickled through the cold damp branches as Phil sat there with his arm around his friend's shoulder and let him sob his heart out. It just flowed and flowed until Tony felt like a rag doll in his mate's arms.

It seemed like an eternity before Tony wiped his eyes, looked at Phil, smiled weakly and spoke. 'All right. What's the name of this world-saver that I have to babysit?'

'Max Tyler. His reputation has preceded him, though. His old man used to be in the job. Remember Frank Tyler? That friendless bastard who used to be in the Internal Investigations Branch years ago. Anyway, his son's a real hot shot according to the drill instructor who rang me the other day. The drilly reckons Max Tyler needs sorting out real quick and I think you're just the man for the job.'

Tony groaned as he looked at Phil. 'Not another self-declared hero of the free world, I hope?'

Phil stood, then turned slowly in the direction of the front door. 'Worse, from what I hear.'

Chapter Five

Tony finished his shift at three o'clock and threw a tracksuit top over his police shirt.

He had only been to his desk once since his talk with Phil Stone, and that was to fling the Jim Beam into the rubbish bin. Besides the dressing-down he had been given, something was telling Tony his time was now. He had stared down a tunnel into the metal rubbish bin for what seemed like an hour. Eventually, he walked out of the station up to Cardigan Street to see Susie.

Approaching the credit union, Tony saw a familiar figure sitting at an outside table at Vitto's Coffee Shop, known locally as 'Gamblers' Grotto'. It was his uncle, local mafia figure Benito 'Benny' Illarietti. Next to him, and traditionally on his right, was Mickey Midolini, Benny's 'muscle'. Benny's black seven-series BMW was parked in the 'No Standing' zone directly outside the café.

Tony smiled to himself as he looked at Mickey. He'd been known as 'Mickey the Mouse' ever since Tony had apprehended him about two years earlier in a drug sting in Bouverie Street near the old Carlton and United Brewery. Mickey had been so quick to squeal on his associates to Tony that, outside his direct circle, he was immediately dubbed Mickey the Mouse. He daren't squeal on the inner circle, less Benny Illarietti found out and had him fed to the sharks at the aquarium in Flinders Street for a midnight snack. Mickey had received a one-year good behaviour bond from the local magistrate, whom Tony knew drove a brand new Aston Martin Vantage. Very strange on a magistrate's wage.

Benny Illarietti was Tony's uncle on his father's side and he had little to do with him. It was well known, not only around Carlton but at headquarters, that he was one of the 'Carlton Boys'. Benny was into drug running and many other illicit operations. However, Tony doubted Benny would ever be caught at any of these trades because of his web of associates and store of alibis.

Since Tony's father had died some years before, Benny had tried to look after Tony's mother Sophia from a monetary aspect. Sophia had gratefully declined the offer and, although she loved her brother-in-law, she would never take money from him because of his 'occupation'. There had been several family functions where Benny attended with his only son Saverio and everyone had got along fine. Benny had been presented with Sav by his now-deceased wife late in life, so there was not the usual family connection between the older Tony and the much younger Sav. Tony knew there would always be that 'line in the sand', that coolness between him and his uncle because of the opposites they represented. Both respected that. It would come to a head one day and Tony hoped he'd be out of the force by then. It would be all-out family war otherwise.

Benny put down his short-black coffee and looked up at Tony.

No hand was offered in greeting by either party.

'How is your mother?' Benny asked.

Tony looked directly at his uncle. 'Fine.'

'You will pass on my love?'

'As always.'

As Tony stood there, Mickey visibly squirmed in his chair. Tony had never passed on his ratting to Benny, and Mickey knew why. One day Tony would call in favours and, if they weren't given, he could just imagine the conversation between Benny and his nephew the cop. Tony scared Mickey and justifiably so. Mickey sat there wishing Tony would move on – and quickly.

Tony started to walk away, then quietly turned to face Mickey. 'Don't move around so much, Mickey. Your chair's squeaking.'

A chill ran down Mickey's spine as Tony walked away.

Benny cocked his head and asked, 'What did he mean by that?'

'Dunno, Boss. Want another coffee?' Without waiting for an answer, Mickey stood, picked up both cups with his dainty little fingers, and walked quickly into Vitto's. He was as scared of Benny as he was of Tony. He had to be very careful with his latest enterprise of 'skimming' Benny, and especially of using Benny's son Sav to courier his Merchandise around. If Benny found out that Sav wasn't the perfect second-year Melbourne University law student that he expected, and Sav in fact had an ever-growing dependency on the same illicit drugs his father peddled around Carlton, Fitzroy and Collingwood – due to Mickey's generosity – then Mickey would be dead and not even buried. He would never make it to the Melbourne General in Cemetery Road. The five a.m. street sweeper would use Mickey as a speed hump in some dark, damp back alley. He calmed himself slightly with the thought that a few more months would see him set up beautifully, then he would be gone. Out of Carlton, out of

Melbourne, out of Victoria and out of Australia. The Seychelles or perhaps Trinidad and Tobago was looking good.

Tony turned into the Police Credit Co-Op building. His day brightened immediately when he saw Susie at her desk, talking to one of the many uniformed members who banked there. He loved the rock that she represented in his life, and at the same time hated the fact he took her for granted sometimes.

After waiting for the member to finish his business, Tony quietly stepped around behind Susie. As she got to her feet, Tony gently put his arm around her waist, forcing Susie to spin and face him.

Her look turned from indignation to love inside three seconds. 'Oh, it's you,' she said.

'It's Thursday. Pay day. Just come up to get some money out. I can't leave you with all these cashed-up coppers.'

Susie looked him right in the eye and shot back, 'They pay more attention to me than you do most times. Except for five minutes last night, I haven't seen you in days. Just remember, mate, I have as many "fizzes" around here as you do, and some of them happen to be barmaids at pubs – local ones. I'm hearing stories about you and they're not funny anymore. Tony, we have to talk… and soon.'

Tony knew for sure he had to get his act together and his life sorted out. And that he could only do this with Susie's help. Looking at her made his heart still jump like it did when he first met her.

'You're right, we have to talk. I'm booking Dominic's for tonight. I'll pick you up at seven-thirty, okay?'

'All right,' she said, 'but only one glass of red. I'm worried about you.'

'You don't have to anymore. Phil Stone had a one-way conversation with me today. All downhill and aimed at my little house in the valley. I know what I've got to do. See you at seven-thirty.'

Rounding the desk, Tony winked at Susie, then he walked out onto the pavement. He felt better in himself now that he had made up his mind.

He didn't even look at Benny or Mickey as he strode lightly past the café.

'Who's in there that he knows?' asked Benny, noticing his nephew's smile and light step.

'His girlfriend, Susie Doherty, is the manager in there. I enjoy keeping tabs on any cop's squeeze,' said Mickey slowly, as a safety net was woven like a web inside his spidery mind.

Chapter Six

For the first time in months, Tony woke up feeling alive. He peered out from under the doona and realised his mouth didn't taste like the bottom of a bird cage, which had become a custom of late. He touched Susie's dark hair and felt her stir slightly. The double bed was in a mess and he warmed to the fact that it had nothing to do with the screaming, sweat-soaked nightmares he had been having about burning cars and screaming people. Knowing that he had just gone through one night without getting up and dry retching was a beautiful feeling.

He had explained everything to Susie at Dominic's the night before. The accident, the feelings, the nightmares, the drinking. She held his hand as he went through every little gut-wrenching detail. She knew most of it. The accident months before was common knowledge around Carlton. She coaxed him through every word as they sat there at the red-and-white checked table on the footpath of the famous Lygon Street institution.

Dom Santino had known Tony and Susie for years, along with Tony's mother Sophia, and he considered them all to be as much a part of his family as his wife Maria and his three beautiful daughters. Dom waved the waiters away from them all night, since he knew it was time Tony poured out his feelings. Things were going well because, for the first time in many months, Tony wasn't calling for another drink.

Dom had been through many after-shift visits from Tony. The Santino Bistro was home to many a party and celebration of the boys in blue at Carlton. Weddings, births, promotions. Dom knew everything that happened in Carlton and never let anything that was said or done in his restaurant past him. Recently though, Tony's visits had nearly finished off his supply of bourbon. Dom had driven him home after every session and checked on him the next morning. Tony was family. End of story.

Susie had insisted on only one glass of Chianti each, and Dom noticed Tony hadn't even touched his. He was pleased and made sure there were empty tables next to them, giving them some space and peace. Losing money by sending customers next door to his old friend Bernardi was irrelevant. The favour would be returned tenfold over time. That was the Italian way in Lygon Street. It was a cold July night and Dom had the overhead heater going. So as far as he was concerned, the restaurant would stay open for as long as his young friends talked.

Towards midnight, Susie and Tony stood and held hands. Dom watched as Tony slipped a small diamond ring onto Susie's left hand, then kissed her gently.

'I don't know if a beautiful name like Susie goes with Signorotto,' Tony said, with a smile. 'Would you like to give it a try?'

Susie could only manage a slight nod as her eyes filled with tears.

Dom rushed to embrace them. 'You will have the reception here,' Dom gushed, in his heavy Italian accent. 'No arguments. You are family. This will be my present to you both.'

'I've got to get him to the altar first, Dom,' said Susie, fixing Tony with a look of absolute love.

Dom waved a pudgy right index finger in Tony's face. 'Listen, Mr Policeman,' he said, with a wink, 'you do the right thing by Susie or I will give you a personal tour of the kitchen, eh?'

'No complaints from me,' Tony said, putting his hands in the air in mock surrender.

Susie looked on with puzzled amusement at Dom's comment.

Dom embraced Tony, lifting him off the ground and squeezing the air from Tony's lungs.

Dom was on a roll. 'Of course, Gina, Rosa and Silvana will be your bridesmaids, eh, Susie?'

Tears rolled down Susie's face, smudging the make-up she had so carefully applied for this dinner. She nodded her head *pronto* and gave Dom a big kiss on both fat rosy cheeks of his happy Italian face.

Dom turned a bright shade of red and laughed.

Susie and Tony said their goodbyes and walked slowly hand-in-hand down the wet footpath as the evening mist engulfed them, until they were out of sight past the yellow streetlights.

Dom turned to see his two white-aproned waiters who were standing by the front door smiling. 'What am I paying you for, eh? Get this place ready for tomorrow's lunch!' He pushed both waiters inside, grabbing them by their shoulders and hugging them to his big barrel chest.

A little later, the rain became heavier as Dom looked out the front window while locking up. He hoped and prayed this was not a bad omen for the pair. His body gave a slight shiver as he remembered his dear, departed mother saying this feeling was like 'Someone walking over your grave.'

Chapter Seven

Jill Norton stared at the figure standing in the doorway of the watch-house. Nothing surprised her anymore. After all, working at the Carlton Police Station for twenty-five years left little room for surprises.

Not that she was a cynic as such. It was just that as a uniformed Senior Constable there was virtually nothing she hadn't seen or done over this time. Everything from taking reports for a missing bicycle to trying to hold together the pieces of skull and brain that remained of the shattered head of a fellow officer when a drug-crazed, hallucinating heroin addict had pulled the trigger after a simple 'pat-down' for weapons had gone so horribly wrong some years ago, when Norton was younger and 'on the road'.

No, nothing surprised Jill anymore, but her work still fascinated her. That's why she dreaded the thought of retirement and digging in the garden, knitting or watching her grandchildren grow up. Not that she didn't adore her grandkids, but after thirty years in 'The Job', retirement would be like going cold turkey.

It stood there. Reflective Oakley sunglasses pushed up on top of the spiked and gelled hair. Uniform so new that you could cut your hands on the creases. Neat as a new pin. Boots so spit-polished the wearer could look down and see his pearly white teeth in the reflection. The

Guardian-of-the-Free-World had arrived in all his glory. The only thing missing was the red cloak with the big 'S' on it.

Jill said nothing as the vision in blue strode to the counter like a uniformed John Wayne and moved in next to a young, bespectacled university student who was reporting the theft of his laptop from his rusted-out Volkswagen. He had left it – possibly, most likely, almost certainly – unlocked in a clearway in Johnston Street that morning. Damn lucky he still had the car!

Normally, Jill would have chewed this dumb-arse to pieces and let him wander out into the sunshine with a ticket in each hand – one for parking in the clearway, the other for dumping rubbish, namely, the Volkswagen. But not this time. This time she played it with a straight bat. She wasn't about to let her guard down in front of Supercop.

Writing down the details of the incident, Jill couldn't get over the never-ending naivety of the average punter who walked through the door, expecting their missing property, husband, wife or child to be waiting for them all safe and warm in the bosom of the law.

'Was the property insured, dear?' she said, dripping with sarcasm as she leant her ample figure on the watch-house counter. She gave the scrawny youth a motherly but stern look over the top of the steel-rimmed glasses perched on her nose.

'Nuh, I couldn't afford that,' Uni-Lad replied.

'Not insured, not locked and in a clearway,' Jill continued. 'Not exactly off to a flying start, are we?'

'You *will* find it? You *will* send some detectives out looking for it, won't you? After all, I pay my taxes. It's got my whole four years' work on it. My thesis. Everything.'

'What are you studying?' asked Jill, thinking it must be a Masters in Stupidity, but withheld her acid-tongued comment.

'Politics and Law,' Uni-Lad said.

Right again, thought Norton looking at one of the country's future leaders. 'Not a problem, son. I'll give the Police Air Wing a ring right now to see if they can have a good look at the area with their three-million-dollar up-close camera lens. If the perpetrator of this crime is out in there with your laptop open they'll be able to read your thesis from two thousand feet. Leave it with me.'

Uni-Lad left with a spring in his step, musing that he really should not entertain bad thoughts about the police just because one of them tried to choke the living shit out of him while demonstrating outside the World Economic Forum on globalisation a couple of years ago.

Screwing up Uni-Lad's report and throwing it into the 'round filing cabinet' in the corner of the watch-house, Jill shifted her gaze to the pristine, blue-uniformed, world-saving apparition who had recently materialised in front of her. 'You lost or something? The ones in uniform stand on this side.'

'I'm stationed here,' came the reply. 'Name's Tyler. Max Tyler.'

Jill Norton turned slowly, lifting the station roster off the bent wire coathanger by her side, then slowly scrolled a finger down the thirty-three names until she got to the very bottom of the list. 'Ah, yes, here we are. Probationary Constable Maxwell Tyler. Sorry it took me so long to find it, but it's down the bottom, you see. Just one above the cleaner's name.'

Tyler glared at Norton. 'It's Max, not Maxwell,' he huffed. 'Am I driving a car or van this morning?'

'Driving? Let's not worry about big boys' toys like police cars and flashing lights and sirens just yet, sonny. Plenty of time to get your jollies later. Don't get your ambitions mixed up with your capabilities. First things first. Go find yourself a clothes locker in the back room, then get upstairs. Inspector Stone is waiting to speak to you.'

Tyler had his own agenda. 'I'll see him later. I have a few things to do first. Where's the car park?' He gestured out the watch-house window at his car parked in the station driveway.

Pointing her right index finger directly at Tyler's face, Jill Norton said, 'No, Mr Maxwell, err, Max Tyler. Listen clearly. What you are hearing is me telling you for the second and last time to get your arse upstairs ASAP, *after* moving your bloody car out of the driveway!'

Tyler's words failed him.

Jill continued. 'Park it in the street like everybody else does. If it's good enough for the Inspector to park out there in the street, I can assure you it will be good enough for you. Or would you like me to do it for you? No, don't say 'yes' to that, because I'll park it right in the middle of the nearest intersection and leave it with the motor running and the doors open. By the time you get to it, every low-life cockroach out there will have dissected your little Dinky toy right down to its chromed wheel nuts. Do you understand me?'

Tyler stood there, his face turning angrier than an undertaker's at a health seminar.

Jill calmly stared out the window at the lowered Nissan sports car in the driveway, blocking in the patrol car. Thank God it was yellow and not black, her mind shooting back to Tony Signorotto's chase. She obviously had to make herself even clearer. 'Another good reason to get *that* out of *there* is because when the court next door breaks for lunch, the boys from the Traffic Branch will be all over your heap of crap like a swarm of flies. They won't have had a booking all morning and will be getting withdrawal symptoms. Even I can see that thing is as roadworthy as a wheelie bin. Move it now!'

Max's eyes bored into Jill's, but were met with an unblinking stare from someone who had met his kind so many times before – and couldn't be out-stared.

Jill could see the young probationary constable was taking an instant disliking to her. Water off a duck's back. If the kid didn't want to follow instructions now, how would he go on the street when he was back-to-back with his partner against some of the scum that the legal system let out of the sewers and cages these days?

Watching him slowly swagger in the direction of the front door, Norton suddenly heard Queen's classic anthem *We Are the Champions* blare from Tyler's mobile phone.

'Don't answer that,' Norton barked, as Tyler reached for his phone. 'Two things to remember here, Mr Tyler. The first is that members don't carry private mobiles in the station and if, for some unfortunate reason, I hear one ring in my watch-house, then I'd better not hear a ring-tone that makes the member sound like the bloody King of Moomba. The Academy is fiction. Carlton is fact. Do you get my drift, Probationary Constable?'

Max Tyler begrudgingly nodded.

But Norton wouldn't let up. 'This is not that dozy place where you were tucked into bed every night by some warm and fuzzy law instructor whispering sweet nothings in your little, pink, shell-like ear.

This is the Carlton Police Station, so forget all the crap you learnt at 'Hyatt-on-the-Hill', and hope like hell you can get through your first week on night shift without being spat at, jabbed with an HIV-infected needle, or told you are the sole cause of every psycho's problems that you find wandering the streets under a full moon.'

Max opened his mouth.

But Jill held her hand directly in front of his face. 'Do not reply. You are here to learn, not teach. Let's get off on the right foot, young Max. When someone or, in your case, *anyone* here says 'jump', you don't ask 'when', you just ask 'how high?' Right now you stand up when Veronica, the Inspector's Secretary, walks in or speaks to you, savvy? Do you have something you wish clarified now?'

Max opened his mouth to speak once more, but realised saying nothing would be the best and safest path to go down with this dinosaur.

'Oh, by the way,' Jill continued, 'tomorrow, according to the roster, you are my assistant watch-house keeper. When you walk in here in the morning, we will start afresh without your "mate" with you.'

Max asked, in a very quiet and subdued voice, 'What mate?'

'Your mate called "Attitude", young Max. Be here at 0700 hours, in uniform and ready to work. Not 0701 hours. When you walk in you will smile as you place my coffee, black with two sugars, gently on the desk next to the picture of my adorable grandchildren. Place the open sports section of the *Herald Sun* newspaper next to said coffee and await further instructions. Do not let me see you enter here with a copy of *The Age* or *The Australian* either. This is a workplace. Now that we understand each other, I hope your day improves when you go upstairs to see Inspector Stone. We do understand each other, Max, don't we? After all, we are in this job as a team.'

Norton put her right hand out to shake the hand of the now suitably chastened Tyler. 'Remember the saying, Max: "There is no 'I' in team".'

Tentatively, Max Tyler shook her hand without a word.

'Come on, son. Move your car now, there's a good boy.'

The stuffing in Max Tyler's ego had been knocked out faster than a phone-book interview in the back room of the City Watch-House.

Max went outside and lowered himself into his low-slung carriage parked in front of the patrol car, where two Senior Constables were now standing and shaking their heads.

'Another one so far up himself he walks on tippy-toes,' the older one said. He ground the butt of his cigarette into the gravel of the driveway, before climbing behind the wheel. He smiled at Jill Norton through the window, then drove out to continue the never-ending fight against the tide of crime. It was a rat race out there and the rats were winning. Today, anyway.

Jill walked slowly back behind the watch-house counter, thinking she should have a quiet word with Tony about his new partner. If the kid had thought she was a bit rough on him, God help him if he crossed Sergeant Tony Signorotto on a bad day.

Chapter Eight

Tony was sitting in the mess room, with a coffee cup raised to his lips, when he heard the phone ring. Others around him were in various stages of eating. A car crew was gulping doughnuts and swilling down mugs of Nescafé in an attempt at some sort of world record for speed eating, but this was the norm when you had between ten and fifteen jobs still waiting.

The least important this morning was the report of two young thugs vandalising the Commission flats up in Princes Street. The number-one job to attend to at the moment was a communication report via the station hot-phone of a drug deal going down in Canning Street, where the perpetrator had decided to use his flick-knife to carve a reminder into the face of some scum-bag dope dealer that it was a bad thing to sell drugs in that area – to anyone else but the perp. Rats always devoured their own flesh.

As the car crew dashed out of the mess room with the remnants of two Krispy Kreme doughnuts smeared around their faces, Tony picked up the hot-phone's receiver, listened for about five seconds, then replied, 'On the way, Boss.'

It was time to show this place that Sergeant Tony Signorotto was still a force to be reckoned with.

He had wanted to keep his engagement to Susie quiet, but Dom had spread the word from Lygon Street to the Carlton Football Ground. Every little old Italian grandmother who knew Tony's mum had dropped into the station and the Police Co-Op to wish himself and Susie all the best... and to give them their recipes for everything Italian – from the old grappa wine to the best way of making Italian ciabatta. His mother had been inundated with callers and was over the moon with the news that her little boy was getting married. Tony realised he owed it to people like Susie and Phil Stone to get his act together and keep off the booze. The question was whether his nerves could handle any big job that he was given.

Tony took a deep breath, bounded up the stairs two at a time, turned left and strode down the mouldy, musty-smelling, plaster-chipped corridor that led to the Inspector's office.

His old friend Phil Stone was trying to grapple with a mound of paperwork that a Flemington steeplechaser couldn't jump over. Gold-framed reading glasses were perched perilously on the end of Phil's nose when Tony knocked on the door. Tony couldn't abide the present-day attitude of some junior members who walked into the office of a superior without knocking. Too many things were changing in this job and tradition seemed to be going out the window. Knocking was a sign of respect for the rank of officer. It didn't mean you had to respect the individual, just the rank. In this case, though, it was definitely the person who earned the respect.

Tony did not go any farther until he saw the smile on Phil's face and the beckoning hand. Phil was performing a brilliant juggling act just keeping all the files on his desk.

'You should be in Circus Oz, Phil,' Tony said, as he peered back out the office door, checking that some pimple-faced kid hadn't heard him call the Inspector by his first name.

'Mate, as long as the out-pile is slightly higher than the in-pile, then I know I'm winning the Battle of the Shovel.' Phil gestured for Tony to take one of two seats on the other side of the 'mahogany foxhole', as he called his desk.

'Okay, where's Superboy?' Tony asked, as he peered under the desk and behind the filing cabinet.

'On his way up,' Phil said, with the hint of a smile. 'Apparently, Jill had to ask him to remove his chariot from the driveway.'

'From the driveway! What is it with these cowboys we're getting from the Academy? You'd reckon they'd knock the stuffing out of them before they hit the real world. Bloody hell, Phil, when we went through the Academy you just did what you were told. Now they seem to think it's some sort of place where everyone has *rights*. God almighty, if they want to be coppers, let them take the heat in the kitchen.'

'Spoken like a true dinosaur, Tony. Stop getting yourself all worked up. He's probably a quietly spoken young lad who just needs a person like you to guide him on the path to righteousness.'

Phil and Tony locked eyes and grinned just as a figure stepped into the room, without knocking.

'You wanted to see me?' asked Max Tyler, as he settled himself into the second chair in front of the Inspector's desk.

Silence engulfed the office.

Phil beat Tony to the opening punch by a millisecond. 'Son. Stand up, turn around and go back out that door you just barged through.

When you've done that, turn around again and stand to attention after, and only *after*, you have gently rapped the knuckles of your right hand three times on the door. When I decide to answer, it will be after you have announced yourself by your name and rank in a dulcet tone, so as not to upset this shuddering pile of reports you can see in front of you.'

Tyler shot upwards like he'd been bitten by a red-back spider, bolted back out the door, tripping on the carpet runner that went under Phil Stone's desk. The slight jarring effect caused a tremble through the paperwork mountain, and before Phil or Tony could perform a Shane Warne-like slips catch, three-quarters of the mound slid gracefully onto the linoleum floor, splaying over the entry area.

'There's your first job, son,' Tony said, holding his hand over his mouth while hiding the smirk spreading across his face. If this had happened a couple of days ago, he would have been a gibbering mess and breaking into a sweat. Tony hadn't realised how long it had been since his sense of humour had departed him.

Max Tyler followed instructions and knocked gently three times.

Stone slowly removed his glasses, placed them where the paperwork mountain had recently been, then looked at Tyler. 'Let's get off on the right foot, shall we, constable? What's your name? Is it Tyler? Because if it is, I've heard of you already. Burning your bridges downstairs with senior members and now continuing the tradition up here. Speak up.'

'Yes, Tyler, sir. Constable Max Tyler.'

Bending down, Tony picked up various files and tried to put them back into some sort of order, at the same time as attempting to hide his tears.

'Well, Max. Welcome to Carlton. I'm Inspector Stone and this is Sergeant Signorotto. What are your ambitions in the job?'

'Just want to catch as many crooks as I can. After I prove myself it will be straight up the promotion ladder, I'd say. I want to end up at headquarters, shaping this job.' Tyler surveyed the overcrowded office with its shabby furniture and an Inspector who to him looked as tired as a wet napkin. Quickly glancing down at the Sergeant picking up the files, he added, 'I don't want to grovel in paperwork for the rest of my career.'

Looking up, Tony caught a slight sneer on Tyler's face.

The constable's head snapped around as Phil Stone addressed him. 'Son, I've got important things to do today and one of them isn't listening to a probationary constable who has an ego problem. If you're as good as you think, Sergeant Signorotto here – who, by the way, has caught more crooks than you've had hot dinners – and myself can gratefully pack up and go home knowing that we've left the station and the inhabitants of Carlton in such capable and experienced hands. I'm sure we will all sleep well tonight knowing you are the captain of the ship.'

Tyler wasn't sure if he should nod or not.

Phil had built up a head of steam. 'I would suggest you eat humble pie and try to learn from people like the Sergeant and Senior Constable Norton. If you finish your probationary period here in three months and have picked up half of one percent of what they know, you will have gone a long way to surviving in a job where the only way to survive is teamwork. Together everyone achieves more. T.E.A.M.

Ever heard the expression, Maxwell?'

Tyler nodded.

'Sergeant Signorotto will be looking after you for the next few months. He will take you downstairs and show you the ropes. A suggestion, son. Think of your mind as a parachute. It will only work if it's open. Understand?'

Max Tyler's face turned white as he stood there being dressed down by the Inspector.

Phil and Tony could feel the bad vibes coming from him as he nodded again, turned around and headed out the door.

Tony called to Max to wait outside the office. Tony smiled and mouthed to Phil, 'Thanks, mate!'

Tony caught up with the new member in the hallway.

Before Tony could speak, Max did. 'What's up his arse? Should be retired.'

The big Sergeant, who was walking slightly behind Max, reached out and yanked him backwards. Tony spun Max around and slammed him against the wall, causing paint chips to flutter down onto the constable's spit-polished boots. Placing his face about two inches from Max's, Tony hissed, 'Three things, constable. Don't ever speak about an officer like that in my presence and, secondly, don't ever speak about one who is also a life-long personal friend, understand?' Tony gradually let go and walked away as Max blinked rapidly.

'You said three things. What was the third?'

'I was going to say "welcome aboard", but I think you're captaining the *Titanic* at the moment, son, and I'm not going to sink with you.'

Tony walked away, leaving Max Tyler standing there looking at his watch realising it was a long time till the end of his shift – but in reality a short time until he brought coffee to Jill Norton tomorrow morning.

Chapter Nine

An evil smile spread across the face of Mickey Midolini as he dialled Sav's number.

It wasn't that he *had* to ring him. It was done out of habit. A habit of checking up on people. He wanted to keep the carrot dangling in front of his drug mules, so their twitching bodies would always crave the drugs he so readily supplied in between his regular payments-in-kind. The cravings bought obedience.

Sav answered with a croaking, 'Who's this?' There was desperation in his strung-out voice.

Mickey used different mobile numbers to contact his couriers. He disposed of them as regularly as others would a packet of tissues. The supply never ran out due to a drug-fuelled Telstra employee who traded SIM cards with him for coke, like he was swapping football cards. 'Sav, my boy. It's your main man, Mickey M.'

'Mickey, Mickey, we gotta meet.'

'You don't sound too well, young Sav. A bit strung out?' Mickey's fat little face smiled knowingly as he toyed with Sav from behind the wheel of his 300 SL Mercedes in a back alley in Collingwood. He had just finished a nice little earner with a fellow dealer from Reservoir, pocketing $10,000 folding for himself. Mickey secreted it next to his nine-millimetre Beretta pistol in the console.

'Mickey, I need it bad, man. I got exams tomorrow and I need it bad. Not much, just a little. Just to get me through, okay, man?'

'Sav, calm down, my boy. Nothing but the best for Benny's son. You know how I've looked after you. But like always, it's gotta stay just between you and me, understand?'

Sweat dripped into the Nokia that Sav was holding. 'No problem. No problem. Where and when. Make it soon, man. Please, make it soon. How about Franky's in Drummond Street. Fifteen. Okay?'

'Sav, Sav, I've told you before. Not around where I do business. You know the rules. Up at the uni café off Swanston Street in one hour. I've got some class A for you and your friends. Go and have a cold shower and calm down. I'll be there. Don't worry about the exams. You'll get through. All you need is a little bit of the goodness I'm bringing you. See you in an hour.'

Mickey flipped his phone closed, sat in his car and thought about the present situation. He had been skimming very small amounts of pure-grade heroin from various shipments that Benny Illarietti's organisations had been importing for some time now. He was forty-five years old and although he had worked for Benito 'Benny' Illarietti for twenty years, he had decided enough was enough. Benny had treated him well up till about two years ago. But now the organisation was expanding, Mickey wanted a bigger share of it. However, Benny had started to deal with families from interstate, and he just wanted Mickey as a distributor at a local level. Benny wouldn't consider giving Mickey any opportunities for expansion or more money. Benny reasoned that Mickey should be grateful to be a lieutenant.

Mickey had taken a lot of heat and chances over time for Benny, both with associates and police. These days he couldn't think of the word 'police' without reminding himself of that stinking Tony Signorotto. He wanted to kill him after Tony made him give up those names of the Coburg Boys. It wasn't that he cared about them. It was the fact that when Tony had taken them down on distribution charges, it left him out of pocket because he had been skimming to them. Now they were all doing time, he had to take more chances and set up sales to others. He didn't want to trade to outside people he couldn't control, so it had to be through someone he knew and could manipulate.

Mickey saw his opportunity the night he had made a drop to a gay nightclub in Russell Street, and spotted a young Sav locked groin-to-groin in a passionate tongue-kissing embrace with another young male, whom Mickey knew to be an addict. Mickey had a deliciously evil mind when it came to storing thoughts of self-preservation… and revenge.

He started his black Mercedes, drove slowly up Alexandra Avenue through North Fitzroy, turning left into Swanston Street, then parked in a half-hour zone. He would be back in plenty of time to avoid a parking ticket, or any unwanted attention from the local demons, because he had no intention of doing anything else but conducting his own rapid-fire business. The last thing he wanted was a search of his car.

Sitting at an outside table of the grotty university café, Mickey looked completely out of place in his Dolce & Gabbana sunglasses, Versace suit and yellow pure-silk tie. He watched the passing parade of youth. Most men of his background would have been looking at only one thing – the young female students. They were either wearing jeans painted on so tight that little was left to the imagination, or skirts so small they reminded him that most well-dressed Australians of Italian descent, like himself, sported bigger handkerchiefs in the breast pockets of their suits. Sleazy thoughts were put out of his mind as he concentrated on the business of the day. Drugs and money.

He recognised Sav long before Sav saw him. The kid was just holding it together as he twitched and shuffled his way towards the café. Mickey had seen him leave a couple of his young friends over near the law building. They were now looking anxiously towards where Mickey was sitting. It really was pathetic to see not only how Sav looked some days, but also the desperation on the faces of his friends. It was just as well that Sav lived in daddy's paid-for flat in Williamstown and only saw his parents about every two weeks. Benny had commented to Mickey recently that Sav was looking very pale and ill because of upcoming exams. If only Benny knew the apple of his eye was floating on a few lines of coke or a small hit from Mickey's stash of heroin to get him through family visits. Benny would go on and on about the day that Sav would graduate with his medical degree and make him proud.

When Sav heard the word 'coke' these days, he automatically thought 'a line of', not 'a can of'.

However, Mickey was worried. Even though Sav had worked up a good client list among his uni friends, it was becoming too obvious that Sav was fraying at the edges from sampling his own wares. A couple more months and Mickey would have over one million dollars stashed away in his Cayman Islands account, even after putting the deposit on his beach-front house in the beautiful tax-free haven of the

Bahamas.

You should have let me run the business, Benny. You're going to suffer soon, my friend. Where it will hurt you most – in your happy Italian family.

Chapter Ten

Sav collapsed into the chair opposite his supplier, spilling several medical textbooks onto the tomato-sauce-stained wooden table. Mickey stared at Sav's pushed-up dirty sleeves. The puncture marks on the inside of both arms were becoming glaringly obvious. Mickey realised he'd better accelerate his last few deliveries to Sav.

Not only did Mickey have Sav selling to his fellow students, but also delivering to some wealthy clients in the affluent suburb of Toorak. One of those deliveries was scheduled for tomorrow night and it was worth a lot of money towards Mickey's overseas retirement plan.

'I've got the cash,' Sav said. He nervously glanced over his shoulder at two skinny males and one anaemic-looking girl skulking in the shadows of the beautiful sandstone edifice of the Law building.

'Business as usual, then,' Mickey said.

Sav slid the envelope out of the medical journal nearest to him.

Mickey thought of the irony when he looked at the magazine. It was titled, *Modern Day Wonder Drugs and the Effects on The Nervous System*. Mickey gazed at the sheen of sweat covering Sav's pale face, and thought, *Nothing wrong with my nervous system.*

Within seconds, three plastic packets of pure -grade Hong Kong horse were surreptitiously slipped into a large pencil case that Sav pushed anxiously across the table.

'Only use the small one,' Mickey said. 'It will get you through the exam and tomorrow night's delivery to Toorak. I'm feeling generous today.' He eyed the pencil case. 'You be generous with your friends, too. After all, they're paying good money.' *More friends, more customers.*

Mickey never told Sav who the Toorak client was for obvious reasons. Never let a junkie know more than is good for him. If he gets caught, he can't cough up what he doesn't know. He was always told to drop the package in a pre-arranged place then vanish.

This delivery was going to a County Court judge, whom Mickey knew not only had a penchant for his high-priced commodity, but also for nocturnal visits from under-age schoolgirls from a very prestigious private boarding college for young ladies in the same suburb. These young ladies were supposed to be tucked up in bed by ten, but it was rarely their own beds they were tucked into.

Mickey could arrange anything at a price. His memory bank was filling up nicely with some very influential names from the world of law and academia.

By clutching the pencil case, Sav appeared to calm himself. 'In the car as usual?'

Mickey gave a thin smile. 'It will be under the driver's seat when you get to it, after your exam tomorrow. Not before, understand?'

'Yeah, yeah. What I've got here will do for a couple of days.'

Mickey knew Sav was in a no-win situation when it came to the delivery. He had to play for two reasons. He needed the free hits that he was being supplied with. He couldn't afford to keep paying cash at the rate his habit was escalating, even on the very generous allowance his father was putting into his bank account each week. Finding out about his heroin habit would just about put the old man in his grave, but not nearly as quickly as finding out his prize student son was gay. Sav would have more than his allowance cut off if that happened. Benny Illarietti would not survive as a mafia Don if word got around that his son was not only as camp as a row of pink tents, but also addicted to the city's dangerous gay and lesbian nightlife sex scene as much as, if not more than, his craving for illicit drugs. Both parts of his lifestyle were being lived on the very sharp knife edge of survival.

'Haven't changed cars this month, have you?' said Mickey, referring more to Benny's inclination for giving his only son whatever he wanted, when he wanted it. *Oh, if he only knew what he really liked.*

'No. Same wheels,' replied Sav, referring to his Audi R8 4.2 litre Sports rocket that was sitting in the undercover Wilson car park across the other side of Swanston Street.

Mickey knew Benny would give Sav anything he wanted. But the only thing he would ultimately get in return would be grief. 'Deliver it between nine and nine-thirty and don't make it obvious. You know the address. Park around the corner, drop the package and go home. When you get back to your flat, there will be a friend waiting for you. I'm sure you will enjoy each other's company for the night. I've told him all about your desires. He's met you before at the Hellfire Club and thinks you're hot.'

Sav shot back a desperate glare.

Mickey gave him a knowing look and wink. 'I might even leave a little package with him for you to share. You can snort, lick and suck the night away to your heart's content.' Mickey dropped his smile. 'This is an important delivery. What's the number again?'

'Nineteen, one-nine, Power Street.'

'*Twenty-four* Power Street, you idiot!'

Mickey had to calm himself for a moment. 'Remember. Do not stuff this up, Sav. I don't want to be the one to show those photos of you and your boyfriend to your father.' Mickey was referring to a set of photos he had arranged to be taken very late one night in the Kevin Bartlett Reserve off the Richmond Boulevard. They were of Sav and a male prostitute naked in the back of his car with a couple of grams of coke, two hard-ons and a ton of lust happening between them. Mickey had only given Sav the copies so as to keep him dangling on the hook.

Sav staggered unsteadily to his feet, staring at Mickey through glazed, bloodshot eyes.

Mickey knew he had Sav trapped. Every way he turned, he had Sav by the balls. Resistance was useless. Mickey was wise to the fact that Sav was weak-willed and couldn't live without his addictions. Could he keep living with them, though? That was the question.

Mickey turned his reptilian-like face away as Sav shuffled slowly towards his nervous, fidgeting friends who proceeded to pounce on him like vultures. Mickey watched as they moved towards various toilet blocks to puncture their veins once more with the substance that would have them soaring skywards for a fleeting time, then just as quickly plunge them into a living, screaming hell. Satisfied customers. *Dumb fucks.*

Mickey smoothed his tie, flashing his right hand covered with gold and diamond rings. He stood, adjusted his coat, then walked quickly away from the university grounds towards the more familiar streets of Carlton.

He wondered idly what time the sun set in the Bahamas.

Chapter Eleven

Sav walked out of the Medicine Faculty building in a daze. He had just completed the mid-year physiology exam for second-year Medicine.

No, he hadn't. He hadn't completed it at all, and the thought of another failure was sitting on his shoulders like an evil gargoyle. After writing non-coherent answers to part of the paper, he had become more depressed by the minute. So much time to look around. So much time and so few answers. He could see two things specifically. The first was the large group of same-year students seated around him with their heads down writing furiously. The second was the reddened, scar-covered tracks on the insides of his forearms. His fellow students were on one track, but he was definitely on another.

Recently, Sav had been injecting into his groin and under his toenails, because he could no longer raise a vein on his skinny arms. Despite finding a way to 'prep' himself for this exam, he began to realise the hit, courtesy of Mickey, had worn off quicker than expected. Sav couldn't write another word, he could only hang out for the finish time.

One of the examiners asked him if he was cold, because he noticed Sav shaking continuously. There was no way he could concentrate on the paper, and he realised his university days would soon be over. It wasn't the first exam Sav had failed or walked out on, and he knew he couldn't hide the results much longer from his father, Benny.

Outside, Sav immediately lit a cigarette, inhaling so deeply that the cylinder of tobacco collapsed with the first desperate drag. It was four-thirty and he knew he couldn't go to his car before five.

Instead, Sav headed towards a nearby vending machine, inserted some coins and grabbed an ice-cold cylinder of Red Bull. Ripping off the top, he fumbled in his jeans pocket and pulled out an assortment of silver foil packets containing a potpourri of tablets and capsules he had acquired via various falsified prescriptions from the university chemist. They tried to be straight at the chemist, but if they called the police every time a false prescription was handed over, they would have to put beds in for the cops.

Sav desperately wanted to get zoned-out before he met his present tonight, so he dropped a combo of bullets into the can and swirled them around. Thorazine, Librium and Benadryl. Should do nicely to help him forget another failure… and his future.

Sav would grab a few winks in his car, do the drop, then get back to his flat. That was the plan at this stage, but if life took another turn, so be it. Not one of his plans was really working too well these days. His head was aching and all he wanted to do was sleep.

After gulping down the cocktail hit, Sav meandered up Tin Alley, down Swanston Street, past the university's security office, and across to the Wilson car park.

Thank God cars had remote opening devices these days. Sav was in no condition to put a key in the door.

Climbing in, he tried to focus on his watch. It looked like five-fifteen. Sav put his head down between his legs, and could see the small box just behind the seat adjuster. *Good, all set.*

First thing first, though. Sav sat back up and reclined his seat, so he could have a quick nap. Just enough to freshen him up before the drop…

Chapter Twelve

Sav's face slid off the headrest, falling between the sports racing seats. Gazing stupidly at the floor of the car, he realised it was dark. Very dark.

'Christ,' his dry throat tried to scream. *What time is it?* Spinning around, his head erupted in a pain-filled, kaleidoscopic light show as the fluorescent bars of the car park whirled before his eyes. Sav moved his hand back and forward in front of red-raw eyes whose lashes were glued partly together from the drug cocktail and its side effects.

The luminous hands on his $10,000 Bulova chronograph shone back at him like two pointers from the lighthouse of hell. *No, no, it couldn't be. It couldn't be nine-thirty! I couldn't have been out to it for that long, could I?*

His right hand fumbled for the ignition. *Where are the keys? Where, where? There they are on the floor. Quick, just go, go! Gotta get there. Mickey will fucking kill me for this.*

Sav's frazzled nerves shot his mind back to another time he had been late with a drop. He knew the kicking he had received the next night behind the Metro night club in Bourke Street had been arranged. Sav couldn't prove who arranged the assault, but it carried Mickey's trademarks. Sav had been kicked in the balls only twice, but the way it was done meant he not only had trouble standing straight for three days, he couldn't even take a piss without screaming out loud. As for performing with his friends, all the massaging in the world couldn't make him upstanding for a week.

The motor screamed as Sav approached the car park exit. The Pirelli tyres had left about 3,000 kilometres of rubber on the second-floor ramp as the Audi slid dangerously sideways towards the exit.

Screeching to a halt, with the bonnet under the boom, Sav spilled the contents of his wallet all over the floor as he searched for his car-parking card. Another gift from daddy. Swiping it downwards through the card reader, he sat there listening to his heart thumping through his chest while he waited anxiously. Nothing happened.

Fuck, fuck. Oh, Christ, Sav! Swipe it the other way. Done. Boom up.

Come on. Quick, for fuck's sake! Out of the car park. Which way? Left or right? Left through town? Right down Johnston Street? Think, think. Get to the South-eastern Freeway, that's it. How? Hoddle Street and Punt Road. Okay, go left, go left. Up to Victoria Parade, down to Hoddle Street and right into Punt Road. Under the silos and go like all fuck down to Toorak Road. Power Street is just up near Glenferrie Road, I think. I'm sure it is. I hope it is.

The thought process was fuzzy but just tracking. Sav was shaking feverishly, his head felt like two jackhammers were going full bore inside his skull, and he was as cold as a stripper with pneumonia. His own death mask danced before his watery eyes when the speedo hit eighty on the tram tracks… and it was the image of a grinning, slimy Mickey Midolini who was handing it to him!

Sav gulped dryly, hanging on with white knuckles to the veneered sports steering wheel, and accelerated faster than a Ferrari on heat.

Chapter Thirteen

Max stood in the backyard of the station and thought about the previous two weeks. He was glad to get out from under the nose of Jill Norton and her demanding ways of running the watch-house. He had never been so closely watched. However, he begrudgingly admitted to himself he had learned a fair few survival techniques.

Paperwork and more paperwork. Surprisingly, though, Jill was adept on a computer… for an old trout. Max had thought two weeks of straight day-shift would have been an absolute drag with nothing much to do, but he had never been so wrong. Jill called it the nerve centre of the station, and she was dead right. Everything happened or was spoken about in the watch-house. It was a bit like the kitchen at home. Everyone seemed to gravitate towards it, and Max realised very quickly that even members such as Inspector Stone had an underlying respect for Jill Norton and her crew who worked the front desk.

It had been quite a few years since the cells at the station were closed due to the twenty-first-century catchphrase of 'occupational health and safety issues'. So Max's duties consisted mainly of dealing with the public and their day-to-day problems, ranging from losing their glasses to the shabbily dressed derelict who appeared at the counter with a Bible in his hand. Looking back on that moment when Jill quietly pushed him towards Peter, as the Bible gent was apparently known to everyone but him, Max realised now it was part of the learning curve. The never-ending learning curve.

While Jill and another senior member quietly worked away in the background with reserved smiles on their faces, Max was at first spoken to and then quietly reeled in by Peter who, over the next forty-five minutes, not only proceeded to quote verses from the Bible to him, but put forward an almost-convincing case for the landing of aliens in the Exhibition Gardens later that day.

Max was totally speechless when, on hearing this piece of news, Jill handed him a set of car keys and told him to take a quick drive up to the gardens with Peter to check out the possible landing site. Max didn't know if he should protest or be overjoyed that he was actually being allowed to drive a patrol car for the first time. As he went out the door, Jill handed Max a twenty-dollar note, telling him to buy Peter and himself a couple of rolls for lunch.

Max didn't arrive back at the station until about sixty minutes later. After he had left Peter happily devouring two of Sammy's finest on a bench near the fountain outside the Exhibition Building.

Jill smiled when she saw Max hanging the car keys back in their place. 'How'd you go with Peter?'

'Okay, thanks, Jill. He seemed to know Sammy well. Don't know why. Doesn't look as though he has two coins to rub together. Funny thing. When I took him to the gardens, he seemed to lose interest in anything to do with aliens. I know he's a bit of a crackpot, so I didn't push it. I just let him sit and have his lunch. Bit of a local celeb, is he?'

'I didn't have a chance to say anything to you,' Jill said. 'He comes in about once a week. Lives rough all over Carlton. Tried to get him into accommodation, but he loves his freedom. Ex-Vietnam vet and is the proud holder of a DSM.'

'What's a DSM?'

'A DSM, son, is a Distinguished Service Medal. One of the highest awards you can get in the military. He was a lieutenant. Went out one day on patrol, took six young fellows and came back with four. Peter apparently saved the other four from being massacred. I checked him out through a mate of mine at Vet Affairs, and it's fair dinkum. The genuine article.'

'Geez, I thought he was just an old derro. By the way, do you want me to fix up the petty-cash entry for the twenty bucks?'

'No, Max. That was my shout. I send him up to Sammy's every week. I thought you should get to know some of the real heroes of this world. It is a pleasure to look after him. How was your lunch, by the way? Did you have it with him? He likes a bit of uniformed company.'

'Thanks, Jill, yeah, it was good. Yeah, I did eat with him.'

Jill raised her left hand in appreciation as she walked away to the other side of the watch-house.

Max cracked a smile and shook his head. *Maybe she's not such a hard-nosed fossil, after all.*

Max was jolted back into the present when Tony Signorotto's voice came out of nowhere. 'You kitted up and ready to go or would you like a little more time to daydream? Can I bring you a coffee or something? Cappuccino, maybe?'

Spinning around, Max saw the Sergeant leading the way outside to the section car in the driveway. Max hurried after him. Tony went directly to the driver's door and unlocked it. Max realised it would probably be a while before he got to sit behind the steering wheel on patrol.

This was the time Max had been really looking forward to, ever since he set foot inside the Academy. On patrol in a busy city. It sent a tingle up his spine as he settled himself into the passenger seat of the Ford sedan. Max adjusted his utility belt, which contained a nine-millimetre Smith & Wesson police and military pistol, can of capsicum spray, two-way portable radio, flick-baton and spare fifteen-round clip.

'Now, before I even start this beast,' Tony announced, 'I am going to run through a few basics with you, okay?'

Max tried not to let his eyes glaze over. *Here we go. He's going to blast me over something that I've said or done.*

Tony cleared his throat. 'First things first. This is an afternoon shift patrol of a busy area and it is your first time out. I expect you will be in fantasy land for the next few hours, because that's how I was on my first patrol. It'll be like first-time sex all over again. Hopefully, it will last a little longer, though,' he said, with a nudge and a wink.

No response.

Tony stared at the now red-faced constable. 'Don't tell me you've handled the butt of your gun at the Academy more times than a girl's?'

'No, Sarge. No. One of the chicks in my squad called me "Max to the Max",' he replied, with more bravado than conviction.

'Yeah, right,' Tony said, with even less conviction. 'Basically, I will either do everything or show you how to do things. On this shift I just want you to get used to being stared at by the public. Every time you get out of this car tonight you will feel like you are naked. You will be stared at harder than a twenty-five-dollar note.'

Max nodded, deep in thought.

'You will quickly realise that every time we pull up at a set of traffic lights, Joe Blow, driving whatever is next to us, will start his guilt trip: "No, I'm not on my mobile phone. Yes, I am wearing my seat belt. No, my girlfriend is only brushing food from my trousers. Yes, my fly is definitely zipped up." You will see a metamorphosis when he has been there for about fifteen seconds and we haven't taken any notice of him. He will turn and look at you like the superior tax-paying member of the public he thinks he is. He may even give you a condescending nod, which in motorist terms means that he is shit-scared of you. He hates being at the lights next to you, and desperately wants you to turn right and disappear up the exhaust pipe of some scumbag P-plate driver who deserves everything we can throw at him. He just wants go home to the 'burbs, watch the six o'clock news, have a beer with his missus, while she has a chardy, and later try the old horizontal foxtrot.'

Max allowed himself a small smile. *Horizontal foxtrot. What the fuck...?*

Tony wasn't finished yet. 'There are two things I want you to do. The first is to ask questions all night long. Don't think that any of them will be stupid ones. They most likely will be, but I am paid to put up with that, and will answer all and sundry. Understand?'

Max nodded, but didn't speak.

'Secondly, whatever thing you want me to pull over – it can be a vehicle, pedestrian or low-flying aircraft – I will endeavour to. My only stipulation is that before we get out to speak to said occupants or hoof-dragging pedestrian, I want some indication of why you wanted them stopped in the first place. I'm not going to approach anyone who is sitting or standing there racking their tiny brain as to why we want them and just grin and say "Hi, citizen. Nice day, eh?" Give me some facts or something I can reel them in with. Doesn't have to be chapter and verse. And remember one thing when you're talking to the dark side: you slide further on bullshit than on anything else. Leave that to me, though.'

Max took all this in.

Tony tried to sound a little more upbeat. 'You've seen the bumper sticker, haven't you? It's the one that says "Get in, sit back, hang on and shut up!"'

Max's head nodded like it was spring loaded.

'Well, it is a bit like that except the "shut up" part. It's not you and me working this car, it is *us*. There is no such thing as Sergeant Signorotto and Constable Tyler tonight. It's just the call sign of the vehicle: Carlton 203. The radio operator will know there are two members on board, but will not differentiate between us. We are one. Just like you and your girlfriend when you get her into your flat. Okay, Max?'

Max looked at the burly Sergeant and realised his head was hurting from nodding. He had actually been spoken to like a fellow police officer by this Sergeant. The same Sergeant who had slammed him against a wall a couple of weeks ago. Finding his voice, Max said, 'Great Sarge. Thanks, Sarge.'

'All right, Max, my man, let the night's entertainment begin.'

Firing up the sedan, Tony nosed it out into Drummond Street and turned north into the asphalt jungle of the United Nations of Carlton.

Tony glanced across at his star-struck pupil. For Max this was clearly like first-time sex: very sweaty and a lot of heavy breathing.

Chapter Fourteen

Max was like a kid in a lolly shop. He was trying to suck it all in. Tony was treating him almost like an equal and had let him handle all the paperwork in the traffic bookings so far. Max was even thinking about leaning back in the passenger seat and placing his size-ten left boot on the dashboard, as he'd seen a lot of patrol members do.

'Don't even think about it,' Tony said, reading Max's mind without so much as a look in his direction. 'You put your boot on the dash and you'll scrub this car out with a toothbrush, understand?'

'How'd you know?' blurted the chastised young constable.

'When I tried that bit of showing-off twenty years ago, son, the next thing my boots hit was the pavement. For two weeks solid. You'll get bloody sick of handing out parking tickets in Lygon Street, mark my word.'

Cruising south down Drummond Street past the Exhibition Buildings, Tony continued. 'You can hang your arm out a bit, but be warned. Don't do it up around the university or you'll find some long-haired freak-show from the student union will go past your open window, probably on a stolen bike, throw in the leftovers from his Macca's, peel off into a side street and pedal like all fuck while you sit there with egg all over yourself, literally, and with everyone at the tram stop pissing themselves laughing at you. It's hard to look cool while you pick shredded lettuce off your Ray-Bans.'

'Oakleys, actually,' Max replied casually.

'Watch it,' came the terse reply.

Max thought about the window scenario and couldn't figure out if the Sergeant was pulling his leg or not. He glanced sideways. Not even a trace of humour on the driver's face. *Must be true.*

Pulling up at the traffic lights on Victoria Street, Max found himself looking up at the green light for the other vehicles, hoping for another traffic offence. They had already handed out two infringements for red lights tonight. He heard a car coming from the other direction at about warp-three speed and he knew, if the lights now turned to orange, whoever or whatever was low-flying towards them had no hope of stopping for the red light.

As the opposite lights turned yellow, there was still no sight of the rocket ship. He was about to speak when he saw Tony move his left hand to the toggle switch for the emergency lights. His heart skipped a beat and his mouth went dry. *A chase. Yes, you fucking beauty!*

The traffic light turned red as a yellow Audi screamed through the intersection, missing the change by a nanosecond, but enough for Tony to hit the black button on the control panel, unleashing the ear-piercing banshee wail of the electronic siren.

Tony threw the patrol car left into Victoria Street, forcing Max to push his hands into the roof lining to prevent himself from crashing sideways into Tony.

Max made a grab for the dash-mounted microphone with the intention of calling Police Communications. Trouble was, he didn't know what to say. He opened his mouth as he pressed the button, but no words came out. His mind was accelerating with the police car while Tony nearly tore out the auto transmission in pursuit.

Max sat there stupidly. Looking up, they flew across Nicholson Street, clearing the tram tracks as they weaved from one lane to another. The yellow Audi had gone hard, but was now jammed in the middle lane as it passed over Brunswick Street.

'Put the radio down,' Tony shouted, above the noise of the haemorrhaging motor.

Gravity forced Max backwards into his seat.

Suddenly, Tony knocked the radio handpiece flying onto the floor as he swerved the police Ford into the right lane, screaming up the right-hand side of the rocket ship. He saw that the driver's side of the Audi and his passenger side were only millimetres apart.

Tony exclaimed, 'Ah, shit! I bloody thought so.'

The Audi's driver had briefly glanced across at the police vehicle, and Max could see the terrified look in the driver's eyes as his face turned blue then red with the reflection of the emergency lights flashing in the night.

Suddenly both vehicles braked dramatically and the Audi was herded into the kerb just outside the Porsche dealership in Victoria Street. Tony had the police car positioned perfectly behind it as he grabbed the microphone, then flipped the switch over to the PA system. Tony's voice boomed out through the roof-mounted speakers, 'Turn left into the next street and switch the motor off.'

Max had done nothing to help his driver, so he went for the microphone handpiece again, with the intention of checking the registration for the owner's identity. The black-and-white personalised numberplate bore the word 'SAVBOY'.

As they pulled around the corner into the factory-lined side street, Tony said quietly, 'Max, there will be plenty of times in this job where, through no fault of your own, you get into a situation you don't want to be in. This is one of them. I will take care of this, and all I want you to do is get out of the car and walk very slowly back up Victoria Street to McDonald's. Take your time and get me some fries. I don't want stale ones. I want you to wait there while they cook up some fresh ones. I don't want you back here for at least twenty minutes. Understand?' The big Sergeant gently removed the microphone from Max's hand, and pushed it back into the holder on the dashboard with a resounding 'click'.

What was going on here? Max wondered. He sat in the passenger seat, confused, while the flashing blue and red lights bounced off the walls of the deserted warehouses. This certainly hadn't happened with the other two traffic stops.

Tony spoke very quietly, 'Family matter. That's all you need to know and you will forget I even said that, okay? Now go!'

Max jumped out of the car, then placed his cap on his head as he glanced back at the nervous driver of the yellow missile.

Max turned the corner into Victoria Street. He was feeling confused but pumped as the adrenaline from the chase coursed through his body.

Chapter Fifteen

Tony waited for Max to disappear around the corner before stepping out of the driver's door and striding towards the Audi.

On any other occasion he would have had his partner standing with his hand on his holstered firearm on the passenger side of the car, and with a clear view of the offending driver's hands. He would not have approached the vehicle if his partner could not see both of the offender's hands clenched firmly on top of the steering wheel. He would have also had a baton-torch in his non-firearm hand, with the beam narrowed and burning a hole into the back of the driver's skull.

Not this time, though. No need. What he wanted was a quiet, dark street with just himself, the driver and no witnesses.

Tony ripped open the driver's door with his right hand, reached in and took hold of his cousin Sav's slicked hair, yanking him out of the seat and propelling him onto the bitumen. With one twist of Tony's hand, Sav was thrown against the Audi so hard he bounced off it. Tony bellowed, 'What the fuck do you think you're doing, smart arse? Just because your old man is the big man in black around Carlton, it means nothing to me. Nothing at all. I'm the bigger man in blue and that's all you need to know and obey. What's your story?'

Sav stood trembling in front of his cousin. He'd sell his soul to him now at any cost... as long as Tony didn't look under the front seat, he'd tell him anything. 'Sorry, Tony. Real sorry. It was stupid, I know. I just can't help it in this thing. It's my fault. Give me a ticket or whatever. I'll take anything. It's my fault, my fault. You know how the old man is with his toys.'

Tony stared at Sav, realising something else was going on here. The kid was terrified and obviously strung out. It wasn't that he had a soft spot for Sav or anyone on that side of the family, but he knew that no matter how hard the kid tried, he would never get away from the tentacles of his father's business.

Tony took a step back and looked at the dishevelled mess who was meant to be a bright university student with an even brighter future. 'What's wrong? You weren't driving like that for the fun of it. What's going on, Sav?'

'Nothing, man. Nothing. Nothing's going on. Zip, Tony. Nothing at all, man.'

Tony's mind flashed back to the day before. A conversation he'd overheard in the mess room between two members of a car crew. For some reason, it had stuck at the time and was now worming its way back into his brain. One officer was doing his law degree part-time at Melbourne Uni and had been talking to his offsider about seeing Mickey Midolini up at the university café. He'd said something about Midolini working with the rest of the 'family'. A chilling thought ran through Tony's mind. 'I saw your father Benny the other day.' Tony tried to sound calm, with the intention of putting the kid at ease momentarily. 'Don't see a lot of you or him these days. How is the family, Sav?'

Sav rested against the driver's door, taking the words at face value.

'Good, good. Don't see a lot of anyone at the moment myself. You know. Uni and all. Living in Williamstown now. You know, head down, bum up. Study and all that shit.'

'But I hear on the grapevine you see that piece of slime, Mickey Midolini,' Tony said, as he put his right hand out and gently slapped Sav on his unshaved cheek.

Sav's body language snapped from a slouch to bolt upright as though he had been hit with an electric cattle prod. 'Nah, nah. Haven't seen Mickey in weeks. Anyhow, why would I want to see that shit? He's trouble. Everyone says he's trouble. Why do you say I've seen him?' Sav's voice was starting to crack with panic. 'Isn't true. No way, Tony. Can I go now?'

Tony's mind was racing. The thought of the traffic offences evaporated into the night air. All of a sudden, he realised he was looking at a boy who had far more serious problems, and underneath the hardened cop exterior Tony *did* care if Sav was mixed up in any way with Mickey. It was a one-way street when you got caught up in the Midolini web. And the only way the street went was downhill.

Tony took Sav gently by the arm, walking him to the footpath. 'Look, Sav. It's just you and me. Not cops and robbers. You and me. Old cousin to young cousin. You can talk to me and you know I won't say anything to anyone.' Tony paused, hoping for Sav to say something.

Nothing.

Tony lowered his voice, 'Tell me you're not involved with Midolini. He doesn't care about anybody but himself. He'll use you and wipe you off his shoes like dog shit.'

Sav's eyes burned into Tony's. *Oh, if only you knew how deep I'm into it, Tony. I wish I'd come to you a year ago.* Sav knew it was too late now. Uni was about to throw him out. He was hooked on any substance he could swallow or inject himself with and Tony was right about Mickey – he *was* involved. Blackmail and drugs. Midolini had him both ways. What was the use? 'Tony, I'll be all right. I can handle anything. I'm all right, really. I've gotta go. Seriously, I gotta go.' Sav went to push past Tony.

Tony shot out his left arm, blocking Sav mid-stride. Tony placed his left hand on Sav's chest and felt the cold sweat through the expensive-looking Ed Hardy T-shirt. 'Do what you like, Sav, but you're not driving. The rocket ship stays here. Lock it up and get a taxi. You're not driving anywhere tonight. I should take you back to the station and drug-test you, and I really don't know why I'm not. Go on, lock it up and come back tomorrow.'

Sav's mind was in a blur. Mickey would kill him if he didn't make the delivery that was sitting like a time bomb under the driver's seat. Now he couldn't get to it. Tony had told him to lock it up and go. Then Sav suddenly realised Tony hadn't asked him for the keys. Maybe if he could just get out of Tony's sight for ten minutes, come back in a taxi, grab the gear and he could still make it over to Toorak. He'd be late, but it would be better late than dead at the hands of Mickey.

Locking the Audi, Sav walked back past Tony and headed towards Victoria Street, hoping he wasn't asked for the keys.

One step, two steps. Closer and closer to Victoria Street. Sav almost broke into a run as he looked back towards his cousin. As he rounded the corner, he nearly crashed into Max Tyler who was carrying a Big

Mac bag in one hand and fries in the other.

Max stepped sideways, only realising a moment later it was the driver from the Audi.

Sav ran up the road. He waved madly at an oncoming taxi, forcing it to slam on its brakes. Max watched as he jumped into the front seat and indicated to the driver to go. The taxi took off east down Victoria Street towards Punt Road.

When Max arrived back at the police car, Tony was just finishing a conversation on his mobile phone. 'What's going on, Sarge? I just saw the Audi driver. Where was he going? Sarge?'

'Just shut up for a minute, will you?' Tony growled. 'I told you to take your bloody time.' Tony drew another breath. 'Look. Inspector Stone is the Duty Officer tonight and he needs a driver for the rest of the shift. He's on his way to pick you up now. We're swapping cars. I'm taking his unmarked one and you're going to drive this. Okay?'

'I want to know what's going on,' Max said. 'I'm down for a patrol tonight, not ferrying around the bloody Duty Officer.' Max's tone was demanding.

Tony spun around, almost grabbing the constable by the shoulder. 'You've got no damned right to know anything, son. You're down for anything I give you. Just do what you're told. The boss will be here in a minute.'

Minutes later, an unmarked blue sedan drove around the corner, then pulled up behind the marked patrol car. Tony went to the passenger door, sat himself inside and spoke quietly to Phil Stone.

Max stood on the footpath, watching them talk.

Minutes later the Inspector got out of his car. Tony slid across to the driver's seat, started the engine and quickly pulled out into the street and disappeared.

Phil Stone, laden down with his briefcase, laptop and some books, walked to the passenger side of the patrol car and stood there looking at Max. 'It's good to be inquisitive, Constable, and I know you have a million questions about what is going on. Unfortunately, not one of those questions will be answered tonight. So be a good lad and open the door. Look on the bright side. You're going to drive a real police car tonight and you've got me for company. What a couple of bonuses.'

As Max slowly pulled away from the kerb, Phil Stone continued, 'I know your father was ex-Internal Investigations, Maxwell, but do not speak to him about the interception tonight. I do not want any phone calls from the Old Boys' Club tomorrow questioning my judgment. Understand?'

Max Tyler was not only confused but angry as well. Angry that he was being kept out of something. Kept in the dark. *Unfair!*

In the end, though, it would make no difference. Circumstances would unfold that would soon drag Max into a world of crime and retribution that you would normally find only in a crime novel.

Chapter Sixteen

Tony parked the unmarked police car in an undercover factory car park, giving him a good view of Sav's Audi, some sixty metres away.

Tony stepped out of his car and climbed onto the bonnet. Taking out his handkerchief, he quickly unscrewed the fluorescent light in the concrete ceiling. The area around his car was plunged into darkness. He prayed that what he suspected was about to happen, didn't.

The thoughts that raced through Tony's mind scared him. Should he just drive away, like he'd been doing since the crash or should he see this through? Staying in the car park would take his investigation beyond Sav. It would most likely lead him right to his own uncle… Benny! Christ only knew what his own mother would say about all this. Was he up to taking on part of the family and probably the Carlton crew that slithered around his uncle's patent-leather shoes?

It had been a week since Tony drank his last Jim Beam, but now his throat was as dry as the Simpson Desert and his nerves were as twitchy as a taser. The Vine Hotel was just around the corner. Even though it was closed, Tony would have no trouble acquiring a couple of cans of Jim Beam. The owner's liquor licence was far more valuable to him than a couple of freebies for the boys in blue.

The thought was chopped off midstream when Tony saw a taxi crawl up opposite the Audi. No choice now. He felt a twinge of sadness for Sav… but only a twinge. Leaning forward, Tony put his hand on the ignition switch, ready for the inevitable. His heartbeat quickened and the old familiar tingle of anticipation went up his spine, just like it used to when he was onto a good drugs bust.

Sav stumbled over to his car, unlocking the door.

Tony saw him look under the front seat. *Oh no, Sav. He's got you, too, hasn't he? That prick Midolini.* Tony's mind shot back to a year ago, when he had intercepted two of Mickey's couriers with a stash under the front seat. Neither had given up Mickey as the supplier. It was better to do twelve months inside than put the finger on one of Benny Illarietti's men. An informer always came out a mental and physical wreck. To make matters worse, they nearly always came out with the added bonus of AIDS from being someone's 'girl' during their time inside.

Tony sensed that Sav was on a run. He hadn't bothered to look up and down the street. The Audi swung a U-turn. Tony crouched down as the headlights washed across the police car. He could see the yellow car waiting at the stop light on Victoria Street. As it turned green, Sav turned left.

Tony gunned his car and turned left as the traffic light turned red. It wasn't so bad now because there were plenty of cars around and the dark night helped. He didn't know where this would lead, but if he ran any speed or red-light cameras, he would have plenty of explaining to do if he didn't have a fish on the hook by the end of the night.

Sav was pushing it pretty hard along Punt Road and onto the South-eastern Freeway. Tony wondered if he should keep up with him. If Sav twigged to Tony's pursuit, he didn't know what the outcome would be.

Tony kept his car in Sav's blind spot, away from the Audi's mirrors. He thought about how to keep pace.

Suddenly, his problem solved itself. A set of flashing blue and reds ran up behind the Audi. Sav had been sitting on about 120 kilometres per hour, but the police van was coming at about 130 or 140. Tony hung back in the other lane, hoping that Sav would not panic and jump on the brakes. His prayer was answered as the Audi pulled into the left lane, leaving the van to use the clear lane like a runway. The police van kept going. They weren't interested in Sav. The crew must have been on their way to a hot job and just wanted a clear path.

Passing the old Kooyong tennis stadium, it seemed that Sav had no idea anyone was tailing him. Tony didn't know where Sav was headed, but he hoped he didn't have to tag him through a Navman's nightmare.

The Audi swung off the freeway and barrelled up the Toorak Road hill towards Glenferrie Road. Tony closed the gap, not wanting to be stuck at traffic lights. Sav braked suddenly, crossed the intersection, and slowly turned right into Power Street.

Pulling up in Toorak Road, Tony switched off his headlights and watched the Audi stop outside a double-storey Edwardian mansion. *Get the street number and check the electoral rolls. Bread-and-butter stuff.*

Tony watched Sav almost trip as he flew out of the Audi, clutching a package to his chest. Not a large packet, but obviously one worth protecting. Sav stuffed it in the letterbox, then shuffled backwards while looking up at the mansion. After jumping back into his yellow roadster, Sav accelerated away. Tyres squealing.

Throwing on one of Phil Stone's old coats, Tony locked the car and walked along the footpath of the street where the Audi had stopped. Number twenty-four. He ducked into a laneway opposite the house.

The street was quiet except for high-pitched female laughter and voices coming from the second storey. Abruptly, the front door opened. A middle-aged man, wearing what appeared to be a silk shaving coat, walked to the letterbox. He retrieved the parcel and returned quickly to the porch.

Tony watched as the porch light came on and bathed the man in bright light. Almost dropping the package, the man headed towards the front door as a teenaged girl stepped outside. Tony could see she was wearing only a bra and G-string.

The man bellowed at the girl, 'Get back inside, now!' He shoved her viciously backwards through the doorway. Stepping inside, he closed the door quietly and turned off the light.

Tony crossed the street and ran back to his car. He jumped in and caught his breath. He'd recognised the man as soon as the scantily clad girl had switched on the porch light. It was His Honour Paul Webster, the Chief Judge of the County Court of Victoria.

Tony knew a few other things about His Honour. Webster was single and had no children, so he wasn't yelling at his teenage daughter. He had recently been the presiding judge in a cocaine-trafficking case where there was overwhelming evidence against the two accused. They were both acquitted on Webster's direction due to the most minor of technicalities. The defendants being Benny Illarietti and Mickey Midolini.

Tony knew he had to follow this through. He wondered how much Benny Illarietti knew about this drop. Benny was a crook, but he wasn't silly enough to make a drop at Webster's home. And surely he wasn't using his own son as a courier? No, of course he wasn't. This had all the earmarks of a Midolini operation. No wonder Sav was scared.

As a light-headed sensation came over Tony, he had another feeling about tonight. It felt good to be back on track. Stalking the prey. Thinking back to when he started the car at Collingwood, he had two choices. Let it go or go for it. He still had that chill running down his spine and it felt good. The hunt was on again. He felt alive. He had to have a win.

Why had he stepped back over the previous months? Fear. Fear of being wrong, that's why. Fear of what could happen. People had told him he hadn't been at fault in that chase, but the boy died anyway. Now it was Sav who could die at Midolini's hands. Like it or not, Sav was family – and Midolini was scum!

Get real, Signorotto. If Sav is hooked up with Midolini, he will probably die from the drug leftovers that he was thrown. Sav would be a loser both ways.

Tony realised sweat was now pouring from his face. The overwhelming need for a drink hit him like a vicious punch in the guts. Susie's face flashed in front of him. He couldn't break her heart. No, get on with it. Do your job. You're here now and you've seen enough. You could go back to the station and tell Phil Stone that you lost the tail. You could – but you won't.

No. Wouldn't it be good if Mickey Midolini got busted… or killed? He didn't care at all. Now that was more like the old Tony Signorotto!

Chapter Seventeen

Tony tossed and turned like a washing machine in bed that night. He didn't know which way to go about it. Did he go for Benny or Mickey? By morning, the Italian in him said go straight to the problem: Mickey. Tony was going to have serious words with that piece of shit.

Arriving at the station for an eight o'clock shift, Tony waited impatiently for Phil Stone to arrive. He started the morning crew on their jobs and fixed up a few counter enquiries. When Phil came through the back door, Tony motioned him into the kitchen where two trainees were sitting – both talking on their mobile phones.

Phil glared at Tony without asking the question on his lips.

Tony needed to clear the room first. 'Put those bloody phones away,' he barked. 'Seeing that you've got nothing to do, kit up and do a foot patrol of Lygon, Faraday and Rathdowne Streets. But leave Cardigan Street to me. Now move!'

Nearly falling over each to get away from Tony's wrath, one of them shot back, 'Right, Sarge.'

After they had cleared out, Phil asked, 'Cardigan Street? Why are you going up there? You're the morning-shift sergeant. Can't a visit to the Co-Op wait till after you've finished?'

'Just had a couple of station files I wanted to tidy up,' replied Tony.

'Listen, mate. You call me in here like you're the Inspector and I'm the Sergeant, snap the heads off those young kids, then give me some crap about files. We have a permanent Senior Constable at this station who handles the files. Had you forgotten that, Sergeant?'

Tony looked at him, not knowing what to say. His mind was thinking about one thing only. Finding Mickey Midolini at the café and having a little close-up and personal chat to the slimeball.

'Sorry, Tony. I've got a lot on my plate at the moment. The Superintendent's coming over today for a sniff around. Something about funding, apparently. But getting back to Cardigan Street – don't bullshit me, mate. Driving in this morning, I saw the black Beamer is up there. Midolini will be there all morning. So he can wait. Tell me what happened last night. You sure left me with one very disgruntled driver.'

Over a coffee, Tony told Phil the full story from the night before.

When Tony dropped Judge Webster's name, Phil nearly choked on his Nescafé. 'Is that the same Webster who let Midolini and Illarietti off those drugs charges a while back?'

'The same.'

'Shit, Tony. You'd better be careful about this. If we don't have proof and this gets out, we're going to be drawing our pensions sooner than we thought. That prick has big-time connections upstairs. He was a nothing when he started in the Labor Party five years ago. A failed barrister. Word from a good mate of mine, who's doing some time as the Chief's Staff Officer, is that some of the ministers around Spring Street know about Webster's personal habits but don't want to admit it. The Labor Party kicked him up to the County Court because he was going to blow the whistle on a female minister. After parliament had finished one day, seems my mate and Webster found her and a young female clerk locked together on the back bench – but not in conversation. She's now the Minister for Female Affairs.'

However, Tony was more interested in the local players. 'Phil, I want to start with Midolini. I know Sav's not much, but he doesn't deserve the shit sandwich that's coming his way. No one does. If I go straight to Benny Illarietti, he won't believe me. He'll think I'm backdooring him with some bullshit story because he knows I hate Mickey. I've gotta do something now. If I can get Sav out of this shit, then that's good. If I can't, I'll take Midolini and Benny down. How about it?'

'You sure about this? I don't want you playing Supercop. You and I know you've taken a few backward steps of late. You haven't exactly set the world alight with arrests or anything else for that matter.'

The look of painful reality on Tony's face forced Phil to stop and think.

Phil paced the kitchen for a good minute before he spoke to his old friend. 'Okay. Go after Midolini for now. See if you can warn him off using Sav. We can't prove connections. Don't mention Webster or you tailing Sav last night. I'm sure you can get the message through to Midolini – he's scared shitless of you. But I can only back you so far, Tony, so be bloody careful.'

'Thanks, Phil. I won't get anyone else involved, I promise.'

'Famous last words. I'll go and write that up on my whiteboard for when I'm trying to get your arse out of a sling with headquarters.'

Chapter Eighteen

Tony stepped up behind Midolini without saying a word. He didn't care there were several of Mickey's associates at nearby tables. He didn't care he had on his police blues with just a tracksuit top covering his shirt. He saw only red when he looked at Mickey Midolini.

Tony had promised himself he would try to convince Benny's henchman to back off from Sav. Unfortunately, once Tony saw Midolini's flash suit and his shiny Mercedes by the kerb, he knew he was past talking.

Midolini was putting a short black to his lips when he turned and saw Tony. 'On your way to the Co-Op, eh, Sergeant Signorotto? Say hello to the squeeze for me. She can serve me anytime she likes. She could handle my deposits. You'd only be good for withdrawals, wouldn't you?'

Laughter rang out among the four well-dressed rock apes who were sitting around the tables.

Tony's Italian temper cracked. The red mist came down like a broken curtain.

Midolini let out a yelp as Tony slapped the coffee cup out of his hands, sending hot liquid spilling over his pin-striped Versace suit and hand-made Italian shoes.

By the time the cup smashed on the footpath, Tony was lifting

Midolini out of his seat by his tie. Tony put his face hard up against Midolini's and spoke in a voice that oozed menace, 'If you've got something to say, little mouse, then speak up. You're among friends here, so squeak away.' Tony stared daggers at the slack-jawed hoods looking on in disbelief.

Midolini tried to take a step backwards, but he was only touching the pavement with his toes. His stumpy legs pumped up and down on thin air. 'Get your hands off me, you fucking pig, or else,' Midolini squealed in a barely audible voice, as the knot of his tie strangled his fat throat.

Out of the corner of one eye, Tony saw a skinny Midolini associate step forward and reach inside his black leather jacket. Swinging his right arm sideways, Tony collected him flush on the nose with a backward fist, sending the hood crashing into a table and knocking the large Vittoria Coffee umbrella onto the footpath. The hood went down on his knees, clutching his face as claret poured through his fingers and pooled on the ground.

Any ideas that Midolini's associates might have had of coming to his rescue disappeared like a wallet at a kleptomaniacs' convention. The only movement they made was to back away from the sight of the bloodied, moaning hood at Tony's feet.

Tony kept Midolini dangling by his tie, while he brought his face up to Midolini's ear. 'That piece of shit there is going to need some surgery. What you have to seriously think about is how much surgery you are going to need, if you don't keep your greasy fucking hands off my cousin. Understand?'

With that, Tony threw Midolini sideways into a chair, then watched him cower there. Passers-by were hurrying onto the roadway to dodge the café rather than become embroiled in the confrontation.

Midolini managed to rasp, 'You're dead, you prick. You've come near me for the last time.' He sat there shaking and pulling out the knot in his tie so he could breathe again.

Sniffing the air, Tony looked down at the gibbering mess and then saw the damp stain spreading outwards from the crotch of Midolini's pin-striped pants. Tony couldn't resist. 'Hey, boys. Step up and look at your business partner. He's pissed himself.'

Midolini's associates were suitably repulsed.

Tony fixed the remaining black-clad heroes with a glare that said 'fuck with me, if you dare'. He decided it was time to draw a line in the sand. 'If I see any of your faces around here again, you'll be in the back of a fucking police van faster than you can say "What the fuck?" I don't give a damn about what the charges will be. But I promise you this: you get on the shit-list in my patch and I'll be in your face twenty-four/seven. In case you don't know me, the name's Signorotto, *Sergeant* Tony Signorotto, and I only work Carlton. If I was you, I'd leave right now and never come back. Rip page forty-three right out of your street directory. Now fuck off. Before you all need your pants dry-cleaned.'

The only sounds that followed were the shufflings of chairs and feet as a phalanx of dark-suited, drug-trade wannabes scuttled like rodents past the slumped figure of Midolini.

'Take this dipshit with you, too,' Tony barked, pointing at the bloodied hood who was holding his nose together with both hands. 'Otherwise I'll throw him into one of your limos and let him bleed all over it.'

Two hoods quickly dragged the jelly-legged hero to his feet, pushing him towards a black BMW with even blacker windows. The sound of disappearing motors was like the beginning of the Italian Grand Prix.

Turning back to Midolini, Tony spied Benny Illarietti at the café door.

Benny walked over and calmly looked down at his lieutenant, who was now trying to hide the dark patch on his trousers by dragging a tablecloth over himself. 'To what do we owe the pleasure, nephew?'

'Nothing you need to trouble yourself about, Benny. Not yet anyway.' Reaching down, Tony pulled Midolini out of the chair by his lapels and smoothed down his shirt and tie. 'Let me walk you to your car, Mickey. You look a little unsteady. You want to be careful in those elevator shoes. You'll get nose-bleeds at that altitude.'

Tony pushed the bedraggled Midolini over to his black Mercedes. Out of Benny's earshot, Tony stood with his arm around Midolini's neck and squeezed as hard as he could. 'I pulled Sav over last night and it didn't take Einstein to figure he was on some sort of errand for you, slimeball. I don't know what you're up to, prick, but be warned: if you're taking him down the drug track, then you know damn well where it will end. And I promise you, it won't just be his death. You'll be joining him. Don't forget his surname, you slimy little piece of shit. It's Illarietti, the same as Benny's – your boss!'

Midolini glared at Tony, but kept his mouth shut.

Tony had one more point to clarify. 'You won't have to worry about me, Mickey, my boy. It's Benny who'll come after you. Now why don't you turn around and say your goodbyes to your boss? You need to get home and change your nappy.'

With an ashen face, Midolini glowered at Tony. 'You think you're so fucking tough, don't you? I've got plans for you, Signorotto, and you won't know what they are until a moment before your fucking lights go out.'

Tony grinned and opened the driver's door of the Mercedes.

Before Midolini could react, his head was slammed sideways into his car's roof with just enough force so, as he bounced off it, he slid downwards into the driver's seat. He let out a squeal and covered his face with both hands.

Tony leaned in the door. 'I could take you to the station and charge you with making threats, but I won't. I'm not going to waste my time with the small stuff, you arse-wipe. I'm going to deliver you to a top court and watch you fucking dance. By the way, call me if you want a good panel beater. Your head left a dint like a fucking bowling ball in your car.'

Starting his car, Midolini looked across at Benny, who hadn't moved from the doorway. 'You're all finished, Signorotto. All your fucking family.' Hitting the accelerator, Midolini sped off down Elgin Street.

Benny Illarietti walked up to his nephew. 'What was that all about? You come here and rough up two of my boys on my doorstep. You show me no respect at all.'

'Respect! Don't talk to me about fucking respect. Just because he's a good salesman for you, it means nothing to me. He's nothing but garbage. Your garbage. You are killing kids around here with what you're doing and you don't give a damn. Well I do. Forget the family stuff, Benny.'

Turning to walk back to the station, Tony stopped mid-stride and spun around. 'One thing, uncle. It's not just me you have to worry about.' He jerked a thumb in Midolini's direction.

Benny Illarietti stared at the back of his departing nephew, then at the blood and upturned umbrella and chairs on the footpath. Tony obviously knew something he didn't.

That was of concern to Benny.

Chapter Nineteen

Back at the station, Tony looked at Max Tyler sitting in the correspondence area, busily working on a computer. He felt a sudden pang of guilt. Tyler had gone off with Phil Stone the night before, without Tony seeing him again.

Tony was on his personal crusade against Mickey Midolini and it was going to become a war of attrition. But the war, which had started as a battle the night before, wasn't just about Tony and his hatred of Midolini. After all, stopping Sav's car had involved Max, yet Tony realised he'd acted as though Max hadn't existed. Just a nuisance to be told to go away. That's what he'd done, all right. He had dismissed him like an annoying fly.

Stepping into the correspondence room, Tony walked over to the constable. 'G'day, Max. What's the paperwork? Anything I can help with?'

Max's glare cut into Tony like a tracer bullet. He had been given the push last night and the look said it all. Not fair, not fair at all. At the same time, though, Max knew he did need a hand with some of the paperwork. 'Just trying to type up a speeding brief from last night. The one in the orange Ford in Pelham Street. The second one we got for the night. Remember? He was doing just under 120 k's an hour.'

Tony had forgotten everything about last night that wasn't

connected with Sav and the subsequent tail to Toorak. 'Mate, I'm sorry. I don't remember it. I got tied up a bit with young Sav. I'll tell you what…' Tony pulled his wallet from his back pocket, and laid a twenty-dollar note on the desk, 'head over to Sammy's and grab us both something to eat. When you get back, we'll eat together, then get stuck into the 'corro' – together. You did all right last night, Max, and I owe you an apology. Let's talk when you get back.'

Max picked up the note. 'It's all right, Sarge. I can do this by myself. I've gotta learn.'

'Listen, mate. It's not often I buy anyone lunch, so don't look a gift horse in the mouth. After lunch, we'll knock over this paperwork. There are a few shortcuts I'll teach you.'

Max stood and walked towards the door. He looked back for a moment to add, 'That'd be great, Sarge. Thanks.'

Tony called after him, 'You drive and take that new trainee who arrived yesterday – seeing you're no longer the junior man around here. And don't get him into trouble. By the way, don't tell him or anyone else that I'm buying you lunch. I have a long-held reputation to keep up around here of being a tight-arse.'

Tony knew he had to look after both jobs. Nailing Midolini was a priority, but so was not letting Phil Stone down when it came to looking after the recruits. Especially young Max Tyler. The kid was keen as mustard and he'd hate for the young rookie to leave Carlton with Tony knowing he hadn't passed on his knowledge to someone so eager. There was something about this kid. He didn't know what just yet, but *something*. Did he have to overcome the stigma of his father being from Internal Affairs? Did he relate to Tyler because he himself had to overcome being the wog boy when he started? Perhaps it was because Max didn't sulk after being admonished. Or was he just looking for someone to drag into this onrushing vortex with Benny Illarietti and his crew? Couldn't he handle it himself? The demons were still haunting him. Tony pushed these thoughts aside and concentrated on trying to make his own out-pile of paperwork bigger than the in-pile.

When Max returned, he found Tony in the mess room, sitting with Phil Stone and Jill Norton. Max stopped at the door, not knowing where to sit.

'Sit down, son, and have your lunch,' Phil said. 'This is everyone's mess room, not just the old fogeys'. By the way, you did well last night. You were right on the ball with those jobs we had to help out with.'

Standing up from the table, Jill Norton put her arm around Max's shoulder and said quietly into his ear, 'Don't let him con you with that old line, Maxy. Or you'll end up being his bloody chauffeur all the time. If you want some excitement in your life, stick with the Sergeant here. He'll show you how it's done, eh, Tony?'

Tony grinned and said, 'Get back to the watch-house, mother.'

'If I start getting called "Mother Norton" around here, Sergeant, you will live to regret it,' Jill huffed, before departing with a smile on her face. She waved a mocking finger at Tony.

Max handed Tony his Sammy's Special triple-decker sandwich dripping with mozzarella cheese and an assortment of hot and spicy salamis. Sitting down next to the senior men, he opened a veggie burger.

Tony was struck dumb at the sight.

But Max kept a straight face. 'Look, I was going to get something a bit tastier, Tony, but you only gave me a twenty. By the time Sammy emptied the shop of cheese and half of Carlton for your salamis, this was all I could buy with two dollars. I wished I'd ordered mine before he got your usual cardio house-brick ready.'

The departing Norton burst out laughing near the end of the corridor.

Stone was open-mouthed.

Max winked at him.

'You cheeky young bastard,' Tony said. He leaned over and gave Max a friendly clip across the ear.

Phil Stone could see a good rapport building between two different policing generations. He smiled inwardly. 'Different from the Academy, eh, son?' said the Inspector.

'Yes sir, a little bit. Different pace. New things all the time.'

'The Sergeant here will look after you. Just take guidance from him and you won't go wrong. Just do your best.' Stone stood up and headed back to his office.

'Righto, Max. Food then paperwork. We'll knock off the stuff from last night, then I want to tell you about a certain little crook we're going to pursue right to steps of the County Court.'

Tony could see the word 'crook' brought a smile to the young constable's face. *There will always be recruits. Cannon fodder. And with this job, there would be fire from some bloody big cannons.*

Chapter Twenty

Sav looked up slowly when the front door to his flat opened and Mickey Midolini walked in. *What's he doing here?* Sav thought, as he lay on his couch in a drug-induced stupor, the result of a self-administered hit of smack a short time before.

Sav's nerves were totally jangled. He knew something bad was about to happen. Nothing good ever came from an unexpected Midolini visit. Rolling onto his back, Sav looked up into Midolini's eyes. It was like looking at two shiny black pebbles.

Midolini measured his words. 'Sav, I'm going to give you a chance to tell me why you were late the other night. My client was not happy. You cut his pleasure time, so I had to discount him ten percent. That ten percent is going to come out of your next stash, Sav. Only fair, eh?' Midolini gently rubbed Sav's shoulder with his black-gloved hand.

'My fault, Mickey. I was running late and then Tony…'

'Tony *who*? Did you have someone in the car with you?'

'It's all right, Mickey. I was going a bit quick and Tony Signorotto pulled me over. It's okay. He's my cousin. You know him. Nothing happened. Just a warning.'

'A warning for fucking what? What did he say? What were you doing?' Midolini asked, with an increasing edge to his voice.

'He just pulled me over because I was going a bit quick through a red light, that's all. I think.'

'You fuckwit. You run late and then attract attention to yourself. What were you on? What did he do?'

'It's all right. He's family. He told me to lock the car and get lost, so I did.'

'Did he take the keys from you?

'No.'

'Idiot. He would've known you'd drive again. How long before you went back to your car? Did you look around? Did you see him when you came back?' Midolini's voice rose higher and higher, taking on a dangerous, threatening tone.

Sav was terrified. He inched himself backwards across the couch.

Midolini tightened the grip on his shoulder and slowly forced Sav from the couch onto the bare floor.

'What are you saying, Mickey? I got a taxi, did a couple of blocks, came back and he was gone. I finished the job. What's wrong?'

'What's fucking wrong?' Midolini screamed. 'He lets you take the keys. He knows you're high and he doesn't even search the fricken car. Are you fucking stupid? He's followed you, all the way to fucking Toorak. He's a cop. He's dumb, but he's not fucking stupid.'

Sav's face dripped with perspiration. He could feel his guts turn to water as his eyes pleaded with Midolini's. Sav knew from past experiences that he was about to be on the receiving end of a Midolini temper explosion. Sav sobbed, 'Don't, Mickey, please don't. I'll make it up to you, I promise.'

Sav's plea was to no avail.

Out of nowhere, a silver nine-millimetre Beretta semi-automatic pistol appeared in Midolini's free hand. He brought the butt of the gun down, smashing two of the fingers on Sav's right hand that were flat on the wooden floor.

The sound of shattering bone was mostly masked by Sav's piercing scream. 'Nooo! Oh fuck, Mickey! You've broken my fucking hand! For Chrissakes, Mickey, I did the fucking job for you.'

'I oughta kill you right here and now for getting me involved with that fucking arsehole cousin of yours.' Midolini looked down his nose at Sav, then suddenly realised he had smashed what Benny would think was the most precious part of his son – the future doctor – his right hand. His surgeon's hand. 'You tell Benny about any of this and you're dead. Understand?'

Sav nodded.

Mickey bared his teeth. 'You fucking fell down the back stairs, you understand?'

Sav gripped his broken hand, wailing with the pain. Between sobs, he nodded again. Anything to stop more of the beating.

Lying halfway between the couch and the floor, Sav felt the intensity of the pain increase and wash over him like a tidal wave. He slipped down the long black tunnel into unconsciousness.

*

Sav didn't know how long he'd been out. But when he opened his eyes, still terrified, he was relieved to discover the front door was wide open and no Midolini.

Sav lay there, chest heaving, as he sobbed to himself and looked at his swollen, disfigured hand. *Got to get out of here. Or he'll probably come back and finish me.*

Chapter Twenty-One

Susie was madder than a cut snake, and Tony was going to pay. Two nights ago he was supposed to come by after work. No show.

Susie hadn't planned anything special that night, but she did want to talk about their future together. If Tony thought he could sit back and run both their lives, he had another thing coming. They had talked briefly about going interstate for a holiday, and she wasn't going to let it drop. Stuff Sergeant Tony bloody Signorotto!

Susie pushed open the station door and saw Jill Norton behind the watch-house counter. She loved Jill. She was everybody's mate.

Jill peered around the head of an elderly lady at the counter and gave Susie a big grin and a wink. 'With you in a tick, love. Good timing. I need a brew. Tony's on arvo shift, but it'll be a nice change to have some female company in the back room. The behaviour in there's rougher than a hessian sack.'

Susie smiled and drew breath.

Jill continued her patter with the elderly lady. 'Now, back to you, Mrs Rawling. You know we'll look after you here. Just wait a minute while I get one of my young virile constables to drive you back home. Don't forget to have a good look on your kitchen table for those glasses. They'll be there somewhere. If not, just give me a ring and I'll arrange to get you down to the local optometrist for some new ones. I'll make sure they look after you price-wise. But it will cost you one of your home-made pies. That recipe you gave me works a treat on that husband of mine. Not that he deserves it, of course.'

With a smile that lit up the room, Mrs Rawling gave a high-pitched giggle. She turned and said to Susie, 'She's a lovely one, that Jill Norton. Known her and her husband for years. They've always looked after me around here. Nothing's a problem to Jill.'

'Jill is indeed a gem,' Susie replied, as the elderly lady took a seat to wait for her taxi.

Jill looked towards the back and called out, 'Constable Tyler, come here, please.' Her voice boomed down the passage to the muster room like a footy coach giving instructions at training. Disobey and God help you.

Max appeared around the watch-house counter, just as a set of car keys sailed through the air. Grabbing them with his right hand, he asked, 'Job?'

'Yes, Max. Mrs Rawling over there needs to be taken home to the Commission flats in Drummond Street. Be a good lad. If she needs to do a bit of shopping along the way, just give her a hand.'

At that moment, Inspector Stone came down the stairs. But Max failed to notice and protested to Jill, 'Home? Shopping! What am I, the local yellow cab?'

'Yes, Constable, right now you are,' Inspector Stone interrupted. 'You can catch a crook on your way back.'

Max swung round and gulped when he saw a serious-looking Inspector Stone.

'This taxpayer wants to see her taxes at work,' Stone said, deadpan.

'All ready to go, Mrs Rawling?'

The old lady stepped up slowly to Max Tyler, put her arm through his, and led him through the doorway. Max looked back at the two police officers wearing grins like Cheshire cats.

Phil Stone's smile broadened further when he saw Susie. 'G'day, Susie. I think Tony's on afternoon, today.'

'Yes, Jill's just told me that,' she said, with a concerned look on her face.

'Come on,' Phil replied, 'This policeman needs a coffee. Hold the fort will you, Jill?'

'No probs, boss. Bring us back a cup, will you? I'm not a camel, you know. We'll have some girl talk later, Susie. We won't bore the Inspector with wedding-dress stuff.'

Phil indicated the way to the mess room and followed Susie through. Phil lowered his voice and said, 'That was a definite "I've got a problem look" that you had on your face. Can I help?'

'I'm really mad with him, Phil. I know Tony's cut down on his drinking, but I can't seem to get through to him at the moment. He's got problems, but he won't tell me about them. He seems so far away all the time... you know, distant. He was meant to come around the other night to talk about his leave and our holiday away from this.' Susie gestured to the dull yellow paint peeling from the mess-room walls. 'We both need a break, Phil. Especially him.'

Stone guided Susie to a chair in the corner of the mess room, and started to make a coffee for both of them. 'Susie, I know what you're saying. I suppose, from where I sit, it's good and bad news. He's given the booze away, which is starting to get him back to the hard-working cop we both know. However, he's sunk his teeth into something big that could turn nasty – real nasty.'

'Phil, I know what he's like when he's fired up about something. If it's a big case, can't you get him to turn it over to one of the other sergeants?'

'I would if I could, love.' Phil paused and looked towards the door. 'What I'm going to tell you now doesn't leave this room, okay?'

Gripping her cup with both hands, Susie lowered her head. 'Go on, what is it?'

'It's a drug bust. Or I should say, it *may* be a drug bust. It involves some prominent people. But what makes it so close to home for him is that he's found out one of our local scumbags is using his cousin Sav as a courier. This scumbag, Mickey Midolini works for Benny Illarietti, Tony's uncle.'

'I've met Benny at the odd family get-together,' said Susie. 'Tony and Benny stand on opposite sides of the room and glare at each other like a couple of bullfighters. I know he's mafia, so I just keep clear.'

'This could get messy,' Phil continued. 'I've given Tony my word that I'll back him all the way. He's determined to nail Midolini, and I don't think he cares too much if Benny goes down at the same time. I suppose what I'm saying is to cut him a bit of slack at the moment. Between you and me, we'll get him through this, then he's all yours. Wedding, holiday and a break from this place.'

Phil and Susie chatted a few more minutes before Susie went to leave.

'What, no time for a secret girl's business?' Jill asked, when Susie returned from the mess room.

'I'll come back after work with some wedding dress magazines, Jill. We'll leave the dinosaurs out of it, eh?'

'Excuse me, ladies, this dinosaur is heading back upstairs to his swamp.'

Before Phil could leave the room, Susie waved goodbye and went out the front door.

Phil stood silently for a moment, looking after Susie.

Jill turned to him and broke the silence. 'If Tony doesn't bloody well look after her, I'll knock his teeth so far down his throat, he'll be eating his breakfast through his bum when I get through with him.'

Phil Stone rubbed his jaw. It was an unusual sight to imagine, but he had no doubts that Jill Norton was as good as her word.

Chapter Twenty-Two

Sav stared at the back of the doctor's head examining his mangled fingers. He knew his old man wanted him to not only be a top doctor, but also a top surgeon. Sav thought it was ironic that even if he decided to keep up his studies, stop using and stick to dealing, Midolini had made sure he could never be a surgeon. Sav couldn't open his fly to take a piss, let alone operate.

'Tell me what really happened,' the emergency-department doctor said. 'I know you've told the nurse and me that you got it caught in your front door, but that's rubbish. It's obvious that you've been assaulted. It looks like someone has smashed your fingers with an iron bar. Two of your fingers are broken in two or more places, and the middle knuckle of your ring finger looks as though it's been crushed. You won't be able to pick your nose with this hand, even when it comes out of plaster.'

'Can you just give me something for the pain?' Sav pleaded, as the nausea ebbed and flowed from his stomach. 'Just plaster it and give me some pain killers.' *Any minute now, I'm going to throw up.*

'It's a bit worse than that. You'll need surgery on that knuckle or you'll never use it again. Lie back and I'll give you a shot for the pain.'

Sav put his head back on the pillow and tried to remember what had happened. After Mickey had left, he remembered staggering to his car with the thought of driving to his parents' place. Why his parents' place, he didn't know. Probably because he knew he was at rock bottom. Right now he was flopping lower than whale shit. He was going to tell Benny he'd been jumped in town, but that would have caused his old man to call in the henchmen to give every young kid around the area where it had happened the flogging they so richly *didn't* deserve. He didn't want a lot of innocent kids getting a hiding for nothing, so he gave Benny the door story.

Benny was now in the emergency-department's waiting room, anxious for news on his son's future. His hands.

As the doctor slid the needle into Sav's skinny arm, he looked closely at the track marks from previous needles.

Leaving Sav in a morphine heaven, the doctor went out into the waiting area and found Benny. 'Mr Illarietti, it's obvious to me that your son has been badly assaulted. He could not have possibly had that sort of damage done to his fingers by jamming them in a door. I've got no choice but to call the police. This is a definite assault case.'

Benny Illarietti stood toe-to-toe with the doctor, slowly leaning down to whisper in his ear, 'No police. I will take care of it.' With a hand firmly on the doctor's shoulder, Benny reiterated, 'No police. Let the boy sleep. I will be back soon. One of my employees here,' he indicated two heavily built, black-suited gorillas nearby, 'will remain. Anything the boy wants, he gets, understand? I will arrange for a surgeon myself. He will be here before morning. There will be a sizeable donation to your hospital's building fund for your continuing inability to involve the police.'

The doctor went to speak, but Benny turned and gestured for the steroid twins to follow him out the sliding doors. As they went to exit, Benny was nearly knocked over by two paramedics pushing a gurney carrying a young teenage girl.

'O-D!' one of the paramedics called to the charge nurse. 'Not looking good.'

Benny looked down at the pale face of the girl. She had vomited over the pillow and her tongue was hanging out of her mouth. Pushing thoughts of his own evil trade to the back of his mind, he headed for his BMW. Benny would get the truth from Sav when he came around. Those fingers had to be fixed. With more connections than a Lego set, it would be no trouble to find the animal that did this to his one and only son.

Chapter Twenty-Three

Sav had the feeling he was floating somewhere near the ceiling of his cubicle. It was the combination of his own smack with the methadone the doctor had given him. Sav's right hand was throbbing so much, it felt like someone was jumping up and down on it, but at least the edge had been taken off the absolutely excruciating pain. He knew it wouldn't be long before things started to wear off, so he tried not to think of his world when he came around. His old man would be back and looking for answers. Sav couldn't even remember exactly what he'd told Benny about his fingers, but he knew he had better have a believable story for him. One that was a lot better than the fricken door story!

Amid his floating thoughts and looming terrors, Sav realised there was something going on in the cubicle next to him. Somebody had yelled for a stomach pump. He heard the sound of metal crashing as things were pushed around a corner in a hurry. Voices were being raised by the medical staff, including the same doctor who was looking after him.

'C'mon, Carly! Stay with us, stay with us,' the doctor called out. 'You've gotta try keeping your eyes open. Don't go to sleep. C'mon, c'mon.'

Sav could hear the bed sliding. It sounded as though the staff were turning the girl on her side. 'How much smack did you do at the Eureka?' the doctor asked.

No answer.

Sav's blood turned to ice. *Carly? The Eureka? No, no way. Couldn't be Carly from uni. Not Carly Watson. Couldn't be the same one.* He knew that Carly from uni sometimes liked a hit, and he'd seen her sometimes at the Eureka bar in Lygon Street. *But no, it isn't her. Is it?*

There were mumbles coming from the girl, but it was all incoherent crap until one word passed from her lips – the word penetrated Sav's floating world louder than an exploding stick of dynamite – 'Mickey!'

Sav slid off his bed, and felt his pain return with full force as he peered around the edge of the curtain. All he could see was the blue shirt and pants of a paramedic working frantically, pumping up and down on the girl's stomach.

Suddenly all activity stopped.

'Too late, boys. She's gone,' the doctor announced. 'Twenty years old and she's gone. What a waste.' He turned and slammed his foot into the cubicle wall. 'These fucking drug dealers. I'd kill them all if I had the chance.'

A paramedic led the young doctor out of the cubicle. He'd seen it all before on the streets of Carlton. The worst part was knowing he would see it all again and again.

Sav's breathing stopped when the other paramedic stepped aside.

The death mask of Carly Watson was facing Sav in a true-to-life horror show.

He stared in frozen disbelief. Carly was a fellow med student in his year. They hadn't been close friends, but they were friends.

The paramedic left the girl's cubicle and drew the curtain.

The pain coursed through Sav's body as he mechanically walked around the corner and unsteadily drew back the neighbouring partition. Carly's body was lying there in only a pair of vomit-stained jeans.

Why didn't she sit up and talk to him? She couldn't be dead. Not Carly. She was a top student who was going to be a great doctor. C'mon, Carly, wake up! No, don't tell me that Mickey has done this to you?

With his eyes locked on her young body, Sav could see track marks on the inside of both her arms. Her eyes were clouded over and her mouth hung open. There was a large tube protruding from her throat, which was connected to a bag hooked to the side of the bed. Whatever was in the bag had just been pumped from her stomach. The last time he'd seen her, about two weeks ago, she was the life of the party at the Eureka. Bubbly and attractive. Now this. *Oh, God, Mickey. Juicing me up is one thing, but this, this shouldn't be. A beautiful kid with everything in front of her. But I'm a beautiful kid with everything in front of me... or I was.*

Sav could hear footsteps coming back down the hall, so he quickly scurried back to his cubicle and sat there shaking.

'Clean her up,' somebody said. 'Strip off her clothes and put a gown on her. Make sure it's a long-sleeve one. Don't let her parents see those needle marks. She didn't give herself much dignity in life. Let's see if we can give her some in death.'

Sav could hear Carly's body being moved around. He looked down when her jeans and T-shirt were thrown on the floor. He started to cry. Tears flowed down his cheeks and his whole body shook with convulsions. It wasn't his own pain that caused it, but the pain he felt for Carly. Gone, and for what? Just so Mickey could get rich.

Suddenly, Carly was wheeled out of her cubicle. All Sav could see through his open curtain were her two feet, one with a toe-tag on it. A white one. He remembered Carly laughing at a dissection lecture at the morgue about six months ago. All the bodies had white toe-tags. When she was asked why she was laughing, she replied that if she were on the gurney, she'd want a pink toe-tag.

Sav forgot about his hand, went to the break in his curtain, and stared at the receding gurney. As it rounded a corner, an arm flopped down the side, but was quickly thrown back up under the sheet. There was no dignity in death, even if you had been beautiful.

Chapter Twenty-Four

Sav didn't have many more places to look for Mickey. He had been through all the local Carlton haunts that his tired brain could think of. Since discharging himself only hours earlier, without telling anyone, Sav had been walking the streets. He couldn't get the picture of Carly's face out of his mind. One way or another, Mickey was going to pay for this. He didn't know how, but he was past caring about himself. Fronting Mickey was all Sav could think of. What he was going to say to him hadn't entered his dulled senses.

Around five a.m. Sav was staggering past a gay bar in Cambridge Street. His hand was throbbing. Even though it was in a sling, the pain was almost unbearable. Just as he was about to head home, Sav looked up to see the rear of a black Mercedes jutting out from the next laneway.

There were two young guys leaning against the roof, blocking Sav's view of the driver. As he shuffled towards the car, one of the guys shifted and there he was… Mickey Midolini. He was doing business as usual, feeding the hungry, drug-craved, early-morning locals.

Sav now had to find the courage that had always deserted him. Standing a little way back from the driver's door, he yelled, 'Mickey! Mickey Midolini. I want to talk to you.'

The other young guy at the car door stepped quickly away and disappeared down the alley.

Mickey's ferret-like head turned to face Sav. Then the rest of Mickey's body emerged from the driver's seat. Mickey stood and faced Sav on the footpath. 'What do you want? Not enough pain for one night? Remember, son, I *own* you. Your arse is mine, excuse the joke. I know it probably belongs to some of your boyfriends from time to time, but as far as our business goes, it and the rest of your body obey me. Capice?'

'Carly Watson was a friend of mine, Mickey, and you fucking killed her!' Sav screamed at the top of his voice, his bandaged hand waving to one side of his body. 'Why, why?'

Before Sav could react, Mickey had him hard up against the side of the black Mercedes, twisting Sav's T-shirt tight up against his throat. 'Don't you come into my patch screaming like a whore telling everyone I killed some slut girlfriend of yours. Understand, you dope head? Don't you fucking dare. Who the fuck are you talking about, anyhow?'

'Carly was a classmate of mine. You got her hooked just like you got me hooked, Mickey. My life's fucked anyhow, but why Carly? She was such a good kid.'

'Listen, prick. I don't know every drugged-up, little skinny-arsed hooker on the street and, frankly, I don't give a shit who she was. If she was buying from me or one of my boys, it was lucky she only did drugs and not tricks. Some of my associates in other patches make them dance for their score – and I don't mean a fricken foxtrot. If she's dead, that's her fault. She didn't have to buy from me and I sure as hell didn't hold her down and shove the hypo in her arm. Now fuck off. You're bad for business around here. I've just about had you and your big mouth. You and I are coming to the end of our acquaintance. Go home or wherever you go to get your head together.'

Sav's body was starting to wind down. The pain, together with the emotion over Carly and the strain to find Midolini, had taken its toll. He slid down the side of the Mercedes and balled himself up on the ground. Tears started to stream down his face as he lay there on the footpath.

'When I want you, I will call you, Sav. Get that through your head. You will never come looking for me again. Do you understand me?' Mickey kicked Sav viciously in the stomach with one of his black patent-leather shoes. 'You can't live without me now, so you will come when I call.'

Sav heard a car door slam, then dirt and rubbish spattered his tear-stained face as Mickey drove off down the alley.

Sleep and pain were winning the battle as Sav dragged himself into a doorway and propped against a wall behind a dumpster. Vivid thoughts ran through his mind, but one stood out more clearly than the others while he lay there trying to catch his breath from the kicking. He might be lying in a dark alley, but at least he had stood up to Mickey and he was still alive. Others who had dared question the little slimeball had never done so again. Some had died and others had ended up with permanent disabilities. He hadn't, and it could be down to one thing only: Mickey needed him. It was probably just for another run. He didn't care, though. If Mickey needed him for anything, it gave Sav another chance at him. Now all he had to do was figure out how to use that other chance. He knew it couldn't be by himself, and he wasn't about to go to his father. There was only one other person Sav could talk to.

Chapter Twenty-Five

Max Tyler looked at Tony as they stood in the front bar of the Lincoln Hotel in Drummond Street. After they had arrived twenty minutes earlier, Jimmy the barman had gone into fits of laughter when Tony had ordered a coke for Tyler and a lemon, lime and bitters for himself. Everyone in the bar knew the big Sergeant's drinking habits and what he was like with a few Jim Beams in him. Most had witnessed him lose his temper with the odd patron – or two – whom Tony either didn't like the look of, or just didn't agree with.

However, the outbursts had been getting worse recently, and the local hoteliers were wondering how they would arrange a possible banning of one of the boys in blue. Would he still turn up when they wanted him in a hurry once a brawl had broken out in one of their pubs? None of them really wanted to dip their toe into that trough.

Tony had simply stared through the bartender while Max stood quietly behind him. The laughter suddenly subsided when Tony walked around the end of the bar, then reached for the bottle of bitters and a glass. Tony grinned at the retreating barman and the slack-jawed patrons, and said, 'From now on, Jimmy, this is the only thing you will serve me in here. I don't care what time of day or night I come in here, this is what I'll be having: L-L-B. And I don't think any barman worth his salt will get that mixed up with a bachelor-of-laws degree or even a JB.'

There were some relieved sniggers among the listeners.

Tony continued, 'Most of you know Susie. We're now officially engaged and I am officially on the wagon. And I know I've probably made an arse of myself in here before, but that is now finished.'

Some of the patrons came up to Tony, as he re-emerged from behind the bar, and slapped him on the back. They were never against him because word had gone around the traps about the demons he had been suffering since that car crash. Shit, they all had demons to purge at some time in their lives. The locals who sat in these pubs weren't your young up-and-coming hipsters who were starting to infiltrate the corner pubs, turning them into all-night boom boxes of noise and light. No, these were your average hard workers, and they could imagine how difficult it was to be a uniform cop in this inner-suburban United Nations melting pot.

A few of the drinkers who congratulated Tony, realised Max was one of the new rookies at Carlton. They all told Max that he could learn from none better than Tony. The big fellow would always have his back covered. More importantly, to these locals, Max would never have to pay for a drink while Tony was his partner. More than one of the people in the bar owed Tony a favour for sorting out things from minor behavioural slip-ups to friendly advice, instead of a couple of hours in the local lock-up.

Tony managed to break away from the well-wishers, so he could sit Max down at a window seat. Tony took the seat where his back was to the wall. Old habits die hard.

A relieved Jimmy put the drinks in front of the two cops, then sighed as he returned to his duties. The general night-time chatter resumed in his little domain.

'Mate, I know I'm taking a chance with this,' Tony began, 'but I really need to know if you want to partner me on this job. I've run it past Inspector Stone and he realises it could all go belly-up. If that happens, it won't be a problem for me because I'm at the other end of my career. You're a different case, because the job is about as shiny as a new Porsche to you at the moment, and I'd hate to see you dropped in the shit because you're following my every footstep.'

Tony had previously filled in Max about everything from Benny Illarietti being his uncle, right through to his history with Mickey Midolini, and the other night when he had followed his cousin Sav to Toorak.

'I've ignored Midolini for too long. That good-behaviour bond he got was a crock of shit. If I get that bastard again, he won't be going up before that in-pocket judge or some other magistrate who's as bent as a car crash. His bloody Honour, Judge Webster, will have bigger problems to deal with than trying to save little Mickey. Webster will end up playing the schoolgirl in the can, and he won't like his boyfriends in there one little bit. If you and I play our cards right, we'll get a big legal fish and a squirming mud crawler on the one hook.'

Max smiled as he took a sip of his drink.

Tony straightened himself in his seat. 'You'll have to put up with a bit from the boys at the station, because they all think I'm past it and couldn't catch a Collins Street tram, let alone a crook. But if you're willing, you'll learn more in a couple of months than they will in two years. It could fast-track you into the CIU or some other plain-clothes area. Don't ask me why I'm putting my faith in you. Probably feel sorry for you having an old man who used to be in the toe-cutters or something. You'll still be pulling some patrol shifts, but Inspector Stone will re-arrange the roster so we'll get a fair crack at Midolini. What I don't want you doing is acting like John Wayne at the station in front of the other trainees, just because we'll be doing our own thing most of the time. What do you think? You wanna get on board?'

'If you think I can handle it, then I'm willing,' Max replied quietly. 'I don't give a stuff what hours I work, cos I'd love to fuck them both over. I mean, I'd like to help you "nail" both of them. What made you pick me, though? There are some other good trainees at Carlton.'

'Who said anything about wanting a good trainee? I just want someone who's good with a computer, so he can handle all the paperwork. There will be reams of it,' Tony said, with a sly smile.

The young constable looked him in the eye and raised his drink. 'Whenever you're ready, Sarge. By the way, who's John Wayne?'

Tony slowly took their glasses and walked to the bar.

Taking two refills, he looked at the bartender and said with a resigned voice, 'I'm getting too old for this shit, Jimmy.'

Chapter Twenty-Six

Mickey Midolini was doing some serious thinking while he drove his Mercedes along Nicholson Street. He knew things would come to a head soon. It wasn't just a matter of keeping Sav quiet. That wouldn't last much longer. Sav was a mess, which meant sooner or later he would do one of two things: die from an overdose, or spill his guts while trying to get help to save himself. Mickey didn't want to hang around to find out which it would be. If Sav died from a needle, all hell would break loose around Benny.

Mickey's world would be turned upside down quicker than a pole dancer when Benny searched for the dealer who killed his beloved future doctor of a son. Mickey didn't want to be anywhere near Benny if and when some drug-addled piece of shit dropped his name in it. Those scum would say anything to save themselves from a bigger beating by Benny's apes looking for the killer. No, get things organised and get out soon.

It wasn't just trying to keep Sav from crawling to his father, either. The thought of Sav opening his mouth to Tony Signorotto sent a cold shiver up Mickey's spine. Or was that a 'shiv'? At least with Benny it would be quick. A bullet behind the ear. Mafioso style. But with that prick Signorotto, it would mean jail time and there was no way Mickey Midolini was going inside. He couldn't remember how many times he'd had cases dismissed because of a pay-out to a juror, magistrate, or judge, but at his last court appearance he'd graduated to a good-behaviour bond.

On a drugs charge there would be some serious stir time to do. He couldn't survive in jail no matter how short a time. Benny would make sure he was the jail hooker, and in the end Mickey would end up with a knife sticking out his back. The thought of bleeding to death, with his pants around his ankles on a cold wet concrete floor in the shower block of Barwon State Prison, gave him a dose of cold sweats.

A car horn blasting from behind shook Mickey completely. He had been sitting at a red light, thinking about prison and had missed the change of lights. A car load of young wannabes in a battered old Ford Fairlane was screaming abuse at him from behind.

One stepped out of the car's passenger side, ready to have a go.

Mickey's left hand slid down to the cold steel of his Beretta pistol next to the brake handle. *Come closer, you dumb shit. Make my day.*

The scrawny young guy ran up to the Mercedes and thumped his fist on the passenger window. 'Open yer fucken window, dipshit. C'mon… open it!'

Mickey slowly lowered his passenger-side window, enough for the punk to place his head inside. Before the hood could speak, Mickey's left hand snaked across the narrow distance and smashed the Beretta into a shocked face. The bones of the punk's nose were shattered by the first blow.

Before the bleeding shit-for-brains could recover, Mickey grabbed his shaggy head and pulled it so far inside the car the punk's legs were off the ground. Swapping his grip to the butt of the black pistol,

Mickey rammed the barrel through the closed teeth of the trapped and screaming prisoner. Broken and bloodied front teeth dropped to the passenger floor like a pocket full of spilled change, as Mickey jammed the barrel deeper down the punk's throat.

Some of the punk's mates had come up behind the gagging, air-dancing figure, but stood rooted to the spot when they saw the gun so far down the retching throat of their friend that the hammer was flush with the place where his nose should have been.

Mickey extracted his Beretta and brought it down viciously on top of the punk's head. He shoved the toothless, bloodied mess back out the window. As the body crumpled on the passenger side of the Mercedes, Mickey stepped out of his car and quickly walked around to where the punk was lying in front of his mates.

With the pistol in his right hand, Mickey spun around and fired two shots into the headlights of their car. Glass shattered and fragments exploded like an invisible hand had thrown them everywhere. The sound of screeching tyres and smell of rubber was all you could hear and see as vehicles in the vicinity vaporised into thin air.

Mickey turned heel and strode over to the prone punk. Mickey lined up his patent-leather right shoe, then kicked the mess as hard as he could in the groin. The punk began to vomit on the ground.

His three mates didn't move. They didn't speak. They were quieter than the tombstones in the Melbourne General Cemetery – which was where they would probably end up if they did speak.

'One of you get me the fucking numberplates off your car, now.'

No one moved.

Midolini's arm flung sideways. A third shot rang out. A bullet penetrated the grille of the Ford Fairlane. Coolant started to flow from beneath the steaming radiator at the same time as human coolant started to flow down the legs of one of the terrified punks. Walking to the side of the Ford, Mickey shot off another round into a front tyre. Hissing air sounded as the right bumper bar sank slowly towards the ground.

'I said fucking now, arseholes!' Mickey screamed.

By now the busy street had totally cleared of all foot and car traffic. Two of the shaking loud-mouths ripped their fingers apart taking off the front and rear plates. Horizontal punk lay groaning on the bitumen and held his crotch tightly as blood seeped from his jeans over his fingers and formed a small pool next to him.

Pointy shoes are not only cool, they're fucking handy! Mickey spat on the retching punk, grabbed the plates and threw them into the open window of his Mercedes.

The three hoons waited for the next demand.

'Whose fucking heap of shit is this?' Mickey barked, pointing at the Ford.

'M-mine,' stammered one of the terrified, piss-stained hoons.

'I want all your names. Do you have fucking licences, you heroes?'

The three hoons began nodding in unison, as Mickey delivered another vicious kick to horizontal boy whose head nodded slowly between groans.

'Give them to me.'

One of them grabbed the licences from all the wallets that were produced. No pity was taken on horizontal boy. His wallet and licence were snatched from his pocket by his friend.

Mickey put all the licences in his pocket. 'Open the bonnet of that heap,' he said, waving the pistol under the nose of one shit-scared hoon.

Once it was open, Mickey continued. 'Now that I know who you all are and where you all live, I know that none of you shit-bags will even think about going to the cops, will you?'

Three bobble-heads turned left and right like clown heads at a carnival sideshow. So did horizontal boy after another kick to his swollen balls.

'Stand your de-balled friend up, then lean him face-fucken-first over the motor. The rest of you can then also lean in like the good gutless wonders you are. After you take your fucking jeans and jocks off.'

Horizontal boy stayed where he was because he had now passed out.

His friends hauled him up and managed to place him, then themselves, face-first across the motor, with their bare arses pointing to the street and their fouled clothing lying on the road.

Once they were all in position, Mickey slammed the bonnet down as hard as he could on their heads.

Despite their screams of pain, Mickey still wasn't finished. 'Now, I don't want any of you to move a muscle, understand? Otherwise people will think you're playing with each other and call the cops. Do you fucking understand?'

The hoods howled their agreement.

With that, Mickey went over to the still intact front tyre and put two shots through it. The sound caused three nude butts to jump and smash their heads into the bonnet again.

Mickey stepped up behind each of the punks and ran the barrel of his Beretta up the inside of their legs one at a time, letting it touch their fingers as he did. 'This is the cold, hard steel of the barrel, boys. Now I'm going to do it again, but I might let a shot go this time. One of you might just lose a finger or gain a second arsehole. If he's lucky. I wonder which one it will be.'

All three started to shake uncontrollably and piss themselves.

Midolini burst out laughing. He opened the driver's door of the Ford, then ripped the cover off the fuse box under the dashboard. The ear-piercing sound of an air horn blasted from under the bonnet.

Mickey yelled, 'Don't you fucking move for five minutes. And next time you see a Mercedes, you show respect, understand?'

After one more slam of the bonnet and another kick to horizontal boy's head, Midolini climbed into his car and slowly drove away, laughing. *Respect. It's all about respect.*

He drove down Johnston Street, parked at one of his favourite restaurants, strutted inside and was greeted like a king by the owner.

As he took his usual seat by the wall, Mickey's mobile phone rang. 'Who's this?'

'Your legal friend from Toorak. I need some of your supplies for a little party I'm throwing next week.'

'Ring back tonight,' Mickey snapped, and hung up. He had one last run for Sav.

As Mickey's eyes devoured the menu, he muttered to himself, 'All this work makes a man very hungry.'

Chapter Twenty-Seven

The rain trickled down the back of Sav's worn shirt. It felt like worms crawling over his skin. But he didn't attempt to take cover. Being soaked through was the least of his problems. Getting wet was nothing compared to where he should be. He should be bone dry like Carly. Lying inside her coffin twenty metres away, next to the open grave.

The rain cascaded off the polished brown casket, pooling on the fake grass matting that was surrounding and partly covering the large mound of wet clay. The clay had a pasty look to it and was clinging to the shoes of the people close to the grave. Clinging like death itself. Like the shroud Carly was laid out in.

The flowers that adorned the coffin now looked bedraggled and very sad. As were the thirty or so mourners who were huddling around the gravesite, supporting each other for comfort under large black umbrellas.

Sav stood back, not just because he didn't want to talk to any of the people, but because he knew if he moved any closer he would be peering down into the grave itself. He was scared that some uncontrollable force would drag him towards the yawning mouth and hurl him down into the pit. His mind wouldn't let go of the picture where the lid of the coffin opened, and the voice of Carly Watson crawled over him saying, 'It was you. It was you.'

Sav knew exactly what the voice meant. It was he who first introduced Carly to Mickey Midolini about eighteen months ago.

Eighteen months ago, when the world was bright with new friends, a new life at university and all the possibilities that were open to them. He thought he could control his habit, and a gift from Mickey now and then, which he could share with his new-found friends, would all be okay. Carly hadn't been that hard to convince about her first hit. After all, it was free that time. It was just an experiment. They didn't really need to. It was just something they thought they had to do as part of the university scene.

It was amazing how many friends Sav could gather around himself with a free hit and some bravado about mafia people who owed him. He had acted like a partner of Mickey's at that time. It was so stupid to think he could keep getting it for free, even though Mickey did work for his father. But his father wasn't a drug dealer, just a businessman. Wasn't he?

A couple of months into university, when their grades started to go down a little, Mickey began hitting them all with a small price for his goods.

Mickey hadn't worried too much at first when some of his new clients couldn't pay. After all, they were friends of Sav's, and Mickey had them hooked. But a little later things started to spiral downwards. One of Sav's classmates turned up for lectures with a face that looked like he'd been on the receiving end of a sledgehammer. Then came the deals to replace some of the monetary payments. Not everyone was offered a deal, though, because some of Sav's friends were useless to Mickey.

Chapter Twenty-Eight

Jill Norton stood at the window that looked directly onto the front door of her 'Fortress Blue', as the Carlton Police Station was known to all and sundry. The morning had been interesting but not overly busy. She had a feeling in her bones that the afternoon would have more in store for her and her watch-house crew, namely Max Tyler and a young female probationary constable. She thought back to the days when policewomen were considered good for only two things… one of which was minding lost kids. Oh, how times had changed for the better.

'Jill,' Max called, in a pleading voice from where he was standing behind the counter. Max was facing a fat little prat waving a traffic fine in one hand and what looked like a large, rolled-up set of plans in the other. 'Can you give me a hand? I've got this fellow here complaining about his fine, as well as two phone lines on hold.'

'Where's Wonder Woman gone?' asked Jill, as she turned to look for the young female trainee.

'Probably on the computer in the back room, updating her status on Facebook.'

'Bloody Facebook! Oh, don't worry about it. Deal with the phone calls first, I'll look after this bloke. Hang up on the least important call. When they ring back, just blame Telstra,' Jill said, with a smirk.

The little prat, who was nattily dressed in a shiny black suit with an attitude to match, started to arc up when Jill returned to the counter. 'I want some respect and some service, and I want it now and in that order! I pay your wages, so fix this right now!'

Jill raised one eyebrow. She slowly leaned across the counter, putting her face right up to the motor mouth. 'And how can one of Her Majesty's finest help said citizen on this rainy Melbourne day?'

Prat slapped the traffic fine down with his left hand, gritted his teeth and growled. 'I'll tell you how. That bright boy in blue there,' he said, gesturing towards Max Tyler, 'slapped me with this 250 dollars' worth of "Get Fucked", as he put it, two days ago for going through a stop sign in Parkville. The prick was obviously waiting behind a bush or something. I couldn't see the stop sign because of a tree. I've got the council plans here to prove it. So fix this!'

'Where was this, *sir*?' Jill said, emphasising the word 'sir' with ironic exaggeration. Before Prat replied, Jill was visualising the intersection of Park Drive and Boyles Street. It was the corner she had sent Max and his partner to, a couple of days prior, in order to enforce the stop-sign rule with some traffic fines. Jill had already arranged the cutting down of the liquid amber tree, which had been blocking the sign up until a month ago. Her members had been to two accidents in the past few months because of that tree.

Holding the traffic fine right up to Jill's face, Prat said, 'If you can read, it says Park Street and Boyles Street. Can any of you lot read?'

Beckoning Max Tyler over to the counter, Jill said, 'I hope you haven't been handing out traffic fines lightly, Constable? The department would take a dim view of that behaviour. As she spoke to

Max she gave him surreptitious wink, then turned back to Prat. 'Could you roll these plans out for me, please?'

With Prat thinking he was winning the argument, he rolled out the plans. There was enough gold flashing on his fingers to make the pencilled streets of the plan look like the fabled Yellow Brick Road.

'Most interesting,' Jill said. 'Just one little problem with this plan. As you can see by the date in the top corner, it is over one year old. And for your information, *sir*, I had that tree cut down long ago. If you like, I can give you the phone number and the name of the company that did the job for us. By the way, did you pay for these plans?'

Prat was not happy. 'Pay? I don't pay for nothing. I have contacts. Good contacts. Why do you want to know?'

Leaning over the watch-house counter, Jill took hold of the edge of the rolled-up plans and proceeded to tear them from one side to the other. The Prat's jaw dropped floorwards.

'That's good then, *sir*,' Jill said, tossing the remnants in the rubbish bin. 'We wouldn't want you taking the old plans to court when you try to get out of the fine, would we?'

'Who do you think you are, you old bitch?' said the Prat. 'Like I said, I pay your wages. I'll have you for this. You can't do this. If you think I'm paying that fine, you've gotta be fucking joking.'

Jill stood up straight. She could feel the presence of her two young watch-house members step up behind her. 'Don't worry, sir. You won't have to worry about paying that fine.'

'That's more like it,' huffed the Prat. 'Good to see you know your place in life, pig. You fucking coppers think you can get away with anything. Well, you don't scare me. You're all shit. I earn more in a day than you do in a week.'

Jill kept her cool. 'That's very handy for you, *sir*. That extra money will come in handy for both fines.'

'What the fuck are you talking about?'

Jill put out her large arms to block the two young constables as they tried to go around her towards the enraged Prat. Max was set to jump the counter, and the young female probationary constable was readying a set of handcuffs by opening out their ratchets.

'Don't any of you touch me,' the Prat demanded.

Jill casually added, 'You'll also have to pay the fine that's being put on your car by the Traffic Police.' She pointed towards the scene unfolding outside the rain-spattered window. 'I would presume the ticket is for parking in the "Police Only" zone.'

The Prat gasped.

'Why don't you quit while you can, *sir*… and while I can hold back my boys and girls here from dragging your sorry arse over this side of the counter and down to the cells. It will save me charging you with offensive behaviour and indecent language in a public place – the public place being the police station you are now standing in.'

Prat's mouth opened and shut like a goldfish as he turned a deep shade of purple. He turned around and charged towards the exit, with parting words relating to the dubious ancestry of Jill and her young members. He swung the door open. The rain and wind blew in as he blew out.

Jill grinned at her two staff. 'I hope for his sake, he doesn't take on that Sergeant putting a ticket on his car. He's the Department's welterweight boxing champ. I don't know him too well, but they reckon he'd book his grandmother if he was short on his quota. By the way, team, thanks for the back-up. But I think I could've handled him if he'd started to play up.'

Max and his colleague winked at each other.

As Jill went to close the front door, there was an almighty crash. A saturated young man collapsed on the station floor at Jill's feet. 'Quick, you two, give me a hand. This young fellow looks about dead.'

Chapter Twenty-Nine

It was late morning when Sav staggered nervously up to the old red-brick police station in Drummond Street. The rain hadn't let up during his long walk from the Melbourne General Cemetery. He stood, dripping wet, with his hand outstretched centimetres from the doorplate. He remembered something Tony had told him years ago about police stations never needing doorknobs, because they were so busy the doors never had time to close. The rain fell on Sav like shots of lead as he stood, almost statuesque, while people scampered in and out of the door with their minds on their problems and hands on their umbrellas. Time stood still as the ever-increasing rain pounded off his aching body.

Sav felt himself being pushed aside. He'd been shoved by a small, fat, well-dressed man swearing at the top of his voice as he came out of the station.

Sav's knees crumpled and he fell to the ground.

He tried to get up, but he couldn't. A combination of Mickey's beating, his grief at the graveside that morning, and a complete sense of helplessness were crashing into his body and shutting it down. Sav actually felt as though he was drowning. He was soaked and there were voices spinning around his head. He felt as though he was being pulled at from different directions. He knew he was talking, but didn't have any control over what he was saying. 'Wet… Carly… help. Mickey, Mickey…'

Max Tyler leaned over Sav and took him by the arm. 'It's all right, mate. It's all right. You're safe now.'

'Get me a fire blanket from under the counter, quick,' Jill said, directing the young female constable with a jab of her finger.

Jill wrapped Sav in the silver sheath. Max and Jill lifted, then carried the limp figure into a nearby interview room. As they propped him in a chair, Jill looked at the young man's face. She'd seen him before but couldn't think where.

When Max raced off to fetch a warm drink, Jill knelt in front of the young man. 'I know you, don't I? You've got a familiar face.'

Sav remembered back to the few times he'd been taken to the station, when his cousin had dropped in for a chat after they'd watched Carlton play football at Princes Park. It had only been a few years ago, but now seemed like a lifetime. He vaguely remembered the large middle-aged lady who was standing over him now. Not for anything bad, though. He remembered the good feeling among the people who worked in the station. Good memories. Trusting memories.

While Sav sipped on the warm drink the constable had brought him, he started to think back to why he was there. He said quietly, 'Tony Signorotto. I-is he working today?'

'I never forget a face,' Jill said. 'You're Tony's young cousin, right?'

'Yeah, I'm Sav. Sav Illarietti. Is Tony working? I need to see him.'

'He's on a day off, today. But I can get him to call you.'

'I need to see him. It's urgent,' Sav replied, in a quivering voice. The cup fell from his broken hand. His body began to convulse violently.

Max reached out to steady him. It took a few long moments for the convulsions to subside.

'Please, just get him here, will you?' Sav said, still shaking. 'I know he'll want to talk to me.'

Max tapped Jill on the shoulder and pointed to the corridor. Out of Sav's hearing, Max said quietly, 'Jill, the Sarge and I pulled this guy over just the other night. He was driving like an idiot. The Sarge didn't want me to know about anything at the time. But I'm sure this is the guy who's connected to a drug case I've been assigned to with Sergeant Signorotto.'

Jill nodded, remembering Phil Stone marking Max's name off the station roster that very morning. Phil had said Max was going to be working with Tony on a permanent basis for the next few rosters. She never questioned an Inspector. It was his station and she knew that it could be for whatever reason he wanted.

'All right, Max,' Jill said, 'you keep him happy and warm, and tell him I've gone to contact Tony. If he tells you anything of importance, get it down on paper as soon as you can. Not in front of him, mind you. He might clam up. We'll let Tony deal with it, if and when he gets here.'

Jill sent Max back into the interview room. She went back to the watch-house counter and looked up the private phone numbers of the staff listed on the computer. She dialled Tony.

After three rings, she got through. 'Tony, Jill Norton here. I'm sorry to bother you on your day off, but you'd better come down to the station, if you can. We've got young Sav Illarietti here and he wants to talk to you, A-S-A-P. I'll keep him in the back interview room. Just one thing, though. Is young Tyler in with you on whatever this is?'

After getting a roundabout answer from Tony, Jill put the phone down slowly. She didn't know if she should be pleased or afraid for Max.

Jill returned to the interview room and saw that Sav was a lot more settled than before. Taking Max aside, Jill said to him quietly, 'Son, if this gets as messy as I think it will, you make sure you stick to Sergeant Signorotto's back like shit to a blanket. If you don't, then you're going to be one very lonely and scared probationary constable. Understand me?'

Max raised his eyes to meet Jill's. Her look nailed him to the wall like a knife-thrust.

Chapter Thirty

Tony's car was parked outside a place most males would prefer to drive straight past: Kylie J Bridal Gowns in Sydney Road, Coburg. He had tracked down Susie and her forward-search troops with one phone call.

Earlier in the day, Tony had dropped Susie and her three bridesmaids – Gina, Rosa and Silvana Santino – off farther south in Sydney Road, so they could explore the bridal-wear shops together.

They had obviously reconnoitred, out-flanked and disarmed a lot of shops and their owners as they infiltrated their way north.

Tony had taken the phone call from Jill Norton about Sav. His immediate thought was that, if he did go back to the station, he would be locked into an ugly fight to the end against his uncle's side of the family. That was because Sav wanted Tony, not his father. The stage was set and it would come to a head a lot faster now. He was thinking what he might say to Sav, when Susie appeared out of the rain under an umbrella at his car door.

'We are at decision time in this shop,' Susie said cheerily, through the partly open window. Then she took in the expression on Tony's face. 'What's up?'

'Susie, I've got to go to the station. You know Sav Illarietti, my cousin? Well, apparently, he's there and pretty distressed about something. Jill Norton said he will only speak to me. I know I promised I'd be here to take you all home, but if you want me to, I've got to go now. I'm really sorry, but this sounds urgent. If you want to stay, I'll pay for a cab for all of you.'

Knowing what Sav being at the station meant, Susie also knew that she had to make up her mind between her friends, shopping and her man. There was no decision to make. 'I'm coming to the station with you. I'll shout the girls the cab ride home. I have to talk to you about Sav. Wait here.' She turned and disappeared back through the rain.

The authoritative tone of Susie's words left Tony feeling a little confused.

Ten minutes later, as the big Ford sedan headed south along Sydney Road through Brunswick on its way to Carlton, Tony asked, 'What's this about Sav?'

'Look, the other week when I was worried about you, which has been most of the time lately, I went to see Phil Stone. It was after one night when you didn't show up at my place, after you promised you would. I thought you'd gone off to the pub or something and I was bloody mad.'

'What the hell? What do you think you're doing by going to Phil Stone for Chrissakes?' Tony's voice was growing louder. 'Let me tell you –'

'No, shut up, Tony. Let me tell *you*. Don't come the heavy cop with me. Don't you even think about raising your voice with me, you bastard!'

The volume of Susie's voice made Tony hit the brakes, nearly spearing a car into their rear.

Susie didn't miss a beat. 'You just be damn grateful that you have friends like Phil Stone… and a fiancée. Yes, a fiancée who loves you and has loved you since you first swaggered into the Co-Op too many years ago. And Phil told me that you were working on a drug case involving Sav and Mickey Midolini. I know it will be dangerous, but if you want me as your wife, you'd better believe the fact that you get me twenty-four/seven, you thick-headed wog!'

The thick-headed wog went to speak, but was cut off again.

'I haven't finished. Don't think for one minute that anyone who hurts you won't get it back in spades from this little girl. When are you going to wake up to the fact that it is not all about *you, you, you*? If Midolini or any one of his sleazebag mates wants to take you on, they'd better realise that they take *me* on, too. Now shut up and drive.'

Susie slammed herself back against the seat, her body language leaving Tony in no doubt that he'd better do as she said. He couldn't recall Susie ever speaking to him before in that tone of voice or with such steely determination. His mouth opened and shut. He was as confused as a teetotaller in a brewery.

Minutes later, driving along Royal Parade in silence, Tony dared to sneak a sideways glance at Susie. Her look could have cracked the windscreen. Seeing that face of determination gave him more confidence than bringing a gun to a knife-fight.

Chapter Thirty-One

Tony parked his car about fifty metres south of the station. Before Tony had locked the driver's door, Susie was out and standing by his side.

'Susie,' he said, 'I have to try and nail Midolini. Between Max Tyler and me, we *were* going to keep a tail on Sav, but now it looks like he's come to us. I don't know why, though. That's what I have to be careful about. The last thing I want to do is scare him off, especially if he wants to use me as his "father confessor". When we go inside, I want you to stay in the mess room, okay?'

'Bullshit to "okay",' came the acid-tongue reply. 'I'm not going to sit around with some pimply-faced recruit and run cups of coffee to you. I don't work for you, Tony. You'd better re-adjust that Italian brain of yours and stop telling me what to do. I'll go upstairs and talk to someone whose thinking is a little more attuned to this century. Phil Stone and I get on like a house on fire, and I'm sure he'll fill me in with all the details when he hears about your family chat-room downstairs.'

Slapping his hands in despair against his jeans-clad thighs, Tony walked towards the station.

Susie suddenly called out in a tone that made him turn around quickly. 'Tony, I love you and I know this might get very ugly with your family involved, but remember this: you're mine, not theirs. I want to know all about this crap because it's the only way I can deal with it. If we have a future together, don't try and cut me out, understand?'

Tony stood for a few seconds before he answered. 'Understood.'

Chapter Thirty-Two

The rain had almost stopped as Tony entered through the back door. He felt it before he saw it: Jill Norton's stare. It was like being hit between the eyes with a hammer.

Tony knew what the look was for. It was the look she gave anyone, regardless of rank, whom she thought was going to get any of the probationary constables under her care into any form of trouble. Her concerns this day were obviously for Max Tyler.

Tony chose his words cautiously. 'Jill, I know what you're thinking, but I'll look after him. It's been given the green light by Phil Stone for Max to work with me on a drug bust. At least I hope it will be a drug bust.'

'Looks like a family matter to me,' Jill said, indicating Sav Illarietti sitting forlornly in the interview room. 'Just remember, Tony, young Max is family also. Police family. Uniform family. Look after him.'

It was beginning to dawn on Tony just how many families and relationships there were involved in this that needed looking after. Blood family, future family and the blue family. He didn't dare stop to think about the consequences if it were to go belly-up. It was too daunting, and daunting things made him think about the easy escape – back to the bottle.

Quietly closing the interview room door behind him, Tony eased himself into the chair beside Sav. 'Before you say anything, Sav, remember one thing. I will look after you as far as I can, but I can't and won't break the law just because you're family. Let's get that point straight right at the beginning. Understand?'

Tony watched closely as Sav nodded his head slowly, while shrugging the blanket farther up around his shoulders. It reminded Tony of a protective cocoon. *Appropriate in the circumstances.*

Raising his tired eyes to look at his cousin, Sav started to speak with a voice that was halfway between self-pity and panic.

Chapter Thirty-Three

The next few hours in the interview room were both a torture and a relief for Sav. He poured out all he knew about Mickey Midolini. The way he had been drawn into Mickey's web. Mickey's threats to tell his father of his sexuality, Sav's haunts and, of course, his all-consuming drug habit.

Tony wasn't about to charge Sav with anything, but he made sure it was all recorded. There was one thing missing, though. Sav could point the finger at Mickey – for everything from assault to blackmail, and even top-class drug-dealing with some very prominent Melbourne A-list people – but Sav never came even close to implicating his father Benny Illarietti. Tony didn't know whether to breathe a sigh of relief or disappointment. That was all for another day and another battle.

An hour into the recording, Sav asked for a breather.

Tony knew from experience that he should keep Sav talking without a break. Tony wanted the whole sordid story, not just some tasty morsel that would never get to court, let alone secure a conviction. Tony managed to keep Sav on track with some careful coaxing.

In between Sav's sobs and deep breaths, Tony was formulating a plan for the future handling of his cousin. For it to work, Tony needed to know if Sav would trust his handlers from here on. One handler needed no further introduction. It would be himself. The other was a risk on both sides. Max Tyler had no experience in the day-to-day running of an informant. One wrong move by Max and the whole thing could blow up in their faces. If Sav didn't have confidence in Max, then he could drop his guard and try to get back into Mickey's good books, merely on the promise – real or not – of a hit of smack. This would be a real tightrope job. Tony hoped Max could keep his end taut.

Eventually, Sav finished his side of the story.

Tony excused himself and left Sav with a strong cup of coffee, a pack of cigarettes, and a softly spoken female officer passing his door every few minutes.

Tony quietly gathered Max from his watch-house duties, and quickly guided him upstairs to Phil Stone's office.

Tony knocked at the same time as he pushed open the door. The Inspector was seated behind his desk and Susie was sitting on his couch. It seemed Tony and Max had interrupted an intense discussion.

Phil Stone looked over the rim of his glasses. 'Last time you were in my office, Sergeant, you witnessed me tipping out young Maxwell on his ear for rushing in here. Any reason I shouldn't do the same to you?'

Before Tony could reply, Susie stood and said, 'This must be Max Tyler.' She put her hand out to greet the new constable. 'Susie Doherty. Nice to meet you.'

Max smiled and shook Susie's hand. 'Good to meet you, too, Susie.'

'I've heard a lot about you, Max, and I've convinced Sergeant Dinosaur here that you couldn't be as bad as what he makes out.'

'Well, ah… thanks.'

Susie smiled at Max and crossed the room to pick up her bag.

Max's eyes couldn't help but follow Susie as she walked towards the door.

Tony and Phil shared a look.

Susie turned back to them. 'It's obvious you three have things to discuss, so I'll leave you to it. Next time the coffee will be on me, Phil. Nice to meet you, Max.'

'By the look on his dial, Susie,' Phil said, nodding towards Max, 'you could call him anything but late for breakfast.'

Susie grinned at Phil, then started back towards Tony. As she stepped past Max, Susie gave the now red-faced constable a pat on the arm. She went right up to Tony and put a hand on his shoulder. 'It's all right, Tony. I've had a long chat with Phil, and I understand what you have to do. Give me a ring when you've finished. Whenever. Don't worry about the time.' Susie gave her fiancée a quick kiss on the cheek.

Before Tony could reply, she was gone.

Phil cleared his throat, then said, 'Righto, Sergeant, what have we got going on here? It had better be rock solid. I know the basics. Sit down both of you.'

Both police officers took seats without replying.

'Max, listen up. Brain on, mouth shut for the moment,' Phil said, with a tight smile. 'Nothing personal, but I want the Sergeant here to cut to the chase and come up with enough facts to justify you two playing Starsky and Hutch for the next few weeks.'

Tony went through Sav's story from A to Z.

Phil interrupted on several occasions, with many and varied points of law as well as ideas to help justify what his Sergeant was after. Time and resources. Which in headquarter's-speak meant overtime and money.

When Tony had finished, he was satisfied he'd given his Inspector all the relevant facts. Tony could tell they were both feeling that old tingle up the spine. White hat versus black hat. Us against them. Except that this was no kids' game. It would be a high-stakes, cover-your-arse fight.

Phil stood and looked out the window into Rathdowne Street. After what seemed like an eternity to Tony, Phil turned, placed the palms of his hands on his desk, and looked the big Sergeant directly in the eye.

Max looked on in amazement, realising this was no talk between friends. This was two old-time coppers doing what they did best. Going head-to-head with the Dark Side.

'Sergeant. You want Midolini real bad, don't you?'

'Like a dog outside a butcher's window,' Tony replied, straight-faced. 'Real bad, sir. Not just because of Sav, though. It's what he's doing to all those kids. What he's doing to us. He's laughing at this place. He thinks we don't exist. That the Carlton Police Station is just a bunch of blue uniforms to wipe his boots on. He thinks the suburb of Carlton is his little fortress, and I think it's time we showed him that it isn't.'

Phil paused for a few seconds. He took a look at Max, then slowly pulled the invisible blanket of brotherhood over them. Phil's voice took on a conspiratorial tone. 'You do realise that we could, ah, somehow, get all this information to Benny Illarietti, sit back, watch the fireworks, then just go in with body bags and pick up the pieces, don't you? It would save us all a lot of work.'

Max replied quickly but warily, 'I don't know if you're trying to test me out here, sir. But just because my father is on the advisory board of the Office of Police Integrity, and was a toe-cutter at one time, it doesn't mean anything to me. He does his job and, if given the chance, I'll do mine. I'd like to hunt this prick down… along with Sergeant Signorotto here, of course. This bastard deserves whatever we can give him.'

Without waiting for Phil to reply, Tony cut in, 'Sir, I want him my way. Midolini got off last time. But this time around he won't have His Honour Judge Webster to look after him when he ends up in the County Court. I'll do Webster, too. I'll give them both a hamburger with the lot.'

'That's what I wanted to hear, Sergeant. I want a clean sweep of all this shit.' Phil tapped his desk a few times. 'How will Benny fit into all of this?'

'Right now, I want to pull Midolini out from under Benny. If he falls over, too, then bad luck. If Benny's mafioso brothers-in-arms hear his trusted lieutenant has disrespected him by ripping him off, then Mickey will be disgraced. He will have to see out his days making pasta sauce in his backyard.'

'Do you think you're up to this, son?' Phil asked, looking Max in the eye. 'You've got bugger-all experience, but do you want a shot at the title? Senior Constable Norton said you're looking pretty sharp downstairs, and have brought in some good catches in the last couple of weeks. If you come through this, your old man would be proud as punch of you. Just remember, though, you don't have to prove anything to anybody.'

'Sir, if Sergeant Signorotto thinks I can help him get Midolini, I'd love to have a go. The experience would be fantastic.'

The Inspector was pleased. 'All right, Sergeant. What's our first move?'

'Sir, Sav discharged himself from hospital not long after Benny saw him. He told Benny a pack of lies about how his hand got wrecked. But Benny's not stupid. He'll know there's more to the story. I'm going to have to take Sav home and give Benny the spiel about leaving the investigation to us. Make it as routine as possible.'

Phil snapped back, 'Jesus, Sergeant, if Benny finds out this is all down to Midolini, he'll reel him in and give him the Glock handshake.'

Tony had anticipated this possibility. 'I'll tell Benny that Sav has been done over by some cross-town punks looking to get in on his patch. That might make Benny send Midolini out to look for them. It'll also make Midolini think the heat won't come down on him. He'll just think he has more time to set up another one of his skim jobs. For us, it'll be a matter of keeping Sav on track. I don't know how long he could run in a sting, but we have to get that hand fixed first.'

Phil nodded. 'If Midolini is skimming from Benny, even he knows it can't go on forever. If he gets caught, he's dead meat. There's got to be a safety clause somewhere for Midolini. Maybe he's thinking of skipping town? If you can convince Benny this is coming from another side of the city, it will not only give Midolini some breathing space to dig his grave a little deeper, but it'll give you two enough time to put a plan together to trap the piece of shit.'

'Fair enough, sir,' Tony replied.

Phil leaned over to the other side of his desk to retrieve a report, which he handed to Tony. 'Midolini's running hot around here at the moment. This is a report of an assault up near Johnston Street. However, the complainant isn't one of the victims who were assaulted. From the sounds of it, Midolini never saw this brave individual standing nearby taking his numberplate, while he vented his spleen on a bunch of wannabe punks. He left these four in the middle of the bloody road, after inserting their Ford Fairlane down their throats via the bonnet. Don't know how it started, but Midolini certainly finished it. Shots fired into their car, as well. Broad bloody daylight. I want this added to the list when you nail him. He's out of control. One of these punks will be walking with a stoop, holding onto his balls till hell freezes over. That's if he's got one left after he gets out of hospital.'

Tony and Max exchanged looks.

Phil's voice began climbing towards the ceiling. 'I want Midolini's arse nailed to the wall of this police station, do you hear? If he thinks he can waltz around my Division pulling this sort of crap, he's got another thing coming. This is *my* patch and I won't have this sort of fucking shit pulled here!' Phil thumped his desk.

Max wisely waited a moment to respond. 'Sir, why don't I get back downstairs and play nice guy to Sav? It sounds like it would be timely for him to think he's got a friend. When Sergeant Signorotto comes down, he can talk about taking him home.'

'Not a bad idea,' Tony agreed. 'Sav's been down there by himself for a while now. He needs all the friends he can find at the moment. How about Max getting into some civvies? Bit less intimidating than the clown suit.'

'Okay, Constable,' Phil replied. 'I want a quick word with the Sergeant here, anyway. Off you go.'

Max bounded down the hall, heading for the change room.

Phil Stone's office turned eerily quiet. 'Tony, you're not alone here. Besides Supercop Max, you have me. And after the long chat I just had with your gorgeous Susie, it's as plain as the big schnoz on your Italian face that she adores you. Let's get through this together and, when we do, we'll all raise our glasses at your reception at Dom's.'

Tony went to speak, but Phil put up his hand and continued. 'Yes, I know it's not all over the station… yet! Susie's only told me and she wants me to tell my missus. Second thoughts – no. She'll blab to the Superintendent's missus, and she's not called "Radio Australia" for nothing. It'll end up in the *Police Gazette*. What I wanted to say is this… congratulations.'

'Thanks, Phil.'

'I know it's been a hard road since that kid died in the smash, but you have to keep living and not many people get a chance as good as Susie at your age. Mate, if you don't want her, I'll wrap her up myself and take her home for a spare.'

'Phil, if everything turns out all right, you'll have had a big hand in it. I promise you this, though, my toast will be in lemonade. It's all I could obviously handle… at my age.' Tony grinned and gave Phil a sly look.

'Speaking about fizzes, mate,' Phil said, sliding his glasses back on, 'you'd better get back to Sav's world.'

Tony stood to leave. 'Yes, sir.'

Phil Stone dug himself back into his mahogany foxhole and attacked the latest incoming from his mound of never-ending paperwork.

Chapter Thirty-Four

On the short drive to the hospital, Max was at the wheel of the unmarked police car. Tony sat in the passenger seat, with Sav in the back seat. Tony had to explain to Sav what he needed to tell his father Benny in order to help Tony nail Mickey Midolini.

The first step was going to be extremely hard for Sav. He had to confess his drug problem to Benny.

The second step would make the whole confession slightly easier, by giving it one very important twist. Benny had to believe Sav had been dragged into addiction by some low-life other than Midolini, preferably from Benny's circle of rodent employment. This would not only buy Tony and Max time to start their operation, it would also keep Midolini within reach. If Midolini twigged that Benny was on to him, he could skip the country and they would have nothing.

While Tony was speaking, a sting was formulating in his mind. 'Like it or not, Sav, you're going to have to get in touch with Mickey again. After a few days of R and R in hospital, of course.'

With his damaged hand still throbbing, and the idea of trying to sell his father a lie, Sav felt this demand from Tony was like a slap in the face. 'Tony, I'm never going near that piece of shit again,' Sav cried, on the edge of hysteria. 'I am fucking terrified of him. He's a fucking maniac. No way, no way!'

Tony gave Sav a don't-argue-with-me look. 'You don't have a choice, Sav. Well, actually, you do. But the other side of the coin isn't worth contemplating. You either work with us or we let you out of the car here and now. If Mickey ever finds out you've paid me a visit – and I'm sure he will from somewhere – you can expect to go from Vic Pol's Witness Security Protection Program straight across the big divide to the Mickey Midolini Witness Cancellation Program. One thing I'm sure about, Sav, is that you would become his top priority program.'

Sav was now in a sweat and his voice began to quiver. 'Who'd tell him I've been to see you?'

Max shifted uncomfortably in the driver's seat.

Tony leaned between the seats and put his face up close to Sav's. Despite facing backwards, Tony made sure Max could overhear his every word by speaking in a voice that sounded like gravel being crushed. 'How many coppers were in the station while you were there?'

Sav shrugged.

'By the time you'd left, I reckon there would've been at least ten uniforms and detectives, not including the brass who saw you in the interview room. Coppers are curious bastards, Sav. They all want to know who's been in their bed, if you get what I mean. Your name had to go into the Attendance Register just because you ended up on our side of the counter. If any of them checked the book and saw the name "Illarietti", it wouldn't take much to put two and two together. But I made sure that book was out of reach to everybody there today. At the moment it is in my desk, all safely locked up. Mickey would pay well for that sort of information, and there's nothing a cop likes better than a free night of entertainment with all the trimmings. Think about it, Sav. Work with us or get cut adrift.'

Sav slumped in the back seat. Tony could feel the heat from the look Max was giving him.

Tony lowered his voice, but not his sense of urgency. 'Sav, my cousin you may be, but there's the side with the white hats and the side with the black hats. The white hats can help you. The black hats, or one of them anyway, will kill you. When we get out at the hospital I want an answer.' Tony looked out his window and could see the front of the Royal Melbourne Hospital through the trees along Flemington Road. 'That gives you about one minute.'

Sav glanced ahead to the hospital. He looked worried but said nothing.

Tony tapped his watch. 'Time is ticking, sunshine. As I said, you are either with us, or we let the Dark Side do what they do best.'

Max pulled into a parking space. He jumped out of the driver's seat, then quickly went around to confront Tony as he climbed out of the passenger seat. 'You'd better be full of shit about what you said about the members. You're telling your cousin we're all a bunch of crooks. What are you on about?'

'Of course it is, Max,' Tony replied quietly. 'Don't worry about it. We've got no time left to get Sav to help us. It's right now he has to climb on board. He has to realise he's safer with us.'

'Yeah, fine, Sarge. But what about the members and the Attendance Register? What about that?'

'You and I know everyone at the station is straight. Next time, open your eyes as well,' Tony said wearily. 'If you'd paid attention, you would have noticed that neither Jill Norton nor I even got the Attendance Register out. To get results, Max, there's a time when you're so busy that some things just slip your mind. It's the *result* we're after here. A result for everyone. Right now it sounds as though I couldn't care less about Sav. Rest assured, I do. Now get him out of the car and turn him to face me directly.'

Max thought about what had been said as he pulled Sav from the back seat.

Tony watched on, with both hands behind his back, fingers crossed. 'What's it gonna be, son? Do you want our help or not?'

Time passed slowly before Sav looked up at his cousin. 'I'll do what you want, but you have to promise me that when it's over, it *is* over. You know what I mean, Tony. No more Mickey Midolini.'

'Oh, my word is concrete on that, Sav.' Tony winked at Sav, and the tension eased. 'Now let's get that hand seen to.' Tony put his arm around Sav's shoulder and, with Max walking behind, he ushered Sav through the automatic doors, past the emergency waiting room and straight to a cubicle.

A nurse quickly approached the group of three. 'Back in the waiting room, please,' she demanded, impatiently trying to wave them away. 'Don't you realise there's a queue?'

'Not today, there's not,' Tony said, pulling his police identification from a back pocket of his jeans. 'We're starting work on this lad right now.'

Chapter Thirty-Five

A lot of thoughts were running through Benny Illarietti's mind as he sipped a short black in the rear of a café in Johnston Street. Most of them illegal.

The story that his nephew Tony Signorotto had given him at the house that morning was obviously a cover. Benny hadn't let on that he already had information which put Mickey right in the sights of a nine-millimetre kiss. His nephew wanted to get to Mickey before he did, so Tony had given Benny the line about Sav being dragged into his mess by some shithead from the western suburbs. *No buy, nephew. Sorry, Tony. You may be family and all, but Sav is my only son and I will deal with Midolini. You may be the cop, but I've already discovered what I want to know.* A vicious, thin smile stretched across Benny's tense face.

During a closed-door session with his two henchmen, Benny had been told that Sav had discharged himself via the back door of the hospital. Not a good sign if he was the victim. Benny could blame the two heavies, whose job it was to keep an eye on Sav, but that didn't hide the fact there was a lot more to the situation.

In Benny's world nothing was unfixable. Everyone had their price. Even the good doctors at the Royal Melbourne Hospital. A cold shiver had gone through Benny when the words 'drug addict' were mentioned in relation to his one and only son. Benny had tried to ignore the slur, but something else kept niggling at him. The facts would not go away. Benny Illarietti's world was not necessarily starting to spin off its axis, but it was definitely working up a serious speed-wobble.

One of Benny's smaller customers, a staffer at Melbourne University, had been slowly feeding him information on Sav's academic progress – or lack of it – in return for a drip feed of his own. Namely, a drug concoction to soften the edge after a hard day of tutoring the future doctors and surgeons of the land.

Benny had instigated his inquiry after he noticed Sav had not been talking at all about his studies in recent weeks. This was a total reversal of Sav's first semester at uni, when he was blitzing exams and wanted the world to know. First a feast, now a famine. Benny had tried to question his son on the increasingly rare occasions he saw him, but Sav was always evasive.

To compound matters, the same Melbourne Uni staffer had let it be known that a steady supply of first-grade 'H' was trickling through to the med students on campus.

Benny had one of his henchmen remove a delivery from a friend of Sav's, then return it to Benny. Suspicion turned to fact when he tested his supply against the removed article. Identical. This made Benny quietly re-check his incoming deliveries with what was going out. He was no fool. He had started out very small years ago and built up his trade by accounting for every gram that went through his business.

It soon became obvious Benny was paying for more than what was being delivered. He trusted his suppliers implicitly and had even brought them up to speed on the possible scam. He worked with them on the packaging of each shipment. When the articles arrived on his desk, he saw there were subtle but definite packaging differences.

There was only one answer. It had to be his man who personally handled all his shipments. That fucking rat, Mickey Midolini. His so-called 'trusted lieutenant'. If Mickey was scamming him, Mickey would be taken care of. But God forbid, if Mickey was using Benny's own supplies to turn his son into an addict. If that proved to be true, then there was nothing on Earth that would save Mickey from a very grisly death.

Benny had gone straight to the Royal Melbourne Hospital when he heard Sav had been assaulted. He was deeply worried about Sav and had duly set in place the best care money could buy. The sight of his son's mangled hand and pock-marked arms brought down the crimson mist before Benny's eyes.

Unfortunately, Benny could not see the irony of the situation. His thoughts were too busy turning from black to blood red.

Chapter Thirty-Six

Tony stared down a shaft of light coming from his kitchen. It was beckoning him to the fridge. It was the only light on in his flat. He'd been sitting on the edge of darkness, staring out the lounge-room window across the city skyline. Shaking. Old demons were coming back to haunt him. It wasn't the temperature in the flat. Tony had turned on the heating when he'd come home. Now he was just wearing a pair of boxer shorts. No, not the heating. Just heat from the past.

Too much thinking. Thinking about how he was going to handle this case. His mind kept tossing images of Sav and Mickey in and out of the too-hard basket. One minute Tony convinced himself that he had the right plan and the right people to help him, like Max Tyler. That's what the little man on one shoulder was telling him. Next he heard another voice telling him to forget it all, kick back and go have a drink.

After two hours, Tony's brain was flip-flopping like a hooked fish and his hands were beginning to shake. The demon had gone from his shoulder down to his fingers, forcing him out of his chair, and walking him with faltering steps to the fridge.

He opened it.

Tony took in a vision of light beaming from a can of bourbon sitting at the rear of the bottom shelf. *Where did that come from? I thought*

I'd emptied the whole flat out of grog?

As he stared, a single drop of moisture slid down the outside of the can, leaving a clear path through the chilled exterior, which enveloped the beckoning cylinder of comfort. Gulping dryly, Tony licked his parched lips. His eyes couldn't shift from the can. It was like a naked woman beckoning him to come and be enveloped in a warm sexual embrace. It was mesmerising.

A hand slowly slid from his shoulder to the back of his neck and started to squeeze. Tony was so focused on the can he had now taken from the fridge, he thought the feeling on his neck was just his throat further constricting over his next decision: whether to open the can and pour the contents down his throat or down the sink.

With the mysterious touch now gripping his hair, Tony's centre of attention clicked like the trigger on his gun. The chill went from the can through his whole body. Clenching the cylinder in his fist, so he could use it as a weapon against the intruder, Tony swung around to face his attacker.

Tony's striking hand stopped inches from Susie's face. 'What the...?' Tony exclaimed. 'What're *you* doing here? How'd you get in?'

Susie seemed quietly pleased with herself. 'The door was unlocked. I was on my way home from the office and just needed to see you. You didn't hear me walk in. I've been standing here for ages, just watching you.'

Tony stood with his hand down by his side, dropping the can to the floor, not saying anything back to Susie. The can rolled slowly back towards the fridge, as if heading for home.

Their eyes locked.

Tony reached back with his foot and slowly closed the fridge door. Not a word was said as he walked Susie unhurriedly towards the patio door.

She reached up and ran a fingernail down his naked chest, stopping at the top of his shorts.

Tony slowly slid the jacket of her business suit down over her shoulders, dropping it to the floor. Even in the dim light, he could see her nipples were as hard as peach stones against the tight fabric of her shirt. The only sounds he could hear were his thumping heart and her quick, raspy breathing. With one fluid movement, his hands went to her shirt and pulled the fabric apart, causing the buttons to fly off in different directions, landing metres away and skidding across the polished floor.

Susie stood against the backdrop of the city, reached behind herself and unclasped her white-lace bra, letting it slide down her arms. She threw it over the back of a lounge chair next to her. Stepping forward, she caressed her firm breasts with both hands, holding them up until they brushed gently against the hairs of his chest.

Tony took both her hard nipples between the thumb and forefinger of each hand, and rolled them around gently, causing Susie's knees to wilt slightly.

She moaned with pleasure and dropped her head onto his shoulder, sliding one hand under the elastic band of his boxer shorts, encircling his hard cock with her smooth hand. Pulling the material up and over the straining member, she began to lightly run her long fingernails along the shaft, from the swollen tip down to his balls.

Now it was Tony's turn to moan.

With Tony on the point of climax, Susie moved back and quickly stepped out of the other half of her business suit. Standing with legs slightly apart, she guided Signorotto's hand to the front of her white-lace bikini briefs, placing his palm firmly against her crotch. Then she began to slowly move his flattened hand up and down against the thin material. She whispered in his ear, 'Why are you just wearing your boxers?'

With his erect cock now hard against her flat stomach, Tony replied with the voice of a chastened youth, 'I was thinking of having a quick nap on the couch.'

'Room for two?' Susie asked, as she placed the tip of her tongue in his ear.

With that, Tony reached around her back, swung her up into his arms, her breasts hard against his chest, and with her arms around his neck. He took three steps, then put her gently down on the leather couch. He watched as she tipped her head back and began to slowly pull her knickers down over her hips and knees.

Susie gently lowered them from one toe onto his bare foot.

Tony knelt between her parted thighs as she reached up and pulled his head down between her breasts.

Susie moaned and raised her hips as her lover entered her, and gently slid every inch of him into her wet and waiting sex.

They were immersed in each other. The sounds of Susie's soft, low whimpers, as Tony slid his shaft gently in and out of her, merged with the sucking sound of their naked bodies slapping, gently at first, then in frenzy against the sweat-covered black leather couch.

Susie's grip tightened around Tony's neck. At the same time, she whispered into his ear, 'Screw me. Take me. Do whatever you want with me.'

Their passion built into a final shuddering climax from within each of them. They slid off the now slick couch onto the floor, both exhausted, arms and legs still entwined, with Susie still bucking under Tony's now spent manhood.

Seconds passed as they lay still and silent.

'You screwed me like there was no tomorrow, Tony. It was absolutely beautiful. What was with the darkness thing when I got here, though?'

Tony pushed himself up onto one shoulder. 'I was just shitting myself about what I'm going to do with Sav and that prick Midolini. I was really wondering if I'm up to it.'

Susie slid her hand down to his crotch, gently squeezing his spent cock. 'Well, you were certainly right up to it a few minutes ago,' she said laughingly.

Tony slid his cock out of her hand, stood and walked over to the balcony door. He heard the sound of Susie's feet gently padding over behind him.

She put both her arms around his waist and pressed her breasts into his back. 'You were really giving that can a good stare for a while. Why didn't you open it?' Susie asked, half afraid of the answer she would get.

'I don't ever want to touch the stuff again. If I do, I will be letting you and everyone else down. What I want is you and my life back together. The piss isn't worth it. I want that prick Midolini nailed to the wall of the County Court, and you in my life forever. That's enough for me to handle at the moment, don't you think?'

'You know what I think? I think you're more than good enough to handle Midolini or any of his kind.'

'I need to talk to someone other than work people about how I want to do this sting. All coppers think they can do anything. They will all just nod their heads and tell me to go for it. I want to get the facts from someone else who's looking in from the outside. Know what I mean?'

Susie let go of Tony's waist, picked up her knickers from the floor, and walked quickly into the bedroom.

She returned in Tony's shave coat, picked up his boxer shorts and threw them at him. 'I'm making a coffee and then you can run it all past your trusty lieutenant here. I'm the one who'll give you the lowdown on whether it's safe or not. Trust me.'

For the next hour, they sat side by side on the couch while Tony went over how he planned to bring Midolini to justice. He soon realised that Susie was coming up with some good suggestions about how he and Max could get it done.

'You are so good for me, Susie,' Tony said, eyeing her lovingly.

Susie looked up at the wall clock. 'Oh, God, I'll have to go! It's almost one o'clock.'

Tony grabbed her by the hand and pulled her up to his chest. 'Just two more things to do.'

Susie looked at him with a puzzled expression.

Tony walked over to the can of bourbon he'd dropped before their lovemaking. He took it into the bathroom, opened the shower door and turned on the water.

'What are you…?' Susie began to ask, as she unconsciously tugged at the cord of the shave coat, letting it fall on the bathroom floor.

Tony smiled at her. 'You're staying here tonight, lieutenant. Now obey orders and step into the shower. Stand at the rest position, legs apart.'

Without speaking, Susie stepped into the cascading water.

Tony whipped off his boxer shorts and hopped in next to her. He ripped the top off the can of bourbon. To Susie's relief, he poured it onto the shower floor. They both watched the brown liquid swirl down the plug hole.

Tony looked up and tossed the empty can over the top of the screen onto the bathroom floor. 'Never again,' he said, through the steam.

Tony hungrily kissed the nipple of each wet, slippery breast.

'What else are you good at ripping off?' Susie teased, as the water streamed down her breasts and saturated her knickers.

Tony put one hand on the band of her knickers and gave a short, hard tug. The wet transparent lace gave way at Susie's hips, as he pulled the remaining fabric slowly through between her legs. He picked her up as easily as a feather.

Raising both knees, Susie wrapped her moist thighs around his hips as he lowered her onto his hard, wet shaft.

The steam from the shower enveloped them like a Turkish bath. Their guttural groaning rose to a crescendo above the sounds of gushing water and bodily friction against the wet wall tiles.

Chapter Thirty-Seven

'How are you holding up, Sav? Tony asked, as he stood looking out the third-floor hospital window into Flemington Road. He had arrived ten minutes earlier and checked with the Senior Constable guarding the door that there had been no visitors during the morning or the previous night. Benny had not yet paid a visit to his son.

'My hand is killing me,' Sav whined. 'They're going to operate on it this afternoon and try to straighten the fingers. Mickey has fucked it completely.'

'Mate. The hand will heal… eventually. It's what we're going to do about Mickey and you contacting each other that we have to figure out. The sooner the better.'

'You'd better hurry things up, Tony. One of the nurses on duty last night knows me. She'll tell someone for sure. She's back on tomorrow morning.'

'No real problem in that, Sav. Who's she going to tell? One of her nurse friends?'

'You don't get it,' Sav said, as he twitched and moved around in his bed. 'She's screwing one of my mates from uni. One of my best mates.'

'Sav, the only friends you have are druggies and gays. Don't tell me she is fucking one of your druggy friends?'

'Yeah. He's my best mate.'

Tony's brain was working overtime as an imaginary train of thought cannonballed through his head. Spinning around to face Sav, Tony spat his words out, 'Are they customers of Midolini, like you? Like all your mates at uni?'

'They're not all drugged up, Tony,' Sav said tersely. 'Not *all* of them, anyway.'

Tony bent over Sav's prostrate body, looking directly into his pale sweaty face. 'Are they fucking buying from Mickey? That's what I want to know. Don't play goody-two-shoes with me, Sav. This is fucking big-time serious shit and I need to know now.' Tony abruptly realised he had started to yell at Sav.

The door to the room swung open and the police guard filled the doorway. 'You right, Sarge?' he asked.

'Yeah, yeah, no problems. The boy here is just a bit hard of hearing, that's all,' Tony replied, with a wink at the hulking Senior Constable.

The guard smiled and retreated, closing the door quietly.

Tony lowered his tone but wasn't going to let up. 'Sav, if they are buyers, this can help us set up the sting. Just think. If you know the little bitch, then tell me more. I need to know about her and her boyfriend. If we have to, Sav, we'll work them over without them knowing. You have to start thinking about yourself and how you're gonna get out from Mickey's clutches. Fucking well wake up to yourself.'

Tears started to trickle down Sav's pasty face, followed by racking sobs.

Tony threw his head back, sighed and started to pace the room. *It's either start the sting now or wait till who knows when?* Midolini's leering face appeared all over the walls in front of Tony.

Suddenly, two strides and Tony was beside the bed. He grabbed Sav by his hospital gown, lifting his body upright. A vicious slap was delivered to Sav's face, followed by the violent throwing of his head back into the pillow.

The crying stopped immediately, and Sav crawled backwards in his bed like a whipped dog.

Tony's eyes bore into him. 'Help me, Sav, or Midolini will kill you. Fucking kill you, hear me?'

A full minute went by while Sav sucked in huge breaths and stared at the wall.

Tony waited him out, all the time saying nothing.

Eventually, Sav turned and looked at Tony through red-rimmed eyes. 'Tell me what I've gotta do,' he said, in a low voice.

'Okay. This is how we're going to play it. When this nurse is on next, see if she can get a mobile phone to you so you can ring Mickey. You're going to tell him where you are, and that you're trying to get out because you need a fix and some money. Let him think you just don't care anymore. That you've told Benny everything about yourself because you're at rock bottom.'

Sav absorbed this part of the plan, without saying a word.

Tony sensed he was gaining traction. 'Mickey will shit himself if he thinks you've told your old man about all the sex, drugs and especially the rock 'n' roll with your hand. That's the ace up your sleeve. If Mickey doesn't go along with your plan, you'll drop him in it – with Benny. Mickey won't do anything to you if he knows that

Benny and I have got you in hospital, and he thinks Benny believes your hand was wrecked by some western suburbs shit-for-brains.'

Sav nodded but was still wary.

'Promise this little powder monkey that Mickey will fix her and her squeeze up, if you can get out early without anyone knowing. We need him to pick you up. Don't worry, I'll have you covered everywhere you go and I'll have you wired for sound. If he thinks you shot through from the hospital early, he won't suspect we've got you covered. Tell him you've got one more run left in you for a big delivery with a big cash payout.'

'Who should I say it's for?'

'Give him a story that the money is for Carly's family, to help them with her funeral expenses. And that unless you get the money to them personally, a letter will be left for Benny and me giving the true story about the drugs he's been dealing to you and what he did to your hand. In this supposed letter we'll say Mickey has arranged for you to get out of hospital early via this nurse. Your mate, the nurse's druggy screw, can be the holder of the letter for all Mickey knows. If you come through the run and get back, then the letter will be mailed to Mickey. If not, it will go to your old man. Mickey will think you're desperate, and this will be our chance to get him up front in a big sting.'

Sav's face was beaded with sweat. 'When do you want to do it?'

'We need a couple of days. Today is your operation, so let's try to arrange it for Friday. That gives us three days. Tomorrow you tell her you need a phone to ring Mickey. Let her act as your go-between. Tell him that she has to keep the phone on her because I won't let you have one. If Mickey asks why I am involved, you can give him the story that I am helping protect you on behalf of Benny, because you've told Benny and me there is a dealer from the western suburbs after you. We know this is bullshit, but that is the entire safeguard Mickey has. That you have been mistakenly done over by a west-side heavy. That'll give Mickey some breathing space – if he thinks you're lying to Benny. It also gives him the chance for a delivery.'

'Tony, let's just hope that my old man stays out of this long enough for you to nail Mickey.'

'I've spoken to Benny and he's promised to let me fix Mickey. It won't be long, though, till Benny snaps. He was very cool yesterday, but it's impossible to know what's going on in that mind of his. I might have street smarts, but, Sav, we both know your old man is capable of anything. He'll be able to find out very quickly about some bullshit piece of western-suburbs trailer trash. We have to play our game before he gets on the field. I want this prick put away, not just given a quick behind-the-ear ventilation shaft by your old man. Let's do this for Carly.' Tony gripped Sav's hand and squeezed.

It was returned by a sweat-soaked grip.

Chapter Thirty-Eight

'You are fucking *where*?' Mickey Midolini snapped.

'The Royal Melbourne fucking Hospital,' Sav replied. 'I got put in here a few days ago because of what you did to my hand, you prick!'

Tony and Max were sitting beside Sav's hospital bed. Tony was listening to the phone call through an earpiece attached to Sav's borrowed phone. Both police officers were in plain clothes – jeans and T-shirts.

Sav's operation had not been a complete success. His fingers would heal, but he would never have full movement in a hand that had been inserted with three steel rods. In time the scars would grow over, but simple things like holding a coffee cup in that hand would be an impossibility.

Tony liked to think the steel put into Sav's body was now giving his determination the mettle to avenge Carly's tragic death.

'Who knows you're in there?' Mickey asked, clearly unnerved.

'Benny knows because Tony Signorotto told him, arsehole.'

When Mickey heard those names, he slumped back in the leather seat of his Mercedes and stared through the windscreen. The fact that he'd just let Sav get away with calling him an arsehole didn't even register.

But it did with Tony. *He's shitting himself.*

'I don't care anymore, Mickey,' Sav added. 'I've told Benny everything. The drugs. Why I'm failing uni. Everything. The only thing that's saving you at the moment is that I told my old man and the cops my hand was done over by some phony crook from the west.'

With a touch of bravado returning to Mickey's voice, he said, 'Well, if you have everything covered with daddy and your stinking cop cousin, what the fuck are you ringing me for? Why should I be concerned?'

'Because, Mickey, you're going to pay up big time for Carly. Her family doesn't have any money and you're going to give them some. In fact, you're going to give them plenty.' Sav spoke with conviction, but sweat was dripping from his face.

Max Tyler put a hand on Sav's shoulder to reassure him.

'What the fuck are you talking about?' Mickey barked. 'Why should I be paying up for some slag friend of yours who treated her body like a pin cushion?'

'You started her off on heroin, prick, then just kept selling it to her. You didn't give a fuck about her, Mickey.'

'You're right on that point, Sav. I didn't give a fuck about her and I don't give a fuck about you.' Midolini nervously tried to bend the sports steering wheel with his clammy left hand.

Silence bounced between both phones.

Tony covered the mobile with his hand, so Sav could drink some water from a glass handed to him by Max. But most of the water ended up on the sheets.

Tony whispered, 'You're doing great, Sav. Now let him know you're weighing up whether to tell Benny the truth about your hand.'

Sav nodded.

Mickey's mind was racing at a million miles an hour trying to out-think Sav. *I knew I should've just given him a beating and left his fucking hands out of it.*

Sav took a deep breath and continued. 'I want $20,000 from you for Carly's family. In cash, Mickey. Or I tell Benny… and Tony.'

Midolini's mind raced. *You fucking piece of druggy shit. I'll fucking kill you. The last thing I'll do before I get out of here, so help me, is fucking kill you.*

The silence from Mickey convinced Tony he'd bought the ruse. *You're fucked now, Midolini. We've got you.*

'Where do you think I'm gonna get twenty grand from, Sav? I only get what your old man pays me. Okay, I get paid well, but I don't have twenty g's just lying around. You tell me where I'm gonna get twenty big ones from!'

'Toorak drugs!'

The two-word reply Sav fired back hit Mickey like a couple of solid slugs from a Mossberg pump action.

'That's fucking dangerous shit you're talking, Sav. You don't wanna mess around with this.' Mickey's voice was one octave below panic mode. He grabbed at his tie, then ripped the top button undone from his Italian silk shirt because he could feel his airways starting to constrict.

'Mickey, I know the address and I don't reckon that Benny doesn't know about your delivery there. Tell you why, dipshit. You've been using me as a courier, not one of the old man's boys. If this is as big as I think it is, he would've had you doing it yourself, and certainly not to the client's house. I may be a druggy, but I can still out-think you, prick.'

Midolini was panicked. *I've gotta get hold of Sav and kill him.*

Sav grew bolder. 'I can read you like a book, Midolini. Don't think about coming here. There are cops on the door. Big cops. Now listen to me. I got this phone through a nurse here, who is a girlfriend of another one of your uni clients. A good friend of mine. I'm meant to be getting out of here Saturday, but I'm gonna walk out tomorrow and you can pick me up. Don't even think about doing anything to me, because I'm leaving two copies of a letter for this nurse and my mate. In it will be all the details of what you've done to me. Your so-called "company drug sales" and the address of whoever the client is in Toorak. If anything happens to me, one copy is going to Benny and the other to Tony Signorotto. Get that?'

In his shock, Mickey almost forgot Sav was on the line. *Webster wanted another run. Was it this Saturday?*

'Did you hear me, Mickey? Now your arse is mine,' Sav hissed into the phone.

A more conciliatory Midolini spoke into his mobile. 'How about I pick you up? No more talk over the phone. Never know who is listening. I'm sure we can work on this together for a *mutually agreeable* outcome.'

'I'll be out the front of the hospital at three tomorrow afternoon,' Sav said. 'Pick me up. We need to talk… and fast.'

'I'll be there,' Mickey said, then slowly lowered his phone into his lap. *I need a last payday and him dead. Sav, my boy, you're gonna do a final run.*

Sav hung up.

Mickey checked his phone's contacts, picked a number and hit the dial button. Two rings and it went to voicemail. Mickey left a message: 'Saturday night party goods. Ten big ones for the pick-up.'

Sav lay back in his sweat-soaked bed. He was ashen-faced and short of breath.

Max tried to get him to drink some water, but again, Sav spilled most of it.

'Good job,' Tony said, unplugging the earpiece.

'Good job?' Max piped up. 'I thought Sav was bloody fantastic!'

'Agreed. *Very* good job, mate, well done,' Tony said, with more conviction. But something wasn't quite right. Midolini had given in a little too quickly.

Chapter Thirty-Nine

Mickey gulped down another coffee. *Why doesn't he say something?* He could feel his heart racing as he sat at the back of the café, opposite Benny. It was only an hour after Sav's phone call and Mickey's mind and stomach were turning somersaults. All of Benny's boys were walking in and out of the café like it was the Bourke Street Mall. *Maybe he hasn't said anything to them?*

Benny continued to silently survey his boys.

Mickey couldn't bear it any longer. 'What's on for today, Benny?' Mickey spoke loudly, so all around could hear. 'Anything you want done, or is it business as usual?'

Benny slowly looked up at his lieutenant with a facial expression as unreadable to Mickey as a Braille menu. Finally, Benny broke his silence. 'I want all of you over here, now.'

When Benny spoke, all his henchmen immediately moved in front of him like schoolboys called to the headmaster's office.

Mickey held his breath. He was suddenly surrounded by several well-dressed gorillas. *I'm trapped. I can't get out past these idiots.* He was finding it hard to breathe.

Benny began to hold court. 'You all know my son Sav,' he began, in a quiet voice.

Mickey's arse-cheeks gripped his chair. His breathing became shallow.

The broad shoulders and shaven heads of Benny's boys leaned forward, over the top of Midolini.

Benny scanned the faces around him. 'Some piece of western suburbs scum has done him over.'

Mickey let a breath of air rush loudly out of his lungs. He felt his stomach turn to jelly. He kept his arse as tight as a fish's.

'You right, Mickey?' one of the bullet-heads asked.

Benny's eyes bored through Mickey.

Mickey forced a weak smile. 'Yeah, no problem. Just a bit crook in the guts. I've gotta switch pizza parlours. That one up in Lygon Street has changed its…'

'Enough of the fucking pizza story,' Benny yelled, as he thumped the coffee table in front of him. The jolt caused Mickey's cup to jump from its saucer and spill the contents over a well-thumbed copy of the *Il Globo* newspaper.

Time stopped.

The world stopped.

Eventually, Mickey spoke. 'Sorry, boss.'

'Shut the fuck up, Mickey. This is more important than even you. Understand?'

Mickey's head moved up and down.

Benny adjusted his tie. 'My son has got himself into a little bit of trouble. Nothing that I can't handle, of course. We are, however, going to tighten up on a few things around our patch. The main one is this. If any of you hear of, or see, a piece of shit you don't know who's doing any business on our turf, I want you to deal with it immediately.

You have my blessing and that of the family. Don't contact me. Just deal with it… permanently.'

Shaven bowling balls began to bob like plastic ducks in a bathtub.

Benny continued. 'I especially want to know if any of these are from the west. My son is in hospital with severe injuries because he was mistakenly done over by some future dead piece of scum. Get out now and continue with business. As I said, there will be no questions asked, but there will be promotions given and monetary rewards. Now piss off.'

Mickey's blood pressure began to subside.

Leather jackets rustled and oily skulls glinted under the fluorescent lighting as they headed towards the front door.

Mickey was near the exit when Benny called out, 'Mickey, back here, now!'

Mickey stopped in his tracks, like he'd walked into an invisible wall. *Oh, fuck.* His blood pressure surged again. He turned slowly, looking around the shop to make sure all the goons had gone.

'Sit,' Benny said.

Mickey sat.

Benny continued with his ploy. 'I've got a job for you. Seeing you're my right-hand man, you will take this and deal with it.'

'Of course, of course,' Mickey said, fidgeting in his seat. 'What is it?'

'I've been given a name of the head piece of scum that did over Sav. You will take care of him.'

'Who is it? Do I know him?'

'Stefan Zilmoski. Dealer from St Albans. He'll be at this address tonight,' Benny said, handing his offsider a scrap of paper. Don't ask questions. Zilmoski will not see the sunrise.'

'Who gave you the name?'

Benny stood. 'Sources. That's all you need to know. I'll expect to hear about his demise on the six p.m. news,' Benny said, walking towards the door, leaving Mickey staring at his back.

Mickey's thoughts went into overdrive. *This has got to be a set-up. Even if Sav said he'd been done over by some hood from the west, he wouldn't know any. He's only ever dealt with me.*

He couldn't even find St Albans.

Who's his source, anyhow?

Why'd he come up with this?

Sav reckons Benny and Signorotto know.

This'll be them setting me up.

Benny wants me dead.

There's no way I'm gonna do that.

Phone.

Book the flight for Sunday afternoon.

Mickey walked out into the sunshine, still with the address in hand. He hadn't even looked at it. For a long moment, he stood with both hands on the roof of his Mercedes, staring at the ground.

Slowly getting into his car, Mickey threw the paper onto the passenger seat, then started the motor. He blindly pulled out into the traffic, causing vehicles to come to a sudden stop, horns blaring.

Benny watched the commotion from the laneway opposite the café. He couldn't helping thinking his 'friend' was looking very distracted. He doubted Mickey would turn up tonight, but was prepared to be proven wrong.

Chapter Forty

'Are you sure this will go off all right, Tony?' Sav asked, while holding up his T-shirt so Max Tyler could tape the thin microphone cord securely to his chest. 'What if somebody comes in and finds out that I'm about to piss off out of here?'

Tony replied calmly, 'Sav, nobody's going to find out. Benny thinks you're being discharged tomorrow, and I've made sure that little coke-freak nurse friend of yours is working in another area. She's spending the day in a ward full of drug-dependent zombies, so she should feel right at home. She's probably helping some dope-head roll up his admission form and snort a line or two out of his vomit bowl. We don't need her or her phone anymore.' Tony turned away from Sav, picked up a pair of binoculars, and checked out the service lane in front of the hospital.

Sav said tersely, 'Underneath it, Tony, you're a real prick. You couldn't give a fuck about anyone, could you?'

Without taking his eyes from the binoculars, Tony shot back, 'You'd better believe it, cousin. Don't fret, though. I'm just a prick, but Mickey is a killer according to you. Remember Carly? If you've changed your tune about him being responsible for her death, then let's call the whole thing off. I'll just leave you two to catch up for coffee and doughnuts so you can have a nice little chat, eh?'

Max glared at his hard-edged Sergeant.

Tony didn't notice.

Max finished taping on the pin-sized microphone head, then tapped it lightly. 'Working?'

Tony nodded slowly. 'Just make sure when you go down to meet him, Sav, you don't for any reason get into his car. I don't give a fuck if he points a bazooka at you, you don't get in. He won't do anything out front of the hospital. Tell him you wanna talk deals, but you'll meet him down the road at the McDonald's inside the Royal Children's Hospital. Two window cleaners will be working there. In fact, they actually work for the Department. Both undercover techs. Do *not* stare at them. There will be a table near them, which will be clear. Sit at it and let Mickey come to you. Everything you say will be recorded and videoed. The mike you're wearing is just in case he says anything at the car. Have you got all that?' Tony put the binoculars down.

'Yeah, yeah. Got it,' Sav sighed, adjusting his T-shirt.

'Good, because Midolini has just pulled into the entrance. Let's get going. Run over the deal again.'

Sav took a deep breath. 'I want money for Carly's family. Twenty grand. I don't give a fuck where he gets it from, but I want it soon. I throw in the Toorak connection once more. If I don't get the money, the letter will go to Benny and you. If he asks where Benny is, I tell him that Benny thinks I'm getting out Friday, not today.'

'Right, good. I've got another two under-covers in an oxygen-cylinder delivery truck within spitting distance of where he's parked. They will be filming your meet. It might sound a bit over the top to you, but I want every bit of evidence I can get on this bastard for court. One final thing. Come here.'

Sav walked over to Tony, one arm in a sling covering any possibility of Midolini seeing the wire.

Tony put one hand behind Sav's head and put the other on his free shoulder. 'I am a prick, Sav. I'm a prick because I hate everything about this little slimeball. Always have, always will. You, however, are family. Yes, you've put yourself in a shit-sandwich here, but I know you have it in you to help me get this scum. Between you, me and Max here, we are going to rid Melbourne of a very fat sewer rat. You might've wondered what I would like to do to your old man after this, but let that slide for now. That's all for another day and you won't be involved. Let's go to work, eh?'

Sav walked out of his room to the lift. He hit the down button on his third try, his good hand was shaking that much.

Chapter Forty-One

Sav walked quickly out the front door of the hospital. He first had to see where Mickey Midolini was parked.

Midolini was hard to miss. He was the one standing by the door of his black Mercedes, yelling at an ambulance officer, 'Fuck off, you blood bus driver! I'll stay parked where I want to.'

Two paramedics began walking towards the Mercedes. One of the officers was pointing at Midolini.

Sav hurried over and managed to step between the two parties before they started warring. 'It's okay, fellas. He's meant to be picking me up. I'll get rid of him.'

The paramedics came to a stop. They sized up the situation, then turned and walked slowly back towards their MICA ambulance.

Midolini smirked at the retreating pair, ready to keep calling the shots. 'Get the fuck in, Sav. We're going for a drive.'

It was fight-back time. '*You* get the fuck in, Mickey. I'm telling *you* what to do now. If you think I'm driving anywhere with you, you're mad.'

Midolini's face dropped. He opened his mouth to abuse Sav.

But Sav cut him off. 'Drive down to the McDonald's at the Royal Children's, and I'll see you in the car park. Now piss off down there.'

Midolini's face turned bright red. He stood stone still, with fists clenching and unclenching.

One of the paramedics called out to Sav, 'You want our help now, mate?'

His partner was glaring at Midolini. 'Looks like you're about to have a heart attack, little fella. Got the kiddie-size bed in the back here. Just your size.'

Midolini was furious. He pivoted on both feet, jumped into his Mercedes, then laid ten feet of rubber as he fishtailed and smoked his car into the service lane.

Sav started the walk down to McDonald's. *I hope I haven't snapped him completely.*

Ten minutes later Sav saw the seething drug dealer sitting in his Mercedes outside the takeaway restaurant. Sav pointed inside and walked in.

Midolini stepped out of his car, slammed the door and followed Sav inside.

Sav's breathing became more regular when he saw the two supposed window cleaners near the empty table. He sat down. *So far so good.*

Midolini took the chair on the other side of the table and leaned across. 'Listen, you arsehole, who do you think you're dealing with? *I* give the fucking orders and *you* follow them. You better do what –'

Sav's resolve hardened. *It's me in charge from now on, you piece of shit.* He butted in, 'No, Mickey, you shut the fuck up and listen. Remember the letters? Anything happens to me and you'll have not only your boss after you, but also Tony Signorotto. And I can tell you this, shithead, Tony Signorotto would love to nail your fat little arse to the wall at Port Phillip Prison. Now I'll tell you what *I* want. The first thing is some food. Get me a Big Mac and a coke and get back here fast. Move!'

The blood drained out of Midolini's face as he stared daggers at Sav. But slowly Midolini stood up, turned and walked over to the ordering counter.

Sav snuck a quick look at one of the window cleaners, who winked back at him.

When Midolini returned, Sav pounced on the food like there was no tomorrow. *If I'm starting a war, it might as well be on a full stomach.* He gorged himself on the meal, then slurped down the coke with such a noise that even kids two tables away looked at him in disbelief.

Midolini was now slightly calmer and had not spoken a word while Sav ate. Finally, it got the better of him. 'What do you want, Sav? What's this letter going to cost me?

'I told you, Mickey,' Sav said, as he wiped his mouth on his sling, 'twenty-thousand dollars. Not for me. It's for Carly's family. You sold her the drugs. You killed her. You pay up. That's it in a nutshell. You give it to me and I'll give it to them. You don't cough up, then your arse is Benny's… and Tony's. Remember, the only thing they don't know is how this hand got wrecked.' Sav held up his bandaged appendage.

Midolini replied through gritted teeth, 'I could just do you right here and now, you fucking piece of blackmailing shit.' Under his suit jacket, Midolini could feel the tensile steel of his Beretta pistol pressing into the small of his back.

'You must be worried, Mickey. That's the stupidest thing I've ever heard. What're you gonna do – shoot me here in the Children's Hospital? Have a look around, fuckwit. Kids everywhere and security cameras, as well. Why did you think I wanted to meet you here? Why didn't I get into your car, eh? You *are* going to do this. Once I have given that money to Carly's parents, the old man will send me off for a long holiday in Italy and you'll be safe.'

Midolini had other ideas about where Sav might end up holidaying. 'What makes you think I can raise twenty G's?'

'Don't think I'm stupid, Mickey. You may have got me hooked before, but I know what you're up to. Like I told you. If you were legit with my old man, you would've been doing those Toorak deliveries yourself, not using me. I don't care where you get the money from, but surely whoever has those squealing parties at that house could fix your money problems?'

'It's not that easy.'

Sav waved away Midolini's objection and looked across to the ordering counter. 'Get me a sundae and we'll keep talking.'

Midolini hesitated.

'Go on,' Sav said, growing in confidence as he pointed Midolini in the direction of the counter.

Midolini fumed as he stomped over to order a sundae. His brain was ticking over, trying to think of ways to get the money over Sav's dead body.

Sav stole another glance at the undercover technicians, who were pretending to be focused on some particularly stubborn spots on the windows they were cleaning.

Midolini returned and placed a sundae on the table in front of Sav. 'It just so happens there is a drop tomorrow night back there. I'm owed an amount of money from this customer. You're not much good to me with that hand, though.'

'You didn't worry about that when you smashed it, so don't start now. I'll do the drop. How do I get paid?' Sav asked, raising his voice slightly so the undercover techs could get a good recording of the conversation.

'It'll be a drop and a pick-up. You get the pick-up back to me, and I'll add some more to it. You take it and fuck off out of my life.'

'I'll decide where I drop it off,' Sav insisted. 'Let's make it at La Stazione. It's a little coffee shop in Flinders Street, just near Elizabeth Street. It'll be full of train drivers who've just finished their shifts. Even if you're thinking about something, there'll be too many witnesses. What time is the drop-off in Toorak?'

'My client will want it by nine tomorrow night – no later,' Midolini replied. 'The package will be in your car in the car park, as usual.'

'No. Even with the letter as insurance, I don't trust you, Mickey. I'll leave my car in the car park of the Carlton Football Club. Lots of space there. It'll be there at six tomorrow night. You do the drop, but I'll be watching. When you're gone, I'll do the delivery to Toorak. Now tell me exactly what I'm delivering.'

'Fucking baby powder for his guests – what do you think? Some coke and some hash. That's all you need to know. Enough to keep his girls satisfied.' Midolini's agitation was rising. He wanted to hash Sav's brains and knew his temper wouldn't last much longer.

Sav said quietly, 'Once we leave the coffee shop tomorrow night, you won't see me again.'

Midolini's head was thumping like he was in the front row of a rock concert. At the end of tomorrow night, he would make sure no one saw Sav again. But Midolini held his tongue, stood up and walked to the exit, without looking back.

Sav couldn't move from his seat. His whole body was sapped of any energy he'd had when he walked in.

As the black Mercedes roared out of the car park, Tony and Max entered through the rear door of McDonald's.

Tony walked over to reassure Sav, while Max went over to the two undercover techs cleaning the windows. After a moment, Max looked across the room and gave Tony and Sav a thumbs-up.

Tony patted Sav on the back. 'It's all on tape, mate. Let's just get through tomorrow. Tonight you can stay at my place.'

Sav struggled to his feet. 'Just get me to a bed. I'm fucked.'

Chapter Forty-Two

'You don't scrub up too bad in civvies, Tony,' Jill Norton said.

The jeans-clad Sergeant was climbing out of the unmarked police car in the station's backyard. He grinned and grunted in reply.

Jill shook her head. 'Hey, listen, Lone Ranger, where's Tonto gone?' She had a friendly but steely edge to her voice. 'I hope you're looking after that kid.'

'Don't fret, Jill. I've got him minding Sleeping Beauty back at my place,' Tony replied quietly, as he looked around the yard.

The only other person who knew the real story about Sav and his visit to the station was Jill Norton. Being the permanent watch-house keeper, she was the barometer of everything that happened, not only in the station but also around the suburb she had worked in for over twenty-five years. Nothing surprised Jill and nothing shocked her in Carlton's ever-increasing melting pot of society. If there were going to be any inquiries about Sav, she would fend them off with professionalism and a 'don't ask me again' smile.

'Phil Stone in?' Tony asked.

'Is he ever out?' Jill shot back. 'He's afternoon-shift Duty Officer and he was here at twelve. I think he's having a coffee.'

Tony walked across the cobble-stoned backyard towards the rear of the station, then into the mess room.

Stone was sitting there with a coffee while reading the *Police Gazette* on his laptop.

'Stop looking for other jobs,' Tony called out, as he pointed to the police transfer section of the gazette that was up on the screen. 'You're not going anywhere till this shit's sorted out with Midolini. It's all starting to go a bit quicker than what I'd planned, though.'

'Why, what's happened? How's Sav handling it all?'

'No problem there. But I think Midolini has something planned. Unless he's shit scared of me and Benny, he seems to have given in to our bluff for the twenty thousand pretty quickly.'

'Twenty thousand?' Stone blurted out, spilling his coffee on the table, just as the morning-shift car crew came in with their lunch. 'What have you got me into here, Tony? Have you swapped trams or something? The Department isn't putting up twenty thousand for you to play drug deals with this prick.'

'No, no. How about we go upstairs to your office and I'll explain it all to you? Seeing that you're on afternoon today, I think you're gonna want to know what's about to happen,' Tony said cautiously.

Crossing the yard, Phil looked at the bounce in Tony's step. 'I don't know what's in store for you tonight, Tony, but I can see you're up and about again, just by the walk.'

Phil and Tony were now back within earshot of Jill Norton. She grinned at them.

Tony paused at the base of the stairs to Phil's office. 'It's just my tight jeans, you old pervert. Christ, all the boys around here will think you've got a thing for a good-looking Sergeant.' Tony turned and bounded up the stairs.

Phil flashed a wink at Jill. 'That's the Tony Signorotto I know, Jill. Italian, flash clothes and full of shit… as per usual.'

Jill smiled to herself as she noticed two amused young constables who had given way at the door to both the Inspector and the Sergeant. 'Let's just hope it doesn't turn to shit,' she muttered under her breath.

Chapter Forty-Three

Sav sat in the back seat of Max Tyler's Nissan sports car, his hand throbbing. Sav couldn't afford to take any more painkillers, otherwise he might not make it through the night. He was getting little sympathy from either Tony or Max. Sav looked at his watch. 'My car's been parked over there for an hour now. What if he doesn't show up?'

Max replied quietly but firmly, 'He'll show. There's a run to do and money to be made. That's why he'll show.' Max's eyes again scanned the car park of the Carlton Football Club. Sav's yellow Audi was parked at the northern end. 'One thing about your wheels, Sav. They don't look out of place at this club.'

Football training had finished and most of the players had returned to their expensive chariots and gone. A few of the younger players were still on the track, trying to impress the coaching staff, looking for a senior game in the following weeks. The cars left were mostly Holdens and Fords. Twenty minutes before and it would have been hard to pick Midolini's black Mercedes in the midst of the luxury car lot.

Tony and Max had decided to take Max's car to do the sit-off. Midolini would pick an unmarked police car a mile away, and Tony had been driving the same car for years. Midolini would be sure to recognise it. The Nissan sports, it was.

They had been parked in the same position for almost two hours. For Tony, it was a silent agony. He had been fighting all the emotions of the night of the crash. Max's car might have been a different colour, but otherwise it was the same as the doomed vehicle. It was like sitting in a pressure cooker, and Tony didn't know how much longer he could take the recurring screams in his head and the vision of the burning arm. *For fuck's sake, hurry up, Midolini!*

'Hope we haven't missed him,' Sav said.

'Midolini's fat, little cockroach body won't be hard to miss among the lads at this place,' Tony said, as he cast his eyes past Sav's car and into the parkland.

'True,' Max added.

Suddenly, something caught Tony's eye in one of the driveways. 'Here he comes, thank Christ!' Tony said.

A black Mercedes crept slowly into the car park and stopped in the parking bay next to the Audi, facing in the opposite direction.

The three of them unconsciously stopped breathing as the driver's door to the Mercedes opened and the ferret-like form of Mickey Midolini stepped out. His head performed a 360-degree sweep of the area.

Midolini reached back into his car. He extracted a package about half the size of a house brick. Swiftly, he opened the driver's door of the Audi, offloaded the package and shut the door.

In a flash, the cockroach was back inside his Mercedes, but he didn't start the engine. He sat and waited for something.

All the while, Max was snapping photos of the scene through a long-distance lens attached to a Sony SLR police camera. 'What's taking him so long to go?' Max asked, over the whir of the camera's electric motor.

Midolini abruptly got back out of his Mercedes. He began walking towards the Social Club door, putting on an overcoat as he went.

'Fuck, fuck, fuck!' Tony said, as he slammed his fist down on the console, nearly splitting it in two. 'I knew there was a reason we should've picked somewhere else. Like half his other mafioso mates, he's a fucking Carlton supporter. He's going for a drink at his club. He's a member. But we can't wait here forever. We gotta get Sav back to the station and fit him out for tonight.'

'What'll we do, Sarge?' Max asked.

Pressure, pressure, pressure. Answer, answer, answer. Come on, Tony. What'll we do? Decision. When Tony began to speak, he surprised himself. He realised his voice was calm and his head wasn't thumping. 'Right. I know he might be a member, but he never goes to a match, so he won't be looking at the up-and-comers out on the training track.' That familiar tingle returned to Tony's spine. 'He wouldn't know a football if it hit him in his greasy, little fucking pinhead. He'll be up in the Social Club all right, but I'll bet he's waiting for Sav to pick up his car. The upstairs windows look over the car park. Lizard eyes will be watching to see if you have company when you pick up your car, Sav.'

'Oh shit,' Sav said.

'I was gonna get you to take some pictures inside your car where he had stashed the drugs, but that's too dangerous now,' Tony said. 'You'll have to walk around the ground the other way to reach your Audi. Then, do you know where the Victoria Police Centre is in

Flinders Street?'

'Yeah, why?' Sav replied, starting to sound nervous.

'Go round the back and park in Siddeley Street. We'll meet you there. I have to get you fitted for another mike and a ballistic vest. I trust this prick as much as the average court solicitor. That's why we're not going back to Carlton. I hope you can keep this going, Sav, because we're depending on you.'

'I need the walk,' Sav said. He wiped one sweaty palm on his jeans. 'Let me out, I also need the air.'

Air? You're not fucking wrong there, son! Tony got out of the passenger seat and pulled it forward to let Sav out.

Both stood face to face for a moment.

Sav sensed Tony was distressed about something more than what they had just witnessed. Sav was about to ask, but changed his mind. He headed off towards his Audi at a good pace around the outside wall of the old grandstand.

Chapter Forty-Four

Sav didn't know what felt worse. His right hand, which was lightly gripping the bottom of his sports steering wheel, or the restricted, sweaty feeling of the Kevlar ballistic vest strapped under his checked shirt. He felt like a one-armed bomber in Baghdad. The only distraction he had from thinking about these two problems was glancing at the plastic package sitting on the passenger seat of his Audi. The package made problem number three. Problem number four was farther up the road in Toorak: the drop.

The traffic was reasonably heavy, so Sav had difficulty picking out Tony's unmarked police car. *They said they'd stay within sight the whole time.*

So Tony said.

Sav knew he had to keep things divided up into small objectives for the night.

So Tony said.

The first was to get to Power Street. Second was to do the drop and pick-up. Third was to do the deal back at the café. That's where it would end with Tony and Max grabbing Midolini.

Fuck. They're just doubling my problems for the night.

Sav stopped the Audi three or four doors down from the drop, but left the motor running. With nervous hands, he fumbled for the package, then quickly got out of the car. Tunnel vision guided him towards the letterbox of the house. Everything else was a blur. *Open it, swap it and get the fuck out.*

Sav heard the noise of a party inside the house, along with the familiar sound of girls laughing and squealing. He paused for a moment, just as he pulled the brown package from the letterbox. With his one good hand, he was trying to juggle two packages. One slipped to the ground. He began to panic, thinking he'd dropped the drugs on the pavement. Sav leant down in the darkness and grabbed what he thought was the drop. It wasn't. It was a very small but expensive leather loafer. *What the fuck?*

Sav looked up and saw three eyes in the darkness. The outside two belonged to Mickey Midolini. The middle and largest was the circular business-end of an automatic pistol.

Sav jumped backwards and landed in a sitting position against the fence.

Mickey Midolini's voice sounded like the devil incarnate. 'Your arse has always belonged to me, Sav. Now it's time for you to kiss it goodbye. Two jobs completed at once. Killing you and taking my client's overdue money. I suppose a bonus is that I get to keep the drugs, too. More for little sluts like Carly, eh, Sav?'

Sav was frozen in fear.

'Now get up, there's a good little boy, and walk into the alleyway over the other side. When your drug-fucked, bullet-ridden excuse for a body is found here tomorrow morning, it'll make this area as popular as a vulture at a butcher's picnic. The house prices will drop overnight.'

Sav glanced along the street as he rose to his feet. *Where the fuck are you, Tony? Where?* Sav took a few tentative steps, then felt the cold, hard steel of the pistol pressing into his sweating skull. Tony was going to be too late.

'Come on,' Midolini growled.

Sav stumbled and tripped into the alley. His night turned into day as an explosion penetrated his ears. Noise and light. *What? Dad. Da —*

Sav was thrown backwards into a garage wall. He hit it with such force, he bounced forward like he'd hit a trampoline, then landed spread-eagled more than a metre in front of the wall. In his mind he was spiralling downwards. There was no hurt. No hurt at all. Everything was just getting darker and darker. No more pain.

Benny, turn on the lights. Open the blinds. Come on, Dad! Benny's form didn't move. Sav tried to reach for it, but Benny wasn't there.

Sav's movements slowed. He couldn't breathe. Couldn't move. Darkness. *Why can't I see? Nothing, just darkness. Nothing, just... nothing.*

It's over. It's all over. No more pain.

A cold calm enveloped Sav like a crematorium shroud.

Chapter Forty-Five

In the quiet suburban street, the sound of a nine-millimetre automatic going off even gave Mickey Midolini a fright. *The whole neighbourhood will be out here soon. Get out quick!*

Midolini ran through the dark, as fast as his fat little body could, towards his Mercedes. It was parked almost 150 metres farther along Power Street in the dark. With his mind racing, he fumbled for the keys. Throwing both packages onto the floor, he started his car and drove quickly away from the shooting.

Hysterical laughter overtook Midolini as he thought about the situation. *One dead runner. Twenty thousand in my hand and the drugs, as well. Not a bad night's haul. Not bad at all. Thirty thousand for my passage on the ship on Wednesday, and I'm gone. No more Benny, no more working. Just a life of luxury under the sun.*

Midolini sped across town to his spider-hole in the northern suburb of Fawkner. He picked up a suitcase full of clothes and grabbed a few personal effects, then drove back towards the city via the West Gate Bridge. He exited at Lorimer Street for the South Wharf. This was where his trump card was waiting.

His contact was the captain of a South Korean freighter. Midolini had made a habit over the years of keeping his ocean-going customers happy through visits to the Mission to Seafarers in Flinders Street. He had worked up a very good, cashed-up clientele of Asian seamen, who always wanted some of his Merchandise for a good time when they hit Melbourne.

It was one thing for Midolini to have an exit route for when he departed the Carlton scene, but there was always the chance something could go wrong. He didn't want to be sliding into his first-class seat on a jet to the States, only to find the suits stepping on board with a set of handcuffs. No, he had come to a cash agreement of thirty thousand dollars, no questions asked, for his passage. A couple of weeks lying low in his cabin on a tramp steamer. No one would ever think Mickey Midolini would travel baggage class. That was the beauty of it. They would check the airports and maybe the top-class passenger ships, but not some rust-bucket shit-heap that was heading back to South Korea.

When Midolini pulled up in a back alley near the South Wharf, his nerves were jangled and his hands were shaking. Not with worry, but with happiness. He didn't give a flying fuck about killing Sav. Another couple of hours and he was gone.

Midolini reached into the console of the Mercedes and pulled out the false bottom to reveal a folded white envelope. He opened the envelope and counted the folded notes. *Good, ten G's.*

Midolini then picked up the package of money from Power Street. He ripped off the paper cover, expecting to see the colour of money underneath. 'What the fuck?' Midolini gasped, as a stack of paper fell from his hand across his lap and onto the floor. The only colour he could see was white. White paper. Blank white paper. 'My twenty G's? Where the fuck are they?'

He tore the covering off the drug drop. *Fucking talcum powder.*

Midolini sat with sagging shoulders, white paper at his feet and talcum powder all over his hands. *A fucking set-up. Couldn't have been Sav. He was bringing the package to me. That judge would know better than to double-cross me. Signorotto! It's gotta be him. He'll have it. A set-up.*

A cold chill suddenly ran through Midolini when he realised he only had a third of the price for his passage. The captain would never take ten grand. It was thirty or nothing. All his extra money was now sitting safely in a Cayman Islands bank account. He had to have the money that he was meant to collect tonight. That's all there was to it. It was *his*. Just one burning question: How to get it back? If Signorotto took it back to the station, like the honest prick he was, then it would be in the safe till Monday. They would transfer it to Police Headquarters after the weekend. It was too much money to stay in a hole like Carlton.

Midolini raised his head. The red mist came down. *Sav and Signorotto. They're working together. Sav couldn't have done this by himself. He's hasn't got the guts to see something like this through. Past tense, Mickey. Past tense. The one thing they didn't count on was me silencing that young prick.*

'You think you have me fucked, Signorotto?' Mickey screamed at the inside of his car. 'Well, we'll see. It's my money and my life you're playing with here. You might wanna stay in good old Carlton, but I don't. Whatever life I have in front of me, I'll kill you or yours to get it!'

Chapter Forty-Six

'That was a gunshot, Max! Can you see anything?'

Tony and Max strained for a visual on the noise source through the windscreen of their police car, which was parked in Toorak Road, facing the address of the drop. Their view down Power Street was suddenly blocked by a tram pulling up opposite them, a full fifty metres before its terminus at Glenferrie Road. It stopped dead… right in front of their car. They were blinded.

'Something's gone wrong,' Tony said. 'Get across there quick!'

Max fired up the car and roared out into Toorak Road. By the time he turned left and did a U-turn around the back of the tram, they had lost precious seconds. Max manoeuvred between a parked car and the tram, then swung a left into Power Street just as a set of tail-lights disappeared down the other end. Max powered the car down the street, headlights on high beam so the road and footpath were lit up like the Melbourne Cricket Ground at a night match.

'Stop!' shouted Tony. 'That's Sav by the garage over there.' He pointed at a motionless form lying by the wall.

Max slammed on the brakes in the middle of the road.

Tony leapt out before the car had come to a stop. 'Oh, shit no!' he yelled, as he vaulted across the bonnet.

Max leapt out of the driver's seat.

The big Sergeant slid on his knees to Sav's side and placed a hand under the young kid's head. 'Sav, Sav! Can you hear me? You okay?' Tony ripped open Sav's shirt.

Sav groaned. 'Tony, Tony. It hurts. Real bad in the chest. Real bad.' Sav reached up with his good hand to grab his cousin.

The ripped shirt revealed the damage done to the Kevlar vest that Sav was wearing. A neat gouge in the outer layer of fabric showed the track where the slug had hit.

Max and Tony slowly undid the Velcro straps of the ballistic vest to reveal a large red patch of bruising on Sav, which was growing darker in front of their eyes.

Tony exhaled with relief. 'It's going to hurt, mate, but you're alive. Some real bad bruising, but you'll be okay.'

'Who was it?' Max asked. 'Was it Midolini?' Max unscrewed a bottle of water from the car and handed it to Sav.

Sav dragged himself up into a sitting position against the wall. 'He was just there, like a fucking ghost. I had both the packages in my hand and I dropped one. I had the talcum powder that you swapped for his dope and I'd just got the pack of paper that you replaced the money with. I dropped one because of my hand. The next I knew I saw a shoe next to the package and it was him. Where the fuck did he come from?'

Tony shook his head. 'Midolini must've got here after I swapped the money for the paper. He's grabbed you because he thought he could clean up two hits at once. The money and the drugs. Sometime real soon he'll realise he's got nothing. Nothing but charges for drugs and attempted murder, which are now coming his way like a runaway train. Him turning up here is one thing, but trying to knock you off is unbelievable. He obviously isn't worried about anything or anyone. Even your old man. I reckon this prick is on the run. He's made his money and now he's pissing off.'

'If he's not worried about knocking Sav,' Max added, 'then you'd think he's going to make a run for it sooner rather than later.'

The Sergeant looked at Constable Max Tyler with a smile. 'Now you're thinking like a copper. You're dead right. What's the bet he's got a flight out of here tonight or tomorrow? Let's get Sav into the car. Midolini will think Sav is dead and his account settled. He'll be desperate to leave the country.'

Sav stood up by himself, tightly holding his bruised ribs to cope with the pain.

People were starting to come out of nearby houses. No one was approaching either of the two plain-clothes police officers. No one from this up-market piece of suburbia wanted any involvement beyond taking a glimpse at the other side of life.

Tony looked at Sav. *This kid's had enough. Time he was looked after properly.*

As Tony and Max helped the battered and bruised kid into the police car, Tony noticed a movement in the bushes next to Webster's house. 'Max, stay here and look after Sav. I'm just going to have a look at something.'

Tony withdrew his service pistol from his holster and approached a large bush outside the neighbouring home to Webster's. A few metres from it, Tony took up a combat stance and pointed his firearm directly into the bush.

The onlookers disappeared inside their houses just as quickly as they had appeared minutes before. Discretion was definitely the better part of valour.

There was a slight movement inside the bush.

'Crawl out, hands first,' Tony called in a loud voice. *Tell me it's Midolini. Please, please tell me it's him.*

The bush moved a little more.

Tony pulled back slowly on the trigger. *Come out with a gun, you gutless wonder. You're going to look magic with a third eye.*

Two skinny arms came out first, followed by the rest of a young girl no older than fifteen or sixteen. She was whimpering and holding in place a torn bra. She was wearing nothing else.

Tony instantly released his pressure on the trigger and placed his gun back in its holster. The girl squatted in front of him and began to sob.

Tony turned and called out, 'Max, bring me that rug out of the car – quickly.'

Max appeared seconds later.

Tony threw the rug around the young girl and hugged her to him. 'It's all right. We're the police. You're okay.' *What the hell's going on in this street?*

The girl's body kept heaving with great sobs, which slowly subsided over the next few minutes. Neither she nor the two policemen said a word.

Finally, Tony said, 'Max, go back to the car and look after Sav.'

'Yeah, no problems.' Max ran back to the car.

Tony stared after Max. *No problems? You've gotta be kidding.*

Some other noises caught Tony's attention, and he turned to see some girls gathering in Webster's front garden. 'Do any of you know this girl?' Tony called out.

Just as two girls started to approach, Judge Webster stepped in front of them. He ushered the girls back into his house.

As the judicial figure retreated towards his front door, Tony called out, 'Be prepared, Webster. Your own law is going to come down on you like a ton of bricks.'

The judge stopped in his tracks on his front porch. He looked as though he was about to give this lowly nuisance cop a piece of his mind, but then thought better of it. He hurried inside and slammed his front door.

Tony looked at the frightened girl in his arms. He could see blood on the girl's legs.

'Keep him away from me!' she suddenly screamed, in the direction of Webster's house. 'Get him away!' Tony knelt down and held the girl tightly. He gently asked, 'What's your name?'

'Amy, A-Amy Kennedy,' she croaked, her voice faltering.

'How old are you, Amy?'

'Sixteen.'

'I don't want you to tell me anything right now, Amy, but I want to call your parents and an ambulance, okay?'

'Not my parents. Please, not my parents. Dad will kill me. He doesn't know I'm here. I'm meant to be staying at school tonight, not out here.'

'I've got no choice, Amy. I'm a police officer and you've obviously been attacked. You're under age and I have to call them. We'll sort it all out, I promise. No matter what happens I'll stick with you. My name's Tony and I am a police Sergeant. You'll be all right.'

Amy gripped Tony's arm tightly. 'Okay, but don't let that creep near me again.'

'Again? What do you mean?' Tony knew he was pushing the legal boundaries.

'Nothing, nothing,' Amy replied. 'Get my parents if you like, but I'm not telling them anything.'

'Let's go to the police car and I'll call an ambulance.' *Two patients for the price of one!*

While they waited for an ambulance, Tony took out his mobile phone. 'What's your dad's name and phone number, Amy?'

Amy had stopped trembling. 'My dad's Bill Kennedy. If you're a policeman, you'll probably know him.'

Both Tony and Max looked at Amy in disbelief.

Max spoke first. 'Bill Kennedy – the Police Minister?'

Amy lowered her head. 'Yes.' She gave Tony the phone number.

Looking at Max, Tony indicated for him to step away from the car before he rang anyone. 'The first call goes to Phil Stone, the second to her dad. This mess could either have a real good ending or a real bad one.'

The unmistakable sound of sirens approached.

*

Half an hour later, the scene in the street had turned into what looked like the set from a movie. Police vehicles, two ambulances and a State Ministerial car. Phil Stone had been briefed by his Sergeant as to what had taken place.

'Well, Sergeant, a lot of what is going to happen from here on, regarding Webster, is in the lap of the gods. The parliamentary gods. The last thing Bill Kennedy will want is a scandal involving one of their own judges, especially with what we think went down here tonight. The daughter is saying nothing.'

'Phil, all of us, including her dad over there at the ambulance, know that she has been raped by Webster. But we need her to confirm the story.'

Tony and Phil saw the Minister was making his way over to them.

'I know, I know,' Stone replied quietly. 'Let's hear what Kennedy has to say.'

Kennedy stepped up to Phil and Tony. He said sternly, 'She is being taken to St Vincent's Hospital. I'll be going with her. We'll talk later. Nothing is to be said about this unfortunate situation, gentlemen. Understand?'

Phil nodded, then Kennedy turned for the ambulance.

But Tony took two steps towards the departing Minister. Phil grabbed Tony around one arm. 'Nothing is to be said?' Tony called out, abruptly shrugging away Phil's hand. 'Are you the Minister for Police or her father?'

Kennedy stopped walking.

Tony couldn't help himself. 'Your beautiful daughter has been raped and tossed away like a piece of garbage by that deviate drug-fucked judge in there. Sack me or do what you like, but don't give up on your own daughter. She's a kid. She wants your help.'

Kennedy turned slowly. 'There are ways and means of dealing with him, Sergeant.'

'What? Sack him and let him live with his million-dollar pension while he rapes a few more teenagers and fills them with drugs. Is that your "ways and means", is it?'

'That's enough, Sergeant!' Phil called loudly. 'Get back to your car now and shut up!'

Tony barged past a stunned Max Tyler, and stormed back to the police car. He smashed his fist into the roof, leaving a large dent, before getting inside.

Tears ran down the face of the Police Minister as he looked at his daughter being loaded into the ambulance. He turned back to a very embarrassed Phil Stone. Phil shook his head and said, 'I'm sorry, sir. I'll speak to him.'

'No, Inspector. He's right. What do I do, though? She won't speak to me about it. I know she's been raped, but she wants to protect my job. What do I do?'

Phil Stone looked the Minister in the eye. 'Do you really want my opinion?'

'Yes, I do. I *need* your opinion,' the Minister replied, his head bowed.

'You have been in parliament for over ten years, right?'

'Yes,' Kennedy said, with a puzzled look on his face.

'Retire. If you do, she won't have to worry about your job. You've got the rest of your life to look after her and now is where it starts. She wants you to protect her and stand up for her. The only way is to go after that piece of shit.' Phil threw a hand in the direction of Webster's house. 'And I can tell you, Minister, if there was anyone in this job I wouldn't want hunting me down, it's that Sergeant I just sent away.

Believe me, he will give everything of himself to fix up a rock-spider like Webster.'

Kennedy stared at Phil Stone with a faraway look for what seemed like a lifetime. Eventually he spoke. 'Inspector. I'm going to the hospital with Amy. Tell that Sergeant I want to see him at St Vincent's tomorrow. Tell him to bring an audio recorder.' With a straight back, the future *former* Minister for Police walked directly to the ambulance.

Chapter Forty-Seven

St Albans didn't exist in the world of Benny Illarietti. It was west of everything he knew and loved. As far as he was concerned, anyone who lived this side of Melbourne should have a passport check to cross the Maribyrnong River. He didn't want to know anything west of the Tullamarine Freeway.

Tonight, though, Benny had to go west. The question was one of loyalty. Not his loyalty to anyone, but of one person's loyalty to him. The loyalty and respect he was owed by Mickey Midolini. *Loyalty will come out the barrel of a gun tonight, Mickey. You have not only crossed me, but you have touched my family.*

The name 'Stefan Zilmoski', which Benny had given to Mickey, was true enough. He was a pond-scum dealer from St Albans, all right. But the address was false. Even Benny didn't want this outer-suburbs piece-of-shit to have his ticket punched when he had nothing to do with the situation.

The house Benny had picked out for Mickey to visit was actually one that Benny owned. He'd rung his Brunswick Road estate agent to see if there were any of his investment 'palaces' vacant at the moment. Benny Illarietti had many properties all over Melbourne. So many, that he left it up to his agent to pick up cheap properties and rent them out at exorbitant rates to anyone he could. They were good earners and very rewarding when it came to tax time. His man had come up with the house in this backwater that Benny was now watching from down the street in his car. *This is personal, Mickey. I will wait out here the whole night for you, if I have to.*

Benny had not brought any of his henchmen with him. He had not even let his usual driver take him. He had taken a vehicle from his car rental yard in Lygon Street. Another of his wise business moves down the years. He sat in the vehicle, one hand in his pocket touching the razor-sharp edge of his favourite weapon: a stiletto blade. *Normally you wouldn't feel a thing, Mickey, but tonight I will pierce both your lungs very slowly while your eyes mist over. The last thing you'll see on this earth will be my smiling face.*

Benny had done as he was asked by his nephew, Tony Signorotto, even to the extent that he hadn't visited Sav in hospital. No interference. Nothing. He had contacted Tony once and that was in relation to when Sav would be out of hospital. He only received vague answers from Tony. Benny had played along with the story for a few days, but things had to be set straight. Family honour dictated it.

Benny's thoughts drifted in and out of a very light sleep as he sat behind the wheel of the car. By two o'clock on Sunday morning there was complete silence in the street and still no sign of Mickey. *Where are you, my 'friend'? Do you think this may be a set-up?*

Benny's mobile phone started to vibrate in his pocket. *I told my boys not to ring me. Who's this?* Fumbling for the talk button, Benny recognised the phone number of his café office. 'What do you want?' Benny snapped. 'Who the fuck is this? I've told you all to leave me in peace tonight.'

'Boss, boss! It's me, Stef. Stef from the café.'

'What's wrong? Why are you ringing me? You know the instructions I left for tonight.'

'I know, boss, but this is important. Real important. That cop, Signorotto was in here just before. He wants you to ring him straight away. I told him to fuck off, but he just cracked me over the head with his fist. He said you'd kill me if you didn't get his message. Sorry, boss. I know you said not to ring, but…'

Benny's brain went into overdrive. *Something has happened to Sav. No, no!* 'Give me his number,' Benny said, as he quickly searched for a piece of paper. 'Wait till I get a pen.'

Benny put down the mobile phone and switched it to loud speaker while he took an envelope and a gold Mont Blanc pen from the inside pocket of his overcoat. 'Go on, what's the number?'

Stef slowly dictated Tony's phone number. When he finished, the phone line immediately went dead.

Benny tried to calm himself as he dialled the number he'd been given. Two rings and it answered. Benny broke in, 'What is it nephew? What has happened to my son?'

'He's alive and well, Benny.' Tony's voice was calm at the other end. 'But there's been a situation with Midolini. I'm bringing Sav home to your place. He's coming home, Benny. And you're going to look after him. We'll meet at your house in an hour.'

'Nephew, if you've hurt him, you'll answer to the family.'

Tony shouted into his phone, 'Listen, you drug-dealing fucking prick. Don't talk to me about "family". You've been fucking up families for years with the shit you peddle. Get off your fucking Italian high horse and start to think of other people instead of yourself. It's about time you looked after the family closest to you. You shut your filthy mouth and do what I tell you, cos your time is finished. Just fucking be there, Benny. Capiche? I am telling *you* what to do. Sergeant Tony fucking Signorotto is telling *you* what to do, now just fucking do it.'

Benny Illarietti was speechless. Never had he been talked to with so much disrespect. The trouble was that he had no answer to it. *What is wrong with me? Why don't I want to kill this nephew of mine?* As much as Benny wanted to scream back into the phone, he could find nothing. He suddenly heard his own trembling voice say, 'I'll be there.'

Tony ended the phone call.

Benny was left mumbling to himself. His hand shook violently as he tried to turn the ignition.

Chapter Forty-Eight

For once in his crooked life, Benny did what he was told. He drove to his Carlton North fortress in a daze, his mind whirling between thoughts of Sav, revenge and unbridled hatred. All notions of business deals and upcoming meetings were dismissed. It was time for business of his own. The axis was starting to spin more violently.

Tony and Max were waiting at the Italian-styled mansion when Benny got there.

Benny started first, gesturing at the junior police officer. 'Who the fuck is this?'

Tony immediately jumped onto the front foot. 'Shut up, Benny. He's a cop. He's my partner and you will show him some fucking respect. Max Tyler, this is Benny Illarietti, Sav's father and a noted member of the Victorian mafioso. Not that I give a fat rat's arse about that.'

Benny went to walk past the outstretched hand of Max Tyler. However, as he did so, Max stepped directly into Benny's path.

They were eyeball to eyeball.

Max spoke first. 'You give your son a hard time and I'll take the greatest pleasure in locking you up. I don't give a fuck on what charge, either. This kid has more guts than you'll ever know. A lot more than it takes to be some pumped-up drug dealer like you.' Max pushed his hand into Benny's chest.

Benny stood, eyes flicking from his nephew to the young Tyler. 'Where's my son?' Rage burned in his eyes.

Tony took Benny by the shoulder. 'He's in bed and that's where he's going to stay. At least he's going to remain in this house, with you looking after him, until Mickey is caught.'

Benny's face hardened. He glared at his nephew. 'What has he done to Saverio?'

'The end-story is that Mickey tried to kill him. He took a shot at Sav, but we had him in a ballistic vest. He's okay, just a bit bruised. I'm going to tell you the whole story, Benny. What you have to realise is that all this comes from your stinking fucking drug business. A drug business that has now spilled over into paedophilia, thanks to Mickey and his sordid contacts. You are going to sit there while I give you Sav's life story. The story that you have turned a blind eye to, unless you are completely fucking stupid, which I know you're not.'

'I know my son, nephew,' Benny replied, with an air of bravado. 'There is nothing you can tell me that I don't know.'

'Oh, yes there fucking is, you pathetic excuse for a human being. Now shut the fuck up, so I can fill in the gaps of Sav's life you have conveniently cared to overlook, while your piece-of-shit lieutenant Mickey Midolini not only fucked Sav's life up, but double-played you for the fucking arrogant mafia shit that you are.'

Benny attempted to speak, but was met with a stinging backhand across the face from his nephew. Benny was knocked backwards into his expensive Franco Cozzo winged leather chair. Benny's hand shook as he felt the side of his face.

'Wake up, Uncle! You're not going to like what I tell you, but I have a sneaking suspicion that you've already begun to piece some of it together since Sav's first visit to hospital. Now you're going to hear Sav's story in full and I'm not going to leave out any of the details. I'm fucked if I know why Sav would have anything to do with you. You're as guilty as Midolini when it comes to this. Even more so, seeing that you're his father.'

Tony turned, walked to the front door and locked it. He went to the phone on the hallstand, and yanked the handpiece off so hard that it snapped away from the phone.

Benny stared at Tony in disbelief. In one swift movement, Benny was lifted to his feet by the two police and had his pockets turned out. His mobile phone fell to the floor.

Max slammed his heel down on Benny's phone, so it shattered over the carpet.

Tony hissed, 'There will be no interruptions while you hear this story, Benny. When I'm finished, I expect you to go and see Sav and do one thing.'

'What?' Benny asked, suddenly sounding like a shrunken old man.

'Hug him, you fucking low-life prick. You don't deserve this kid. He's got more to him than you'll probably ever discover. The fact that he came to *me*, and not *you*, sums up what he thinks of you, and how much help he expected you could give him.'

Chapter Forty-Nine

By the time Tony and Max left Benny's house, the sun was almost up. Benny had sobbed the last hour. Sav had come downstairs towards the end of Tony's revelations. Benny seemed to shrink before all their eyes as he was told the blackmail story involving the male prostitute. By the time he'd heard of the drug sales and death of Sav's friend Carly, Benny was a spent force. The Midolini and Webster cases were mere sideshows at this stage. Benny shed what Tony believed to be genuine tears. Tony knew his uncle, though.

Tony took the wheel of their police car, slowly driving himself and an exhausted Max Tyler back to the station.

Max looked over at Tony. 'What do you think, Sarge?'

Tony didn't take his eyes off the road. 'About what?'

'You told him to leave Mickey to us. Do you think he will?'

Tony pulled the car into the gutter. He turned to Max and said slowly and calmly, 'Mate. I could sit here and say there's nothing I'd like more than to catch Midolini. At the very least there is an attempted murder charge he'll face. What I won't do is lie to you. Because there's one thing I would like even better.'

Max took in the world-weary face of his Sergeant. 'What?'

'To find Mickey Midolini dead. And you know what, Max? I wouldn't even go looking for the culprit.'

Max was stunned. 'You've signed his death warrant, haven't you?'

'Shit happens, young Max, shit happens. Drug dealers sign their own death warrants. We now have someone more important to speak to. Let's get back to the station and have a shower and something to eat. Then it's down to the hospital to interview that girl Amy we found in Power Street.'

'What about Midolini? Shouldn't we be looking for him? And shouldn't we leave Amy to the Sexual Offences Squad to deal with?'

'Midolini will surface soon enough. Floating in the Yarra will suit me. Pond scum on river scum. We'll deal with Amy. There is an obvious link between her, Webster and the drugs.'

'Makes sense,' Max said.

'I told the radio operator to notify the airports. Midolini won't be going anywhere just yet. We've got his money and his drugs, so he's not real cashed-up at the moment. He can't get to a bank till Monday, and I doubt very much if any of his scam money is deposited in any of our banking institutions. I reckon he was after a last big hit, then off overseas. He's not stupid enough to try and fly out of the country on a commercial flight now. When he realises he has blank paper and talcum powder, though, he'll know we're on to him. It'll either be a light-plane job or a ship. While we have something to eat, I'll get Jill Norton to contact the Water Police to check what freighters are in and where they're headed to. She's on at seven this morning.'

Max put his tired head back on the headrest. 'How long will this hospital thing take?'

'How long's a piece of string, Max? This is what police work is all about now. You keep going till you have as much information as you can get, and then you go after more. Don't think for one minute that you have to be one of the suited wonders to bring down shit like Midolini. *We* will do it. I want a statement from this kid this morning. Phil Stone rang me hours ago and said her old man wanted to see me this morning at the hospital. Phil's pretty good at getting people to come over to our side. If he didn't want to talk to us, he could've done it via Phil. We go in there gently, but keep *at* him till we come out with a statement that'll sink Webster deeper than the *Titanic*.'

Max smiled at the thought.

'Look at it this way, Max. While we are the ones who can tie up Webster, there'll be plenty of others looking for Midolini. Sometimes it helps having the crooks working for you. If he gets caught in one of his own webs, then we'll let his fellow spiders devour him. We also have a big, fat rock-spider of our own.'

'You don't feel anything about letting Benny know about Midolini?' Max asked.

'Mate, at this time of the morning I don't feel anything at all. They're all shit, and as far as I'm concerned, and society is better off without them all. That's our fucking job. To get rid of this scum any legal way we can. It's like going to a brawl on the street, mate. Never jump out of the car swinging, because you'll only end up on the ground with the sewer rats. Wait till it's all done and then bag up the shit that's left over.'

Max nodded and grinned at the voice of experience.

Tony pulled the police car into the back of the station. Max followed him into the watch-house.

Behind the front counter, a Senior Constable was checking the property in the safe.

Tony asked him, 'Where's Jill?'

'She swapped a shift with me, Sarge. My missus is crook with the flu and I was on night shift. But I've gotta look after the kids tonight. Jill didn't mind.'

'Yeah, no problems,' Tony said. 'While you're doing the property, I have some cash we've recovered from a crime scene to go in the safe.'

'No worries.'

'I'll get it all transferred to the Melbourne City Property Office on Monday morning.' Tony pulled a wad of bills from a pocket of his trousers and counted out $20,000 in hundred-dollar notes.

The Senior Constable double-checked the amount with Tony and Max looking on.

When the total had been confirmed, Tony said, 'Sign the cash in properly and lock the bills away tight.'

'Right away, Sarge.'

When the Senior Constable returned from the safe, Tony handed him the packet of drugs. Together they checked and double-checked the package. The contents were entered into the register, along with the cash, then the drugs were locked in the safe.

Tony had one more request. 'Make sure that you do the handover to the afternoon shift correctly. I want you and the afternoon-shift Sergeant to check it all over again, and then Jill to do the same tonight. Understand?'

'No probs, Sarge. Good bust, by the look of it?'

'Hope so, mate, hope so.' Tony turned to his partner. 'Come on,

Max, breakfast and a shower, then on to the hospital. I want this sick judge as much as I want Midolini.'

Chapter Fifty

Tony and Max waited at the nurse's station while a doctor talked in hushed tones to Amy's father, Police Minister Bill Kennedy.

'How're you gonna tackle this, Sarge?' Max whispered wearily.

'We're not going to tackle it at all, Max. He's called *us* in, so let's see what he wants. If he doesn't support his kid, Max, you'd better hold me back, because I'm likely to do my job with one punch. I'm that stuffed at the moment.'

Minutes passed before the doctor finished her conversation with Bill Kennedy and left.

Kennedy gradually raised his head, turned and walked slowly at first, then with more purpose, towards the two police officers. 'Let's talk over here, shall we?' Kennedy indicated some chairs around the corner.

Once they were seated, Tony wanted to get straight to the point. 'If it's an apology that you –'

But Kennedy cut him off with a wave of his hand. 'Sergeant. There are a couple of things I want to say, so hear me out. First off, there is no need to apologise for what you said. I stood in front of you last night as the Minister for Police, first, and a father, second. I'm ashamed of that. I've done that too often to my family. For your information, I have this morning been to see the Premier at his house.

I notified him that I've resigned my position as Minister for Police and resigned from parliament, effective immediately.'

Tony leaned forward to reply, but Kennedy had more to say.

'It's funny, you know. These past two years I've had so many occasions to talk on police matters and how the community should get behind their police force by showing more control over their kids. Yet here am I, not knowing where my daughter was on a Saturday night. I just presumed she was boarding at school. I haven't even seen her for two weeks because I've been so busy with work. What you said to me last night struck me like a slap in the face. She's my beautiful daughter and I will support her fully over this. I've spoken to her this morning and told her that I have resigned. She and I want this animal put away. Whatever she has to go through with this case or anything to do with the drugs she has been on, I will help her with. Can you help both of us?'

Kennedy and Tony both stood and looked at each other.

'Sir, it will give me the greatest of pleasure to put this dog into a cage of his own. However, there are a couple of things I need first.'

'Name them, Sergeant.'

'Obviously, I need a full statement from Amy. I'll get one of the women from the Sexual Offences Squad to come down this morning and do that.

'Thank you.'

'And what I need from you, Mr Kennedy, is your silence.'

'My silence?'

'Yes, I want Webster to think he's home free. That there are no possible charges coming out of this. All I want you to tell your colleagues is that you have resigned due to poor health. I don't want anyone to know what happened to Amy. That way Webster will think he's got away with it. He'll think that you're too ashamed to lay charges. I want him to keep playing judge until I drop the guillotine on him. And I can promise you, he *will* be walked out of his chambers handcuffed.'

Kennedy nodded. 'You have my word and you have Amy's. One thing, though. I want to be there when Webster is 'cuffed.'

As the conversation between the former Police Minister and two police officers continued, three teenaged girls appeared from the lift and approached the nurse's station.

Minutes later, Kennedy said goodbye and went back into his daughter's room.

Tony and Max were readying themselves to leave, when a nurse walked up to them.

'There are three girls here who have something to show you, Sergeant.'

Tony looked over at the young, very nervous girls. They had their arms linked together. Something about their appearance told him this case was about to take on a whole new twist. He motioned the girls towards him.

'What is it, girls? Are you friends of Amy's?'

The two girls on the outside gently pushed the middle girl nearer. 'Is Amy going to be all right?' whispered the girl.

'I'm not going to tell you lies, girls. She's been assaulted and I think you all know what happened. I'm not going to treat you like kids. You were at the party, too, weren't you?'

'Yes, we all were,' the middle girl said. 'We want to help Amy, but we'll all get into heaps of trouble.' The girls linked their arms together again and tears began to flow.

Tony and Max looked at each other.

Max ushered the girls over to a bench and sat down beside them. He watched one of them fidget nervously with her mobile phone.

Suddenly, she held her phone out to Max and took a deep breath. 'If Amy has been hurt by that old creep, then this might help.'

Max looked at the screen. 'You took photos that night?'

Tony watched on quizzically.

One of the other girls spoke up. 'We saw Webster take Amy upstairs. We thought he just wanted to do a line with her, so we didn't pay much attention. We were having fun downstairs. There was booze, boys and music… and some shit. It wasn't till someone wanted to change the music that we heard her cry out.'

'Hang on,' Max said, 'what do mean by "doing a line"?'

'Coke. Cocaine. Webster supplies as much as we want. Other shit, too. Uppers, downers, you name it, it's there. It's there all the time. Just about every weekend.'

'Do you realise that whatever you're going to tell us won't help Amy at all, unless we get it recorded? And in front of your parents?'

'Amy's one of our best friends and that old prick raped her. Standing up for her in front of our parents is the least we can do. This has scared the shit out of all of us.'

Tony burst in, 'Raped? How do you know she was raped? No one except the police, ambos and her father have spoken to her since we found her.'

The girl with the mobile phone held it in her outstretched hand. 'It's all on here. We went up to the bedroom when we heard her cry out. He didn't know we were looking. The door was partly open. Webster had her on the bed with her dress shoved up and she was trying to push him off. You could see everything he was doing to her. He was just holding her down and fucking her. She kept screaming at him to stop, but he held her by the throat and kept slamming into her. He was like an animal. I grabbed my phone and videoed the whole thing. I knew there'd be trouble after it, and it's all we could do at the time to help Amy. He was laughing all the time in a weird high-pitched sort of way. We wanted to go in, but we thought he'd lock the door and take all of us. He was off his head. After he finished, he wiped himself on her dress, and we thought he was about to come to the door. We ran off. We never saw Amy again. We took off soon afterwards, and we reckoned we'd see her back at the school, but we didn't. We only heard about the rest of it this morning.'

Max opened the phone app and started to play the video.

Tony looked on, shocked. He leaned across and stopped the vision after about ten seconds.

There was stunned silence.

Tony cleared his throat, then said with renewed urgency, 'Girls, you're all going to have to stay here. We have to contact your parents. In the meantime, I want all your mobile phones. I don't want any of this getting out.' *Not until we have our day in court with you, Webster, you low-life prick.*

Chapter Fifty-One

Mickey Midolini was in hiding. Down but not out to the count. He hated the suburb of Fawkner, but had bought a small bolt-hole flat there two years before – just in case.

Just in case had become a reality.

There was no way Midolini could approach the airports, not even the smaller ones. He'd be picked up in a flash. His chances of being caught were now extremely high, not only because that prick Signorotto and the Victoria Police Force were after him, but also Benny and his henchmen. Interstate would be no good, either, for the same reasons. Benny's tentacles would have spread right across the land overnight. No, a new escape route had to be found.

Midolini dialled his mobile and waited anxiously.

A cheery voice with a strong Korean accent answered, 'Korean Kuisine Restaurant. Take your order, please.'

'Kim? Kim Lee?' Midolini asked. 'Is that you?'

'Who is it that wants to know?'

'One of your suppliers. Not one of your food suppliers, though. It's Mickey. Mickey Midolini.'

'Ah, Mr Midolini. To what do I owe the pleasure? Do you want another Korean girl?'

'No, I haven't got the time for that.' *The last Korean whore I had from you nearly killed me after four hours of Korean gymnastics.* 'I wanna know if there's a berth I can buy on a Korean freighter. Is there one in Melbourne or Sydney at the moment?'

'You need it in a hurry?'

'Yeah, I do.' *You shifty prick. You're going to screw me over, I know. Five grand is all you'll get.* 'I have a contact who was thinking of sailing with an old friend of mine, a Korean captain who's in port at the moment. His ship is leaving in the morning… but the *passenger* can't go with him. It has to be a ship in a couple of days. I have to figure some things out… for the passenger. You know, business things.'

'Who is it for and where do they need to go?'

'Listen, Kim. It's for me to go anywhere in Europe or America. Enough questions.'

'You in trouble with your bosses, Mr Midolini?'

Midolini snapped back, 'Enough with the fucking questions, Kim. How much is it going to cost me?'

'I take big chance with this, Mr Midolini. I also take one-third of the price. I will arrange and get back to you.'

'How much, Kim?' *Ten is all I have, for fuck's sake.*

'It will cost you thirty – I think G's, is how you say. All cash. I will get back in one hour.' The line went dead.

Midolini slumped in his chair. He was about to smash his mobile phone into the floor but stopped. He had no choice but to find the thirty G's. He stopped short of destroying the phone because he needed Kim to phone back.

'Where the fuck do I find another twenty-thousand fucking

dollars?' he screamed, at the wall of the near-empty flat. *The only prick I know right now that has twenty grand is fucking Signorotto, and it's* my *twenty grand.*

Cunning started to rise in waves through Midolini's devious brain. He sat up suddenly, talking to himself, 'It's fucking Sunday night. There's a fair chance it'll be in the safe at the Carlton cop shop.'

A plan. A plan. They only work one in the station at night. The other two are out in the car. I'll just have to make sure the car is out when I go in. A nine-millimetre in some skinny cop's fucking mouth should get me that money. Yes, yes, yes!

A delusional Midolini paced the flat, slapping his hands together. 'Fuck you, Signorotto. Fuck you,' he called out loudly, to no one but himself.

Forty minutes passed before Midolini's mobile rang. He recognised the number and nearly dropped it in his desperation. 'Kim. What's the go, man?'

'The *Poong Sun* will tie up at North Wharf on Monday morning. It leaves on Wednesday morning at four a.m. The captain is a friend of some Korean businessmen here in Melbourne. It will be all right… ten thousand for me and twenty thousand for him. The *Poong Sun* is headed to San Francisco. For another ten thousand he can arrange a passport for you. You wish?'

'You fucking wish, Kim. Leave the passport to me. Tell him he gets his money when I lock myself safely in my cabin and we're out the Heads.' *I'll shoot the first prick who tries to get anywhere near me.*

'You are not a trusting person, my friend.'

'This is business, Kim. Trust doesn't come into it. You will get your money at the gangplank.'

'We have done good business in the past. I am sure that with your connections we can continue some operations when you set up base in the United States.'

'I'll keep that in mind, Kim,' Midolini said, as he hung up. He knew full well he would never see or hear from him again after the gangplank handover.

Chapter Fifty-Two

'I'm getting too old to babysit you lot,' Jill Norton said, as she threw a set of police car keys to the lanky young constable on the other side of the watch-house counter.

The catcher of the keys and his partner were preparing to fight crime and evil in the badlands of Carlton. 'How come you scored a night shift, Jill? Where's Eddie Gray? I thought he was on night shift with us.'

'Eddie's little boy is sick and his wife is down with the flu. Phil Stone rang me to see if I could pinch-hit just for tonight. Eddie will be back on tomorrow night.'

'Fair enough.'

'This'll give me a good chance to see what you young fellas get up to during the night. Stone's sent me in as a spy, so you better make sure you come back in with some decent pinches. Understand?' Jill kept a straight face for a moment, before bursting into laughter.

The two constables shook their heads and smiled.

'And I don't mean any little dolly birds from up at the Oxford Tavern. The cells are closed for business… and that means funny business, all right?'

One of the constables gave a groan and held his hand over his heart. 'Jill, what makes you think we'd bring back anyone other than a crook?'

'Two reasons, sunshine. One is that I've been in this job for a lot longer than you've been drawing breath, and there's nothing I wouldn't put past a young copper. Secondly, is that my roast dinner tonight is for three people and not four. Okay?'

'If you're trying to bribe us with a roast dinner, Senior, there's only one thing I have to say,' one of the constables shot back, as he reached into the equipment-issue cupboard.

'What's that?' Jill asked, knowing she'd get the same reply as she had always received over the years when it was her turn in the watch-house on nightshift.

The drooling twins answered as one, 'What time will it be ready?'

'Piss off and fight crime till I call you in.'

One of the constables changed tack. 'Love to catch up with that Midolini arsehole. I read the report Sergeant Signorotto did. Midolini must be on the run from both sides of the law: Victoria Police *and* Signorotto.'

Jill had also read the report Tony had posted on the mess-room board. The picture of Midolini that accompanied it was a pretty good likeness of the little crim she had seen many times around the traps in Carlton. 'Just you two remember to be bloody careful out there,' she said, as she strapped on her equipment belt containing a nine-millimetre Smith & Wesson police and military pistol. 'And don't call Midolini an "arsehole". Arseholes have a very important role in life and are extremely useful. He ain't!'

'No worries, Jill. I'll shoot first, though. I'd rather be tried by twelve than carried by six.' The constable patted the pistol at his waist. 'See you during the night. If you want us, just give us a yell over the bat phone,' he said, pointing to the phone sitting next to the property safe with the direct line to Police Communications.

'Okay, be careful,' Jill said, looking them in the eyes.

'Yeah, no worries, *Mum*. We've both been to the toilet and have our handkerchiefs with us.'

Jill shook her head. 'Go on – git!'

The station door closed and an eerie quietness descended on the old building. Jill did her usual trick of putting an old numberplate up against the inside of the door. This was a simple way to make sure that wherever she was in the station, she would hear the clang of the metal hitting the linoleum floor if anyone came through the door.

Jill walked back behind the counter, noticing the weight of her gun. *Been a bloody while since I've done a night shift. This shooter is heavy.*

She went across to the safe, unlocked it and double-checked the $20,000, which Tony and Max had brought back from the Toorak operation, was still at the back of the safe. *Phil Stone will be glad to get rid of this into Headquarters tomorrow, I bet.*

As she tidied the safe, Jill slid her firearm out of its holster and laid it at the front of the safe, closed the door and locked it. She went over to the gun safe, unlocked it and took out another pistol, loaded a fifteen-round clip and slid the gun into her holster. *Just in case, Jill, just in case.*

For the next few hours, Jill busied herself with overdue paperwork and preparing a roast dinner for her boys on the road. The only thing she had to deal with at the counter was an irate taxi driver complaining about his passenger who had skipped without paying the fare. There wasn't anything she could do about it, except pacify the driver by filling out a report for theft, which, on his departure, was thrown straight into the round filing cabinet on the floor next to her desk.

Two a.m. came. She called Police Communications to get the crew back.

The two constables looked tired when they trudged in. However, as they approached the mess room, their eyes lit up as the smell of roast lamb wafted towards them.

'Jill, you bloody legend,' the tall constable said, as he saw the three plates on the table. Two were laden with enough meat and vegetables to feed an army.

'You both need to put on some weight. The roast's on me tonight. Now get stuck into it before it goes cold.'

The two young constables dumped pieces of equipment and paperwork on the floor and table before pouncing on the feast.

'You're outvoted, Jill,' the second constable said, after a minute with a mouthful of roast lamb.

'What do you mean?' Jill asked, looking up from her own meal.

'It's two to one. You're staying on night shift for the week. Tomorrow night it can be roast beef. We'll alternate for the week. Decision made. Just don't let the crews from Collingwood or Fitzroy know about this feast.'

Jill leaned over the table and gave the lad a light clip over the ear. 'You cheeky bastard. By the looks of the way you two eat, I'd have to do three months of night shift to pay for the meat.'

The two boys laughed as loud as their full mouths would allow.

Eventually, one of them said, 'Thanks, Jill. This sure beats bringing your own sandwiches.'

'Also better for you than Sammy's. Keep eating that stuff and your arteries will clog up.'

Conversation varied between work and Jill's suggestions of how to handle the mounting paperwork the two members had in their correspondence lockers. All ideas from the experienced Senior Constable were gratefully accepted.

'Anything happening out there?' Jill asked. 'Seems quiet on the radio.'

'Not much at all, actually. Couple of drunks up at the Sarah Sands Hotel. Still a few hanging around up at Princes Park after the Blues had a one-point win over Collingwood at the Melbourne Cricket Ground. Generally, though, a pretty quiet Sunday night.' The tall constable sponged the last of the gravy from his plate with a piece of bread.

'There's apple pie for later,' Jill said. 'You're not getting it yet, though. I want you to stay awake thinking about it. Time for a coffee.'

No sooner had the words left her lips than the shrill sound of the Police Communications hotline rang through from the watch-house. 'Spoke too soon, boys. Stay there and I'll get it.'

A minute passed before Jill Norton returned. 'Sorry lads. No time for coffee. Apparently, there's some sort of siege going down in Gold Street, Collingwood, near the freeway. They want you down there quick to block off an intersection. Don't know the full story, but there are kids involved.'

Both members grabbed their gear and ran out the door to the car.

There was no need for questions when kids were involved.

Jill replaced the numberplate against the door and went back into the mess room to clean up after the two-man demolition squad. It didn't worry her. She was as pleased as punch that her culinary skills were wanted as much here as they were at home.

The sound of the falling numberplate suddenly echoed throughout the station. She strode quickly back into the public area.

Looking around, she saw no one. *What's going –?*

The feel of cold steel on her temple sent a terrifying shiver down her spine.

Chapter Fifty-Three

Midolini had bided his time, standing in a darkened alleyway opposite the police station. He'd been there since the shift change at eleven o'clock and observed the coming and going of police and public. He was prepared to wait however long it took to pick the best time for his own personal sting.

In one ear, he had an earbud connected to a handheld scanner, so he could listen to police radio traffic. The calls had dwindled over the past hour. The last person to visit the station had left an hour ago, a disgruntled taxi driver cursing everyone in general before he'd slammed the door of his cab and sped away.

When at last Midolini heard the Carlton crew being called back in for a break, he set his plan in motion. He removed the SIM card from his mobile phone, then rang emergency services on triple zero about a bogus siege in a large block of flats on Gold Street, Collingwood. Even without the SIM card, the emergency call still went through, but the idiots at Police Communications couldn't put a trace on it. Midolini had strategically chosen the location for the fictitious siege to take the Carlton crew far away from its area, as well as drag in all available night crews from Collingwood and Fitzroy.

Not only did the Carlton crew respond, but, just as Midolini had hoped, all cars from Collingwood and Fitzroy were called in, with the added bonus of Collingwood's night-shift supervisor racing to the scene.

The one thing Midolini hadn't anticipated was the numberplate falling at the front door. It frightened the shit out of him and he nearly fell over as he headed to the other side of the watch-house to hide behind a large metal locker.

A moment later, a shadow appeared on the floor, then a middle-aged policewoman came into his line of sight from behind the locker. She was oblivious to his presence. Everything was going his way. Midolini snuck up behind the policewoman, raised his nine-millimetre pistol and placed the end of its barrel squarely against her left temple.

She froze.

Midolini simultaneously unclipped the policewoman's holster and removed her weapon. 'One fucking move, bitch, and you'll stop breathing permanently. I'm gonna tell you what to do, and the sooner you obey, the quicker I'll be outa here. Mind you, I wouldn't mind killing a fat pig like you.'

Midolini thumbed the magazine release on Jill Norton's pistol, causing the clip to hit the floor loudly. He kicked the clip away, then threw her gun as far as he could along the corridor.

His next move was to shove Jill towards the watch-house door, then slam her head as hard as could into the door's framework. Jill's nose exploded in a cascade of red. Blood poured onto the floor. Jill said nothing. She was too terrified.

'Nothing like a stuck pig, eh?' Midolini snarled. 'Now get the safe open and give me back my twenty grand that fucking Signorotto brought back here.'

'What twenty grand?' Norton asked, through bloodied fingers.

Midolini slammed the side of his pistol down on the back of her head, causing Jill to buckle at the knees. More blood flowed onto her uniform shirt.

'Don't fuck me around, bitch. You know what twenty grand. Tell him Mickey has come for what's his. Get the fucking safe open now or I'll put a bullet through each of your knees and then make you crawl to the safe and open it. What's it to be?'

'All right. Don't do anything else to me. I'll open it. It's behind the watch-house.' *Open it slowly, Jill. Don't let him see around you.* Jill moved towards the back of the counter, her blood flowing freely onto the worn floor.

Midolini grabbed hold of her, shoving the pistol in her face. 'Where are all your guns?'

'They're in the safe in the back room. We don't keep them out here with the public.'

Midolini glared at the terrified woman from only inches away. 'Get the money. Be quick. If I have to, I'll shoot you from over here and I'll shoot anyone that interrupts us.'

Jill staggered around to the safe, knelt down and deliberately blocked Midolini's view with her body. *Now I know what you look like up close, you stinking little coward. Give me ten seconds.* She wiped the blood from her shaking hands onto her uniform.

'I said fucking hurry up!' Midolini screamed. His reptilian eyes flicked between Norton's back and the front door of the station.

Jill slowly opened the safe door. *I'm going to shoot this prick where he stands.*

When Midolini turned his eyes away from the front door and back to Jill, he found himself a metre away from the business end of a pistol. Jill Norton had extracted it from the safe. Midolini could only see black steel and an angry blood-splattered face looming behind.

'Your turn, arsehole! Drop that fucking gun and put your two hands on the counter before I blow your little balls off, you fucking coward.'

Midolini didn't move. His arms remained motionless as he stood on the other side of the counter. His pistol was at his side, out of Jill's view.

Jill released her double-handed grip. One hand slowly reached for the Police Communications phone behind her on top of the safe. Her bloodied left hand fumbled with the receiver. As she raised it to her ear, the receiver suddenly slipped from her grasp and fell to the floor. Her natural reaction was to look at the falling object.

Too late.

The booming sound and exploding pain happened together.

Jill was slammed back against the safe and fell to the floor, with one round from Midolini's pistol embedded in her left shoulder. Through a sea of stars and pain, she saw Midolini start to come around to her side of the watch-house counter. *No you don't, arsehole!*

Midolini had made the mistake of thinking that this older policewoman was down and out. Bad call. As he came around to Jill's side, the first round from her gun smashed into the wall, millimetres from his head, causing plaster splinters to embed themselves into his left cheek and nose.

It sent Midolini reeling back behind the counter. 'You fucking bitch. I'm going to kill you for that, you fat fucking slut. Copper or not, I'm gonna shove this gun down your throat and let off every fucking round. Do you hear me?' Midolini screamed, taking a blood-soaked hand away from his face.

Jill had managed to drag herself to the side of the safe, so she could gain some sort of cover. 'You've got nowhere so far, you coward,' Jill yelled. 'Just remember that I have twenty-nine friends around here with me. Fourteen in this gun and another fifteen on my belt. If you've got the guts, which I very much doubt, then show your ugly lizard face around here again.' Jill could feel herself slipping in and out of consciousness. 'Come on, you slime bag. You want a shot at the title? I'm only a girl, you prick. You feel like a hero now?' *Keep talking. The bat phone's off the hook. They know where this is happening. They can hear every word. Every gunshot. Let me hear those sirens.* Please *let me hear those sirens. I don't want to die here.*

Midolini was silent.

'Hey, prick,' Jill called out, 'the cavalry's on the way. What are you gonna do now?'

Suddenly, Midolini's pudgy shape came up onto the bench as he let two shots go at Jill's head. But the bullets slammed into the thick watch-house book to her left.

The terrified policewoman returned three shots.

Midolini screamed again as he fell back to the other side.

Jill tried to breathe steadily. *Come on, boys. Hurry, hurry, hurry!*

What seemed like minutes ticked past.

No sound of screaming sirens or screaming crims.

Chapter Fifty-Four

Mickey Midolini's head was spinning. *This is not happening. It's my fucking money. Just give it to me.* Not just from the plaster in his eye, but that last shot of return fire had literally parted his hair and left a graze mark across his scalp. A trickle of blood was now running into his left eye and his ears were filled with the screaming cacophony of bullets that had just missed him. His head was screaming.

While he lay spread-eagled behind a desk, out of sight from Jill Norton, he started to realise that he'd lost all control of the situation. *This female Signorotto is fucking up my life. One chance left. Around the other side of the counter. Kill the bitch. Get ready.*

As Midolini slowly eased himself up from the floor, a cold chill went through him.

Sirens. The ear-piercing sound of sirens.

Fuck! Midolini spat his words out, 'You think you've fucking won, don't you, bitch? You tell Signorotto that he'll never get me. Tell him it was a pleasure killing his fucking cousin.' He let three more rounds rip into the steel and woodwork of the watch-house counter before he crawled on hands and knees to the front door.

Jill knew the Carlton Police Station like the back of her hand. She could tell from the shuffling sounds that Midolini was trying to get out. She immediately racked the slide on her pistol, automatically ejecting a round and clearing any possible chance of jamming that could happen with her next shot. If that low-life made it out alive, he would be running.

Jill stood bolt upright from behind the counter. She ignored the red-hot pain searing through her shoulder and the blood running down her face and arms. She could see Midolini's feet going through the doorway. She let fly in his direction, unleashing a whirlwind of wood and plaster chips around the doorway as the bullets took their toll on the old building. Forensics later counted ten rounds from Jill's pistol around the doorway.

The overwhelming sounds of sirens and brakes flooded Jill Norton's brain. She collapsed to the floor in tears.

The last thing Jill saw, before a veil of darkness descended on her, was the helmeted black form of a Special Operations Group officer reaching down to put his hand under her head.

Chapter Fifty-Five

Mickey Midolini had dragged himself back into the darkened alley by the time a dozen police cars were skidding to a halt outside the station with their sirens blaring. *End of the alley. Run. Get to my car. Get the fuck outa here.*

Throwing himself into his Mercedes, Midolini felt like the whole world was closing in on him. His overseas dream was a distant thought. Survival came first. But he didn't panic. He started his car as quietly as he could, then drove slowly across Johnston Street and vanished into the Carlton night.

Taking as many of the darker back streets as he could, Midolini picked up the pace and drove for what seemed like forever to reach his flat in Fawkner.

Once safely inside his front door, Midolini went straight to the bathroom. He slumped onto the floor and ripped handfuls of tissues from a box. He held them over his face and head.

It was ten minutes before he dared look into the mirror.

And what he saw was not a pretty sight. There was a red welt across his scalp from front to back. His left eye and cheek looked as though they'd been scratched by a crazy whore. Plaster chips were imbedded into his face.

A further ten minutes of cold water helped Midolini regain some form of composure before his thoughts returned to money. More importantly, how to get some. There was no way he would get close to that ship without it.

He slowly lifted himself off the floor, walked into the kitchen and grabbed a bottle of Black Label Johnny Walker whisky. He stumbled into the living area and fell backwards onto the couch.

Think, Mickey, think! Where do I get cash from? Where do I get twenty G's from?

Midolini took a few slugs of whisky and felt the fire burn down into his gut. His thoughts began pinging around like a pinball machine, one second he was popping with money-grabbing fantasies, the next he was convulsing with hatred towards Signorotto and everything in blue. *He thinks he's so good. But he's not gonna fuck up my life. No, not him or his smart-arsed bitch. She's the next thing to a fucking cop, anyway. A cop's whore. A fucking cop's whore that gives them money. They think they're that fucking good they have their own bank.*

Midolini got up and paced the floor of his flat, whisky bottle in one hand and gun in the other.

Own bank. She's the manager of that Police Co-Op. That's where all their money is. Mickey, you idiot! Why didn't you think of this before? Money and *revenge. Take their money and Signorotto's whore, too. If they get me, it doesn't matter about his bitch. They'll have me for murder of his cousin and hopefully the murder of that old bitch in uniform back at the station. His whore will come way down the ladder.*

Midolini sat back down quietly and dabbed a dirty handkerchief at the congealing drops of blood on his face.

Hit it on Tuesday. Late Tuesday before closing. If any cops come in, I'll use her as a shield. Grab what I want and shove that bitch in my car. Find a deserted place and wait till about two a.m. then head to the docks.

He suddenly yelled loudly, 'She can be my whore for a few hours. What a way to leave the country! Fuck the Police Co-Op and its manager at the one time. She can go for an early swim after I've had my fun with her. Mickey, Mickey, Mickey! You are a fucking genius.' He raised his nearly empty bottle of whisky to toast the dark depths of his night.

Pleased with his plan, Midolini lay back on his couch, shut his eyes and fantasised about what he'd do to Signorotto's bitch.

Chapter Fifty-Six

'Don't know about you, Max, but I'm getting tired of visiting this hospital,' Tony said, as they walked quickly down the corridor to Jill Norton's room.

'You're not wrong, Sarge. First it was Sav, then Amy and now it's Jill. I can't believe that even Midolini was stupid enough to attack the station.'

'Not just stupid, Max. Desperate. He's tried to kill a cop. He won't be looked after by any of his so-called "friends" now. There are detectives kicking down doors all over Melbourne at the moment. Midolini's cornered and dangerous. Obviously wanted to steal the money in the safe from what Phil Stone told me over the phone. Which reminds me, Phil should be here by now.'

'Everyone we've come to see in this hospital has been put here by Midolini.'

Tony stopped dead in his tracks. 'You're spot on with that, Max. If we were coming here to see Midolini, there'd be only one room I'd like to visit. It's in the basement and it's called the morgue. You don't get answers in that room. At least not any spoken ones.'

Both police officers had to weave their way through a phalanx of navy blue when they got to Jill's room.

A fellow Sergeant from the station, who was just leaving Jill's room, said, 'Tony, this prick Midolini is as good as dead. Every member from the station has rung or come in wanting to be put back on shifts. They want to give up their leave, rest days, anything. They'll work twenty-four/seven. They'll kill the low-life for what he's done to Jill. Even members from Fitzroy, Collingwood, Richmond, Melbourne West, Melbourne East, everywhere in the Region. They all want a piece of Midolini. If he's caught, he won't even be given a chance to put his hands up in surrender. It'll be an execution. Frankly, the cop that does it should be given a medal.'

'Yeah, mate. I know and I don't disagree, but the only one who's going to be given a medal is Jill. What she did was unbelievable.'

'Too right, mate.'

'Tell me, is Phil Stone in there?'

'Yeah, Tony, he's just in there with the doctor now. Her husband's also around somewhere – I think in the administration office with their son and daughter. She'll be okay, thank goodness. She's one tough individual.'

Walking in with Max behind him, Tony took in the sight of Jill propped up in the hospital bed, with bandages over her nose and her left shoulder in a sling.

Jill looked up at the two members in plain clothes and gave a faint smile.

'Jesus, Jill. Who's going to run the bloody place with you in here? Don't leave it up to that bloody Phil Stone or we might as well all pack up and go home. We all know who's the real boss of Carlton.' Tony held up one hand between himself and the Inspector.

Phil grinned and shook his head.

Max intervened with a burning question. 'I just want to know if anyone finished that apple pie of yours, Jill? If not, I'm outa here and back to the station.' Max sat down quietly next to her bed and squeezed her left hand gently.

'Ah, compassion from the younger members,' Jill replied quietly. 'Something you wouldn't know about, Sergeant.'

The Inspector, Sergeant and Constable all drew a collective sigh as they realised Jill Norton could still give back as good as she got.

'Seriously, Jill. I'm so sorry,' Phil Stone said. 'We should've realised how desperate Midolini was and put at least two on the night-shift counter.'

'Just get the mongrel,' Jill said. 'No need for apologies. When you join our navy-blue club, you know you're going to spend most of your career stepping through a minefield. I just zigged when I should have zagged.'

'From now on you'll have a full-time guard outside,' Phil said. 'The Operations Response Unit is looking after that.'

'Listen, you lot,' Jill said, struggling to sit up, then falling back onto the stacked-up pillows, 'the main thing I remember he said was Tony's name. Don't worry about me. He's finished with me. His real target is Tony. And also get someone to look out for Susie. He's crazy enough to try anything.'

Phil Stone looked across the room at Tony, who had turned whiter than an Australian beach.

Tony said quietly, 'If he goes near her, Jill, he's signed his own death warrant.'

'I'll pretend I didn't hear that, Sergeant,' Phil said, as his eyes flicked from his Sergeant to his Constable. 'When we get Midolini, we'll do it the right way. If he ends up in court, we'll have our case set in concrete.'

Tony didn't reply or even look at Phil.

Phil continued, 'Tony, it's now Monday morning. I want you and Max here to take the rest of the day off. If the Special Operations Group gets him today, that's fine. If not, we'll all sit down with the Major Crime Squad tomorrow and plan it from there. Go and spend the night with Susie. In the meantime, I'll arrange for a car to sit outside her work till this has finished. I'll ring her and tell her. Off you go.'

Tony was about to put up an argument, but suddenly realised how tired he was after the last few days. He and Max could do with a quick break. 'Okay, boss. I'll go and see Susie now. I'll wait till your boys are in place, then come back at closing time and take her home.'

Tony went over to Jill and self-consciously leaned down and kissed her on the cheek. 'Take care, Jill. Look after yourself. Keep that slug from your shoulder and make a pendant out of it.'

'I'd like to put it somewhere else on Midolini, but I'm too much of a lady to say where,' Jill said, with a grin. 'Thanks, Tony. Look after Susie. We'll all have a laugh over this at your wedding. But be careful. Make sure you look after the young lad with the manners here.' She pointed and waved feebly at the departing Max Tyler.

Jill's eyes closed with exhaustion when the two officers left.

The look that passed between Tony and Max as they exited the hospital was one of pure hatred. Hatred for Midolini and everything he stood for.

Chapter Fifty-Seven

Midolini had sweated through the remainder of Sunday night and all twenty-four hours of Monday. He didn't have the perfect plan, but at least it was a plan.

He'd swapped the numberplates from his Mercedes for a set off an identical vehicle he'd located in a car yard in Sydney Road, Fawkner, earlier that morning. If the cops checked his car now, it would come up as a model of the same year and colour. He figured he could sit tucked away near the Police Co-Op in Nicholson Street, and keep his eye on the flow of customers without being noticed. The heavily tinted windows of his car gave him plenty of privacy.

Midolini's head and face were still red and grazed, but he didn't care anymore. He knew this would be his last roll of the dice to get money. His original $10,000 was tucked away in a small carry bag in the car's boot, along with a change of clothes. The ship was his last and only chance to flee the country. He'd located a nice dark car park under the West Gate Bridge, where he expected to while away the next few hours degrading Signorotto's bitch before his sea 'cruise'. For now, it was a waiting game. He would hit the building just before five. If there were cops around, then so be it.

Unfortunately for Midolini, he wasn't aware his opposition had planted two uniform members sitting in their own private car directly across the road from the Police Co-Op. He wasn't to know that so many members were out looking for him that the surrounding stations were having trouble finding enough cars for all the volunteers.

Seeing the force's stake-out of the Co-Op was a static post, the Senior Constable from Richmond, who was teamed with another from the Melbourne West Station, had no hesitation in volunteering his private Subaru sedan for the job. The other item he had no objection to was pasting the A4-size picture of Midolini taken by the internal CCTV at the Carlton Police Station on the dashboard of his car.

Midolini divided his time between watching the building and cleaning his favourite Beretta pistol. From under the floorboards at his Fawkner house, he'd also retrieved a Glock nine-millimetre that housed fifteen rounds. *If I go down, it's gonna be a pig shoot!*

At 4.55 p.m. it was time. Midolini laid his two guns on the seat beside him and accelerated his car from the kerb. *No one outside. Stop in the cop car park out the front. Grab the guns and walk quickly inside. You know what she looks like. Grab her by the hair. Get the money and get out.*

Midolini's car screamed into the parking space out front, then he executed the first part of his daring plan. He crashed shoulder-first through the glass doors, and was relieved to find only the female tellers cleaning up. The one who stood out from the rest still had her jacket on. Midolini couldn't help himself and let one shot go into the perspex panelling next to one of the tellers. Screams erupted from all the women.

Midolini turned towards his main target and pointed both pistols directly at Susie. 'Ah, fucking Signorotto's whore. I want money now or I'll shoot every last bitch in this joint. Midolini is the name. I'm sure you've heard of me. Now get me money.' He shoved the barrel of his Glock into Susie's chest, causing her to gasp with pain.

Susie tried to stand still and not show the fear that was racking her body. 'The safe is locked. It's a time-lock until tomorrow. I can't give you any money,' she said, her voice shaking.

'It's not five o'clock, bitch. The safe shuts at five.' Midolini stomped towards the nearest young teller, grabbed her by the front of her blouse and flung her sprawling backwards across one of the desks. He stepped around the desk to force the barrel of his Glock into her mouth till the woman almost gagged.

'All right. All right. Wait!' Susie shouted. She ran to the large safe, punched numbers into a keypad and pulled the door back.

'Be a good little bitch and bring me out at least forty grand in hundreds. Bring it over here, count it and bag it for me. Be real quick or this pretty little thing will chew on a bullet,' Midolini snarled, as he slid his slimy little hand under the teller's white blouse. He grabbed her breast so hard, the teller began to dry-retch with fear.

Susie did what she was told, all the time being mindful of the screams of the female tellers and the choking sound of the woman Midolini had flung across the desk. When Susie had finished, she handed the bag to him.

'You see the position she was in, Susie? Yes, I know your name and I know you're Signorotto's bitch. Remember the position, because you're gonna be like that, too, for the next few hours. Only I'll be on top of you. We're going to have some real fun together. There won't be one part of you I haven't touched by the time I've finished with you. Signorotto won't come near you when he realises I've been there.'

Midolini yanked the young teller so viciously by the legs she slid off the desk. She landed with a crash on her back, sending her into convulsions.

Midolini spun Susie around by one arm, put the Beretta into the money bag, then slid the Glock up under Susie's blouse at the back. 'Now we go for a nice little walk out the door and we get into my car. Your fucking hero squeeze wouldn't have ever taken you in a Mercedes before, I bet.'

Midolini looked around from behind Susie just in time to see two cops pull back from the doorway. He yelled at the top of his voice, 'Shoot at me and I'll put the first bullet right through her spine. I'm sure Sergeant fucking Signorotto would love that. His fucking bitch in a wheelchair. Now get out of my fucking way. I'm coming through!'

Chapter Fifty-Eight

There had been no sign of Midolini in the previous twenty-four hours. For most of the day, Tony, Phil and Max had been in discussions with members from the Major Crime Squad and Special Operations Group. A temporary headquarters had been set up in the muster room of the Carlton Police Station. They were organising raids on every place they thought Midolini might set foot. Nothing was being left to chance. Every location where Midolini had been known to leave his footprint was being turned over.

Max had gone for a coffee when Tony looked at his watch. 'Shit, it's five o'clock already. I've gotta head down and pick up Susie, fellas.' As Tony went to leave the muster room, he was grabbed on the arm by a frantic Phil Stone.

'Tony, something's happened down at the Co-Op. Radio reports have just come in from the members that Midolini is there and has fired shots at them. They're all right. But they said he dragged a girl out of the Co-Op and it looks like Susie. They didn't fire back because he was using her as a shield. Wait for me and we'll head down there. I'll get the SOG boys on the road.'

The Special Operations Group men came thundering out of the room, followed by Stone.

'Righto, Tony, let's go,' Stone said, looking around for Tony. But there was no sign of his Sergeant. Running back through the watch-house, Stone yelled Tony's name again.

This time he was answered by the young female watch-house keeper. 'Sir, Sergeant Signorotto just grabbed a set of keys and flew out the back door. What's going on?'

Max Tyler suddenly appeared from out the back, jumped the counter, snatched one of the detective's car keys off a hook, then sprinted out the front door and up the road.

Stone looked after Max, his mind was screaming, *Head him off, Max! Head him off!* Stone turned back to the young female constable and cried, 'A gun, quick!'

She leapt into action as Stone grabbed a portable radio. He took the pistol from her, then raced to his car.

Chapter Fifty-Nine

Snatching Signorotto's girlfriend from the Police Credit Co-Op in broad daylight was fast becoming Midolini's worst nightmare. Trying to keep his distance from the Carlton Police Station, Midolini had headed south from the Co-Op, but the traffic in Victoria Street was heavier than he'd expected.

He was forced to hang a left into Nicholson Street, where the traffic was light enough for him to charge north alongside the Carlton Gardens. However, a police car, with lights flashing and siren wailing, came screaming down the Nicholson Street tram tracks directly towards him.

Midolini was confident he could slip past or beat this prick at chicken if he had to. But at the last second, the police car swung hard off the tram tracks and blocked Midolini's side of the road. Midolini put his faith in the strength of his German-built Mercedes and rammed into the side of the police's Ford.

The middle of the police car's passenger side was smashed badly and its motor stalled. The front end of the Mercedes' Krupp steel was crumpled and its engine groaned, but Midolini was still able to slam his car into reverse and extricate himself from the mess.

At the very moment Midolini hit his brakes to change gears back into drive, he caught sight of Signorotto in the driver's seat of the damaged and stalled police car.

And Susie's terrified face was clearly visible to Tony through the passenger window of the Mercedes.

Midolini saw Signorotto's face turn to boiling rage. The sight of the enraged cop's face would stay with him till the day he died. Something Midolini was desperately trying to avoid as he floored the accelerator of his ailing Mercedes and lumbered northwards along Nicholson Street. He kept one hand on the steering wheel, while his other hand grasped an agonising hunk of Susie's long black hair.

Susie suddenly lashed out with a closed right fist, striking Midolini flush on the nose.

'You fucking bitch!' he spat back, slamming Susie's head into the dashboard. The claret flowed from his nose onto his Armani shirt. 'I'm gonna turn that face of yours into pulp and show it to that piece-of-shit boyfriend of yours just before I finish you both. He's fucked my life, so I'm going to fuck his and yours!' Midolini let go of Susie's hair so he could try to control his lurching and damaged car.

Susie threw herself at Midolini, one set of fingers clawing at his face, the other digging with long fingernails into his crotch.

Screaming in agony as his balls were being crushed, Midolini grabbed for his pistol stashed in the door pocket. Taking it by the barrel, Midolini brought it down on Susie's head, cold-clocking her onto the floor of his Mercedes.

However, the car wasn't going to last much longer. Steam was hissing from under the crumpled bonnet like a Turkish bath in Brunswick. The front right wheel was sending up sparks and the blown tyre was sending up liquorice-like strips of rubber, which were whipping past the driver's window of the once-pristine black mafioso chariot.

As the damaged heap slowly lost speed, Midolini threw a left turn into Carlton Street, along the top end of the Carlton Gardens, in an attempt to escape from the ear-piercing sirens he could hear in the background. About halfway along the street, the Mercedes gave a death shudder, let out a metallic groan and ground to a halt. The crumpled wreck was finished. No amount of frantic key turning was going to change the situation.

Fuck, fuck, fuck!

Midolini jumped out and raced around to the passenger side, furiously wrenching open the door.

Susie fell out onto the roadway.

'What's happening there?' an elderly male voice called from nearby.

Midolini looked up to see a frail man waving a walking stick at him.

Midolini raised his gun. He shot the old man twice in the chest, killing him instantly.

Screams erupted from the tennis courts across the lawns in the Carlton Gardens, as blood flowed from the body near Midolini's feet.

'Not such a fucking hero now, eh, old man?' Midolini wheezed, as he grabbed at his groin with one hand. With the other, he dragged Susie to her feet. 'Start walking, bitch. Walk or you die here with him right now.' Midolini pointed his pistol at the old man's body. Everything in Mickey Midolini's world was now totally out of control.

Susie swayed as she vomited onto the ground.

But within seconds Midolini was pushing and shoving her across the footpath into the park.

Susie whipped her arm backwards, smashing Midolini's nose and splattering blood over his face. 'Why don't you give up?' she screamed. 'You can hear them coming. You're finished you prick, you scum.'

Midolini grabbed at his nose as he pushed her farther into the gardens. 'Maybe, bitch, but not before I shove a gun up your boyfriend's nose and blow his fucking brains through the top of his head. Remember this, you stuck-up cop's whore, when you see it happen – and I'll make sure you do – you'll know you've got about ten seconds to live before I do the same to you. You'll be joining him in hell!'

Chapter Sixty

'Start, you prick of a thing – start!' Tony screamed, while madly turning the ignition again and again in an effort to kick the dead motor of the patrol car back into life.

Tony had done well to anticipate that Midolini would be forced to flee up Nicholson Street after hearing radio reports of his car weaving east through heavy traffic along Victoria Street. But trying to block Midolini's car on Nicholson Street hadn't worked, and now adrenaline coursed through Tony's body as a gut-wrenching fear was beginning to take a vice-like grip on him. Every second Midolini was taking Susie farther away from him. Rage was far out-running every other emotion in Tony, pushing aside the thoughts buzzing in his head: *Why'd I leave Max behind? Why won't the fricken car start? Why can't I do something? I'm a cop, I've got to do something – anything!*

Slamming his fist into the steering wheel, Tony gave the key one more turn. The engine finally jolted back into life. Midolini crashing into his Ford hadn't completely killed the motor, but it sounded sick. Tony simultaneously threw the vehicle into reverse, planted his foot on the accelerator and spun his steering wheel to the left. The police car laboured through a semi-circle as smoke poured from the rear tyres and the smell of burning rubber enveloped the vehicle. Reverse, brake, gears, turn. This tried-and-true police pursuit method returned like a bolt of lightning.

Tony's car whined in protest as it fishtailed back into the chase, the engine's sound competing with the ear-piercing wail of his siren. Midolini had a start on Tony, but a trail of radiator water and shredded tyre from the Mercedes gave Tony hope.

However, Midolini's trail suddenly disappeared. Tony was left with clear daylight ahead. Slamming his foot on the brake pedal, Tony realised that Midolini must have ducked down a side street.

Throwing the police car into a vicious right turn, Tony reached down and pulled the handbrake on fully. The vehicle was forced to skid and turn through 180 degrees.

The thought of a trap was uppermost in his mind as Tony slowed the car and looked left and right into the side streets he had just passed. Only two streets back, Tony spotted the black Mercedes halfway down Carlton Street, wedged against the gutter with its front doors open.

Tony turned cautiously into Carlton Street. His intense concentration was being interrupted by the crackling voice coming over the police radio. Realising it was asking for his location and a situation report, Tony reached down and turned the control switch to the off position.

The twin voices of fear and survival screamed in silence at him to stop and wait for back-up; however, the overriding wave of emotion for Susie urged him on. Tony pulled up behind the Mercedes, and slipped out of his car with gun drawn.

Nothing was going to control his red-hot Italian temper now.

Driver's side. Nothing.

Quick look through the back window. Nothing.

Crouch. Wide circle around the back. Aim for body mass. Sweep left. Sweep right.

Nothing. Wait.

Body on ground. Not Susie. Not Midolini. No, no, a bystander. Midolini's lost it.

Check passenger side. Nothing.

Sweep through into the park. Nothing.

Gun still drawn. Check his pulse. Nothing.

One down. Dead.

Fuck, fuck!

One dead. No Midolini, no Susie.

Tony stood with his gun by his side, his mind racing.

People were appearing from nearby houses.

Tony's gun hand jumped when his mobile phone rang in his shirt pocket. He glanced at the screen. The name 'Max' was flashing incessantly.

Chapter Sixty-One

Max was furious with Tony for taking off without him when Midolini's target became known.

Max had run from the rear of the station, only to see the back of the police car fishtailing into Drummond Street. Charging into the watch-house, he grabbed the only set of keys available, leapt over the counter and hit the front door running.

The unmarked Criminal Investigation Unit car was parked in the street, about fifty metres away. By the time Max had fired up the car and pulled out, Tony was long gone.

Max initially thought he would drive to where Susie worked, but then reports of a failed intercept in Nicholson Street hit the police radio waves.

Max did an abrupt U-turn then powered down Faraday Street towards Nicholson Street. He crossed Rathdowne Street, but when he reached the roundabout at Canning Street, his access to Nicholson Street was blocked by roadworks. Max roared down Canning Street towards the Carlton Gardens. When he reached Carlton Street, he was about to swing left towards Nicholson Street, but instead slammed on his brakes.

Max couldn't believe his eyes. A gun-toting Mickey Midolini was dragging Susie through the Carlton Gardens, not more than thirty metres from him.

Max's training told him not to go in headfirst. If he did, it would most likely end in a shoot-out and, with Susie in the middle, the result could be deadly.

Slipping quietly out of his unmarked car, Max drew his service pistol. Taking cover behind the rear of a nearby parked car, Max checked his gun and the number of rounds on him. He didn't want to use any at this stage.

Holstering his gun, Max took a deep breath and scuttled crab-like into the park, staying well behind the two figures. Max realised he was trembling, but he kept Midolini in sight by ducking behind anything from trees to rubbish bins. Sweat began to trickle down Max's back, underneath his ballistic vest that was feeling heavier with every darting move from cover to cover.

Two things sprang to Max's mind. The first was that the ever-increasing sound of an approaching police siren had stopped. The second was the cold realisation that he was as alone as he'd ever felt in his life. He hadn't told the radio dispatcher where he was. Big mistake. He'd simply forgotten to do it. All he had was a ballistic vest, a gun, his mobile phone and his young copper's belief that he was indestructible.

Max guessed that Midolini wouldn't keep pushing Susie in front of him if they left the park when they hit Rathdowne Street. He was too smart for that. He would have to slow down and keep her close, otherwise he would draw too much attention to himself.

The big question was, where was he taking her? The way they were headed would take them back towards the city and a lot more people. Or did Midolini have another trick up his sleeve?

Chapter Sixty-Two

Tony answered the call in a heartbeat. 'Max, haven't got time to talk. Midolini's got Susie. He's gone into the Carlton Gardens with her. Mate, where the fuck are you?'

Max immediately forgot about any ideas of recrimination against Tony for leaving him behind. 'Sarge, I'm *in* the Carlton Gardens right now. I'll explain later. And I can see them just ahead –'

'Where? Where are they?' Tony screamed into his phone. His wild eyes scanned the gardens around him. He could see people, but not the ones he wanted.

'You're not going to believe this, Sarge. He's dragged her across Rathdowne Street and over to the old Lemon Tree Hotel site. You know, where they're building the new police station. Probably thinks that's the last place we'll look for her – in a bloody police station.'

'Stay where you are, Max. Don't move till… what was that noise? Was that a shot? What's going on, Max? Talk to me!' Tony yelled. He bolted through the gardens towards Rathdowne Street. His phone was glued to his ear and his pistol felt slippery in his sweating hand.

Chapter Sixty-Three

A cold shudder had gone through Max when he'd heard the gunshot. He suddenly found himself sprinting across Rathdowne Street from his cover next to the garden-keeper's house. He took refuge behind a large picture of the Victorian State Premier that was fixed to the hoarding out front of the new multi-million dollar police station. The Premier's beaming face was central to advertising the police station's opening later that year.

Max looked at his shaking hands and he pointed his firearm at the ground. He racked his brain for what to do next. He had to save Susie.

Suddenly, a bulky figure staggered out of the building site. He was clutching a bloodied arm. Max swung his firearm in the man's direction, ready to fire before fully recognising who it was. 'Police – don't move!'

The man dropped to both knees. His construction hard hat, covered in union stickers, fell from his head, and bounced along the footpath into the gutter. 'Help me. Quick. Fucking help me!' the man in overalls pleaded. 'He fucking shot me. He fucking shot me!'

Max darted over, leaned down and grabbed the bloodied figure by the shirt. He dragged the building worker behind the hoarding to what he hoped was relative safety. 'How many people are in there? Quick, tell me,' Max demanded. 'How many, do you know?'

The worker was gasping for oxygen. 'Some guy and a woman, mate. No one else. Stop the fucking blood, will you?'

Max whipped a bandanna from the worker's neck, then began tying the cloth around what appeared to be a long graze on the man's bleeding arm. 'What the hell's happening in there?'

'Those two burst in just after everyone else had left the site to go off to a union rally,' the worker replied breathlessly. 'I was going, too, but I had to turn off the mixer and empty it. We've got a picket line starting at another building site. Orders from the union. Am I going to die?' the worker asked.

'You'll be okay. There's a lot of blood, but not much else.' Max tied off the bandanna. 'Just stay here with me, there are more cops on the way,' Max said, without a great amount of conviction in his voice.

The worker nodded.

Max scanned the front of the site. 'So other than woman and the man who shot you, is everyone else out?'

'Yeah, but they're not friends. He was saying he would kill her when he dragged her out the back where I was working. I dropped my shovel and ran out front to get help. And he fucking shot me, mate. I'm fucking shot.'

'Don't move. There'll be police swarming all over here soon. They'll get you to the medics.' Max got into a crouch, then suddenly sprinted around the sign, gun in front of himself.

Max zig-zagged his way down the side of the site, next to a partially constructed brick wall. He felt himself stumbling over broken bricks and bits of plaster. Stopping at the end of the wall, he tried to listen for any sounds. But all he could hear was his heart beating and blood pounding in his head.

Taking another couple of big breaths, Max slowly peered around the wall into what looked like the nearly finished cells of the watch-house. One large steel door was in place and another was leaning against a wall.

Next to it, with his back turned, was Midolini. His head was peering over a concrete ledge, trying to see what was happening out the front on Grattan Street. Susie was on the ground with Midolini's foot on the back of her neck. Across the room was a large, churning concrete mixer that the builder had mentioned.

As the sound of Max's own heartbeat became more regular, the slopping sound of the wet concrete in the mixer took over. Max knew Tony wouldn't be far away. He could imagine the wild man trying to storm the building to shoot Midolini. However, Tony would be rushing headfirst into a nightmare maze of unfinished rooms and building rubble. The noise Tony would make would be a dead give-away for Midolini. And it would be Tony who ended up dead.

Max could see the pistol in Midolini's hand. If Max called on him to drop his weapon it could become a shoot-out with Susie in the middle. *No good. Second plan, quick!*

Looking up at the ceiling, Max saw his chance. Above him was a large metal pulley set up on a steel crossbeam. The builders must have used this to manoeuvre the cell door into place.

Stepping out from behind his shelter, Max looked at Susie.

Her eyes widened like saucers as Max put his gun back into his holster, then quietly took hold of the pulley and flung it towards the back of Midolini's head.

The sound of the rattling chain attached to the pulley caused Midolini to spin around. Trying to sidestep the huge block of approaching airborne metal, he tripped on a piece of concrete box-work. The pulley hit him with a thudding, bone-crunching blow on the shoulder, forcing his pistol to fall into the mess of building rubble that was strewn across the floor. Falling backwards, Midolini landed heavily on his back in the box-work with a loud grunt.

Max jumped over the tow bar of the churning concrete mixer, yanked Susie up by the arm, then bundled her towards where he had entered. He wasn't going to waste time fighting with Midolini. He just wanted Susie out of trouble. Stumbling out of the unfinished building, Max took one last look at the maddened figure trying to get itself off the floor using his only good arm.

Max saw Susie begin to fall as she picked her way across the rubble. She fell backwards onto him. He hoisted her up, one arm under her legs and another under her back. He could feel her tears wetting the side of his face. With Susie hugging Max tightly, they staggered out into the street, collapsing onto the footpath, then looking up in time to see Tony charging across the road.

Susie instinctively shifted in Tony's direction, but Max refused to let go of his protective grip on her.

Chapter Sixty-Four

Throwing his arms around the prone figure of Susie, Tony quickly realised she was terrified but physically not hurt. With hatred for Midolini burning in his eyes and his voice full of pure venom, Tony asked, 'Did you kill the arsehole, Max?'

'No, Sarge. He's still in there. He's hurt, but he's still got a gun. Wait for the Special Operations Group. Don't go in there by yourself.'

Tony stood up.

Susie grabbed Tony by one arm and pulled him back down. 'No, Tony, Max is right. I'm not going to lose you. Wait for more police.'

The injured worker suddenly called out from where he was propped up against the fence, 'The woman next door has called the cops and the ambulance. You can hear more sirens now.'

Flashing lights started to appear in the distance along with the high-pitched wail of sirens from both directions along Rathdowne Street. Within twenty seconds there was an ambulance and six police cars – including Phil Stone's – screeching to a halt outside the unfinished police station.

Tooled-up police in ballistic vests poured from the vehicles and took shelter at the front of the building.

Phil Stone and a young female constable shepherded Tony, Max and Susie back behind the Inspector's car. Two other police officers covered their mates as the building worker was picked up and carried to one side where the paramedics were waiting.

'Turn those sirens off and let me think!' Phil Stone shouted.

Chapter Sixty-Five

Benny Illarietti had avoided police most of his life. It wasn't that he didn't have any respect for the law, it was more the fact that in his line of business it was a lot easier to get by without their involvement. However, this situation was the exception to the rule.

Sav's life had been ruined by Mickey Midolini. So had Benny's. The disrespect that Midolini had thrown in Benny's face – with the skimming of his product and the virtual destruction of Sav's life by the same traitor – had brought Benny's business and personal life to a door-slamming close.

Benny was no longer concerned that his international associates had told him to retire immediately. He was sixty years of age and money wasn't a problem. In his line of work, if you were told to retire and didn't, then you would be retired permanently with a new lawn-cemetery address.

No, it was Sav's life that was destroying Benny. With the injury to Sav's hand and his ongoing fight against drug addiction, Benny's dream of having a successful surgeon or doctor for a son was finished.

Mickey Midolini had to die. Plain and simple. Where and how didn't matter, but it had to be now. His demise had been ordered from higher up, towards the head of the snake.

Benny had organised for his henchmen and contacts to be regularly reporting back to him during the past week while they searched for his lieutenant. The net was starting to close. With Benny's nephew in blue also searching for Midolini, it would only be a matter of time.

Benny wanted him first, though. Midolini would not be given the comfort of a jail cell to hide away in. However, if it were a matter of Benny asking Tony for any type of help to find Midolini, then it had to be. Benny could use the family ties to try to lever information from his nephew.

Benny's plans for Tony were going through his head as Benny stepped out of the passenger seat of his black seven-series BMW opposite the Carlton Police Station. His train of thought was broken when he heard the screeching of tyres coming from the driveway. Looking up, he saw his nephew behind the wheel of a police car as it screamed past him.

'Boss, boss!' yelled Benny's driver.

'What?' Benny snapped back, watching the disappearing tail of the police car.

'Boss, my cousin Gino. You know him. He runs a café down Cardigan Street. He's just seen Mickey dragging some bird out of her office at gunpoint and thrown her into his car. What the fuck's he up to?'

The rat was trapped!

Benny saw Tony's young partner Max run out of the station and jump into an unmarked police car farther along the street and fire it up. Jumping back into his BMW, Benny shouted at his driver, 'Keep up with that plain cop car. Lose it and lose your job!'

It all fitted together now: Mickey Midolini's last stand. The girl he'd snatched had to be Susie. Benny could see a window of opportunity opening just slightly.

The driver swung Benny's big sedan out into the traffic, determined to keep up with the unmarked police car.

Minutes later, after a wild ride through Carlton, Benny's driver brought the Beamer to a stop at a safe distance behind his quarry. The police car had come to a sudden halt near the corner of Canning and Carlton Streets, opposite the Carlton Gardens.

Benny watched Max leap out of his car and scan the gardens. Benny could not believe his eyes. Mickey Midolini was dragging a dark-haired woman through the park.

Stepping quietly from his car, Benny saw the relieved look on his driver's face when he was ordered to stay with the car. Benny walked slowly up to a vehicle that was parked two back from the unmarked police car, then pretended to search through his pockets for car keys.

It didn't matter. Max was too busy to notice Benny. Max was putting on a ballistic vest as he darted through the gardens, all the while talking into his mobile phone.

Benny could hear the word 'Sarge' being used. Putting two and two together, Benny reasoned that his nephew was not in the vicinity – yet. While trying to stay out of sight, Benny skirted around behind Max and kept his eye on the young policeman, as well as checking to see where the other two were going.

Benny saw Midolini take the girl across Rathdowne Street and enter the site of the new police station. Benny's mind raced as he waited for the blue cavalry to arrive. Admiration and stupidity crossed Benny's mind when he saw Max race across the road after Midolini.

Benny was taking cover near the garden-keeper's cottage when he heard a shot ring out. Next, he saw a building worker come staggering out of the site, then Max charging in. It was time for Benny to make his play.

He quickly crossed Rathdowne Street, weaving through the traffic and cutting across Grattan Street to the side of the building site. Slipping through the rear of the partly constructed building, he felt for the cold, razor-sharp stiletto he had secreted up his sleeve.

A shadow of a smile crossed Benny's face.

Chapter Sixty-Six

Tony wanted Midolini to himself. The arrival of Phil Stone and the approaching Special Operations Group were not factors he was concerned with.

Tony let go of Susie and sprinted into the front yard of the site, gun out in front of him, sweeping from side to side, until he reached cover. No sound from within.

'Get back here, Sergeant!' Phil Stone's voice boomed from the street.

'Got to see this through, Phil,' Tony called back.

There was a sudden scrambling sound.

It was Phil making his way across the broken rubble. He wedged his shoulder up against Tony's, firearm in hand. Phil lowered his voice, 'We might as well get into the shit together on this, mate. You know what I'm like with paperwork. One report beats two.'

The two old mates looked at each other before Tony broke the silence. 'Count of five, we go down the passage behind us. You cover right, I'll do left. If there's a door on the right, I'll start and you cover my arse. Then vice versa. Understand?'

'Let's get on with it.'

On Tony's count of five, the two veterans teamed as one and bolted for the passage.

Tony's voice filled the corridor, 'Police, don't move!' He took the first open doorway. Nothing.

They continued to cross and double-cross each open doorway.

Sweat dripped from Tony's face and hands, making the two-handed grip on his pistol all the more difficult. A quick look at Phil was like looking into a mirror. They were both terrified. Neither of them called out the police challenge again.

Tony could hear machinery rumbling towards the back of the unfinished building.

A muffled scream came from the rear of the site, where Phil knew the future jail cells were being constructed. He'd helped plan the new premises and had visited only the previous week to oversee the construction of his new station. 'Back me up, Tony,' Phil whispered. 'I know where that scream came from.'

Guns in front of them like battering rams, Tony followed his boss to one side as they entered the rear of the building.

Phil came to a sudden stop as he entered the jail cell area – Tony nearly knocked him over.

Stepping around his Inspector, Tony began to sweep the area with his pistol. But his sweep was stopped halfway. Tony lowered his gun.

Both police officers stared at the figure before them.

'What the fuck?' Tony said.

Chapter Sixty-Seven

The gaunt figure of Benny Illarietti stood, hands by his side, staring back across the rubbish-strewn jail cell area at Phil Stone and Tony. There was no sign of Mickey Midolini.

'What's going on, Benny?' Tony demanded, his voice strained, perspiration running down his face. 'What are you doing here?'

'I would say the same as you, nephew. Looking for Mickey. I heard he may have been in the vicinity. As you would be only too aware, I have a lot of local contacts. I want him as badly as you.'

Both Phil and Tony began to systematically search the partially built rooms that led from the cells area. No Midolini.

On their return, Tony noticed that Benny had not moved. Tony beckoned Benny over to himself and the Inspector. Tony watched Benny closely as he walked around the now-silent and empty concrete mixer and the large box form of wet concrete on the floor between them.

'What's going on, Benny?' Tony asked. 'We heard a scream from here seconds ago. I know Mickey was in here with Susie, but young Max managed to get Susie away from this area.'

'Ah, yes,' Benny said, with a casual air, 'the scream. It was me. I tripped over some rubble and fell down. Very clumsy of me, nephew. Now if you don't need me, I'll leave Victoria's finest to do what they are paid to do. Fight crime.'

Tony and Phil looked at each other.

As he went to walk around the two policemen, Benny paused, reached out and touched his nephew lightly on the arm. Benny said quietly, his voice breaking slightly, 'Tony, as of now, I am retired. I have been retired by my brothers. Of no concern, though. I have Saverio to look after. And, nephew, I am grateful to you for his life. I am forever in your debt for saving him. He is my family. You also, Tony. Although you fight it, you are my family, too.'

Tears streamed down Benny's cheeks as he gently placed a kiss on both cheeks of Tony's sweat-covered face. 'You take care of that beautiful girl of yours outside. Look after your loved ones. Whatever it takes, look after your loved ones.'

As he reached the exit, Benny slowly turned towards the two silent policemen. 'This will be a very good place for law and order. From here you can look out over Carlton. You will stand over crime… and criminals from here. Mark my words.' Benny slowly lowered his eyes to the wet concrete slab near their feet. With that, Benny strode from the site and disappeared.

Tony and Phil turned and looked at the wet slab before them. A few drops of concrete were still falling from the mixer, making a light plopping noise on the surface of the setting grey mass.

Like the sound of a wet kiss on the face of a cadaver.

Looking at each other, Tony and Phil knew no words were needed. Now or forever. The look was one of justice served. Blue justice.

Chapter Sixty-Eight

There was only one theme for the wedding: Italian, of course.

There was only one place for the wedding: Lygon Street, Carlton, of course.

During Susie's recovery over the previous four weeks, she had bowed to the red, white and green avalanche that Dom's daughters Gina, Rosa and Silvana brought to her townhouse in Cardigan Street.

They had completely taken over all the arrangements. From the ceremony at St Carthage's Church in Royal Parade, through to the reception at their father's bistro, and to the wedding cars – bright red Holden Monaros.

Susie didn't really mind. It was like having three young sisters and, besides, she just wanted to spend as much time with Tony as she could. Phil Stone had sent him on leave with the ultimatum that he not come back until ordered.

Tony had made Phil his best man, with Max as a groomsman. Tony had to find two more to satisfy the three bridesmaids. One wasn't a problem. It was a fellow Sergeant from the station. The third was a surprise to many, including Tony's mother, Sophia. It was Sav Illarietti.

Sav had a long way to go with his physical recovery, but when Tony had dropped into Benny's house three weeks before and asked him, the look on Sav's face was one of determination and pride. When Tony told Susie of his plan, she let him know his gesture would go a long way to mending some family fences. Tony agreed but told Susie that some fences would never be re-built, and that she had to go along with the fact it was better not to mess with ghosts of the past.

*

Friends from near and far dropped into the reception. It was, according to Dom, one of the happiest nights he could remember at his establishment. It even overflowed into his old friend Bernardi's restaurant next door. The night was a long one.

Tony took time out late in the evening, and concealed himself in the kitchen. Looking out through the doorway, he smiled to himself when he saw Phil Stone's wife playing cupid between Max Tyler and one of Dom's daughters.

On the stairs were Jill Norton and her husband. She was taking aside one of the young constables, who had dropped in, and removing a glass of Chianti from his hand. Jill's recovery was well on the road. It would take a lot more than a bullet to stop her. She had been nominated by the Department for a Valour Award for her courage that night with Midolini.

Max Tyler was also up for a Valour Award in recognition of his daring rescue of Susie from Midolini's clutches. The young constable had been set upon by another of the Santino girls. It was an amazing place, Dom's bistro. If you went into the kitchen, you got into a fight. If you went into the restaurant, you fell in love.

Turning around, Tony saw Dom and Phil sitting in the far corner of the kitchen, on two large olive oil tins. They were deep in discussion, glasses of red in hand.

Tony wandered over. 'Righto, you two. Excuse the pun, but what are you cooking up?'

Instead of being greeted by a look of happiness, both men stared at Tony.

Phil spoke first, 'Dom has been telling me about a group of Asians from interstate trying to muscle in on the strip here, looking for protection money. They've already beaten the crap out of the bloke who owns the Malaysian restaurant down near Queensberry Street.'

'Tony, everyone here knows you. All the owners. They trust you. Can you look into it for us? For me?' Dom pleaded.

'Dom, I'm on holidays. I'm going on my honeymoon. I don't know if I even want to stay in the job. I'm tired. Worn out. I need a break.'

Phil chipped in, 'He's right, Dom. He's tired, old and at the end of his career. Come down to the station next week and I'll get young Max Tyler in. We'll have a chat. Leave old Tony out of it.'

Tony blurted, '*Old* Tony! *Young* Max? What're you talking about? You're not going to throw him to the wolves. He was good with Midolini, but these guys will be different. No way. They'll slice him up for stir-fry.'

When Dom's droopy-eyed stare combined with a shrug of Phil's shoulders, it was all Tony could take. 'Okay, okay. I'll catch up with you when I get back. Max and I will see you at the station when I get back from leave. Satisfied, you two?'

As Phil smiled, Dom stood up and embraced Tony. Dom looked over Tony's shoulder and beyond the kitchen door. Dom quietly asked, 'Why don't we have dinner here when you get back? Mr Stone and his beautiful wife, you and the beautiful Susie, and Max and whichever of my daughters is over the moon with him by the end of the night.'

Tony shook his head, pulled back from their embrace, put his hand up to his face and laughed. 'Wogs, restaurants, love and bloody coppers. Where will it end?'

The three of them raised their glasses in a toast: two reds and a lemon, lime and bitters!

Chapter Sixty-Nine

His Honour Justice Paul Webster stood looking out over William Street, deep in thought. He wasn't thinking about legal matters. He was thinking about what he was to do now that Midolini had disappeared without a trace. He didn't care if Midolini was dead. Webster only cared about where he was going to procure his next nubile party pack from.

Since Midolini's disappearance there had been no one to supply Webster with his insatiable appetite for young girls and drugs. He thought about looking at the legal list to see if there were any large drug cases coming up. *Surely with a lenient sentence for the accused and a note slipped to the defence barrister by my tipstaff, it could prove to be a fresh shopping list.*

A smile spread across Webster's face as his chamber door opened without a knock. Turning to confront the unwelcome interruption, Webster declared, 'Even *you* have to knock, Tippie.'

But two suited men walked into Webster's chamber.

Behind them, a red-faced, puffing tipstaff was tripping along. 'They say they're detectives, Your Honour. They have badges. But, really, the indignity of it!'

The taller of the detectives said, 'Paul Webster?'

'*Your Honour Justice* Webster, thank you. Who are you?'

'As your tipstaff said, we're detectives. I am Detective Inspector Peter Brannigan and this is Detective Senior Sergeant John Collins.'

The second detective nodded with no show of emotion.

Brannigan produced an arrest warrant from behind his back. 'Paul Webster, you are under arrest.'

In a flash, Collins produced a set of handcuffs.

'W-where are you from?' Webster stammered. 'What's this all about?'

'I am from the Sexual Crimes Unit and my colleague is from the Major Crime Squad. You are under arrest regarding sex and drug offences with minors. We'll fill you in with the gory details back at our office. Turn around please.' Brannigan spun Webster around, placing his hands behind his back. Brannigan clicked the silver manacles around Webster's wrists.

'You have no witnesses to anything!' Webster screamed.

'Oh, I think we do, Judge,' Collins replied. 'We have a whole girl's school full of witnesses.'

'By the way,' Brannigan added, 'if I was you, I'd get used to using Webster as your name. Forget the "Judge" or "Your Honour" bits. They'll just get you into deep shit with your new friends at dinnertime tonight at the Remand Centre. If they discover who you are, then you'll be given a practical, hands-on examination of sex offences and what they're all about.'

Brannigan held the handcuffs behind Webster as Collins dragged the white-faced paedophile out of the room.

The tipstaff was abruptly pushed aside and the door was held open for the detectives by a helpful civilian, Bill Kennedy.

The last thing Webster saw as he stared breathless and open-mouthed back into his chambers was his horse-hair wig sitting on his desk.

THE END

About the Author

Phil Copsey served with Victoria State Police Force, Australia, for forty years. His hard-earned experience fighting crime on the streets of multicultural Melbourne compelled him to write his debut novel, *Blue Justice*. His depictions of characters and crimes are infused with authentic operational details, told through the eyes of his composite character, Sergeant Tony Signorotto. Phil is a natural storyteller who returned to study towards the end of his career to begin his Tony Signorotto crime series.

*

You are welcome to email the author via:

philipcopsey@gmail.com

Acknowledgments

Many thanks to all past and present pupils, both girls and boys, of the 'School of Blue'. Writing this book has reminded me of the great characters I have worked with and the many colourful situations we faced together. You are legends, one and all. Always remember the Victoria Police motto 'Tenez Le Droit – Uphold the Right'... but keep the left handy!

Special thanks to Dr Euan Mitchell for his ongoing friendship, professional help and support with the writing of *Blue Justice*. To Mara Bron, my teacher at Box Hill Institute, thanks for the continued interest in my studies and the positivity you always displayed towards my efforts. To Janet Hodgson, my English Literature lecturer, who encouraged me to pursue my writing.

Unlikely inspiration came from the legendary Greg Roberts, alias Gregory David Roberts, the acclaimed author of *Shantaram*, who did time in Pentridge Prison for armed bank robbery before escaping to India. Greg was invited by my teacher Beth Price to talk to our writing class. Even though I was a 'Boy in Blue', when Greg and I sat down to discuss experiences, his road to writing brought tears to my eyes. You are in the legend club, too!

Former fellow police officer, Colin McLaren, reviewed my manuscript at a crucial stage of its development, and his enthusiasm helped motivate me to reach the finish line. Thanks, mate.

I salute the suburb of Carlton. My memories include standing on a wooden box alongside my dad watching legends play football at Princes Park, as well as our family hotels, the Carlton Inn and the Sarah Sands. What better setting for a crime novel could a Melbourne-born-and-bred boy ask for?

Heartfelt thanks to Daniel, Amanda and Elise for all their help in getting *Blue Justice* over the line.

Last, but most importantly, is my long-suffering wife Liz. When I said I wanted to return to study, the teacher in her came straight back with: 'Do it. Don't talk about it, do it!' Liz, you are on top of the legends list.

ω α ω α ω α ω α ω α ω α ω α

ω α ω α ω α ω α ω α ω α ω
α ω α ω α ω α ω α ω α ω α
ω α ω α ω α ω α ω α ω α ω
α ω α ω α ω α ω α ω α ω α
ω α ω α ω α ω α ω α ω α ω
α ω α ω α ω α ω α ω α ω α
ω α ω α ω α ω α ω α ω α ω
α ω α ω α ω α ω α ω α ω α
ω α ω α ω α ω α ω α ω α ω
α ω α ω α ω α ω α ω α ω α
ω α ω α ω α ω α ω α ω α ω
α ω α ω α ω α ω α ω α ω α
ω α ω α ω α ω α ω α ω α ω
α ω α ω α ω α ω α ω α ω α
ω α ω α ω α ω α ω α ω α ω
α ω α ω α ω α ω α ω α ω α
ω α ω α ω α ω α ω α ω α ω
α ω α ω α ω α ω α ω α ω α
ω α ω α ω α ω α ω α ω α ω
α ω α ω α ω α ω α ω α ω α
ω α ω α ω α ω α ω α ω α ω
α ω α ω α ω α ω α ω α ω α
ω α ω α ω α ω α ω α ω α ω
α ω α ω α ω α ω α ω α ω α
ω α ω α ω α ω α ω α ω α ω
α ω α ω α ω α ω α ω α ω α
ω α ω α ω α ω α ω α ω α ω
α ω α ω α ω α ω α ω α ω α
ω α ω α ω α ω α ω α ω α ω
α ω α ω α ω α ω α ω α ω α
ω α ω α ω α ω α ω α ω α ω
α ω α ω α ω α ω α ω α ω α
ω α ω α ω α ω α ω α ω α ω
α ω α ω α ω α ω α ω α ω α
ω α ω α ω α ω α ω α ω α ω
α ω α ω α ω α ω α ω α ω α
ω α ω α ω α ω α ω α ω α ω
α ω α ω α ω α ω α ω α ω α
ω α ω α ω α ω α ω α ω α ω
α ω α ω α ω α ω α ω α ω α
ω α ω α ω α ω α ω α ω α ω

ω α ω α ω α ω α ω α ω
α ω α ω α ω α ω α ω α ω
ω α ω α ω α ω α ω α ω
α ω α ω α ω α ω α ω α ω
ω α ω α ω α ω α ω α ω
α ω α ω α ω α ω α ω α ω
ω α ω α ω α ω α ω α ω
α ω α ω α ω α ω α ω α ω
ω α ω α ω α ω α ω α ω
α ω α ω α ω α ω α ω α ω
ω α ω α ω α ω α ω α ω
α ω α ω α ω α ω α ω α ω
ω α ω α ω α ω α ω α ω
α ω α ω α ω α ω α ω α ω
ω α ω α ω α ω α ω α ω
α ω α ω α ω α ω α ω α ω
ω α ω α ω α ω α ω α ω
α ω α ω α ω α ω α ω α ω
ω α ω α ω α ω α ω α ω
α ω α ω α ω α ω α ω α ω
ω α ω α ω α ω α ω α ω
α ω α ω α ω α ω α ω α ω
ω α ω α ω α ω α ω α ω
α ω α ω α ω α ω α ω α ω
ω α ω α ω α ω α ω α ω
α ω α ω α ω α ω α ω α ω
ω α ω α ω α ω α ω α ω
α ω α ω α ω α ω α ω α ω
ω α ω α ω α ω α ω α ω
α ω α ω α ω α ω α ω α ω
ω α ω α ω α ω α ω α ω
α ω α ω α ω α ω α ω α ω
ω α ω α ω α ω α ω α ω
α ω α ω α ω α ω α ω α ω
ω α ω α ω α ω α ω α ω

9 780648 557111